A STRANGENESS IN THE CLEARING

All around the clearing, hanging from the branches of every tree, is a flock of dream catchers, the kind you can get at the Saturday market in Galway: colorful webbed circles hung with little beads and feathers. There are maybe fifty of them, all different shapes and colors, just hanging there at head height.

"What is this place?" Sam reaches up as if to touch one of the dream catchers but then drops his hand.

I feel a lump forming in my throat. I can hardly breathe past it. My heart thuds in my chest and goose bumps prick up along my arms. "Elsie did this." I turn around and around so that the trees revolve about me, and the dream catchers blur. I can feel my heart beat in my ears.

"But why?"

"I don't know." I stop spinning and close my eyes. It takes a few seconds for my balance to steady, for my breaths to slow, for my heart to beat normally again. I take Sam by the hand and lead him over to the little bush that hid the mousetrap. When I carefully part the branches, we can see it clearly: an ordinary mousetrap, wood and wire, with a tiny little doll sitting on top of it.

Sam laughs, but I recognize it as disbelief rather than humor. "Who *is* she?"

There is a strange sinking feeling in the bottom of my heart. I say it again. "I don't know."

OTHER BOOKS YOU MAY ENJOY

THE
ACCIDENT
SEASON

THE
ACCIDENT
SEASON

MOÏRA FOWLEY-DOYLE

speak

SPEAK
An imprint of Penguin Random House LLC
375 Hudson Street
New York, New York 10014

First published in the United States of America by Kathy Dawson Books,
an imprint of Penguin Group (USA) LLC, 2015
Published in Great Britain by Random House Children's Publishers UK, 2015
Published by Speak, an imprint of Penguin Random House LLC, 2016

THE LIBRARY OF CONGRESS HAS CATALOGED THE KATHY DAWSON BOOKS EDITION AS FOLLOWS:
Fowley-Doyle, Moïra.
The accident season / by Moïra Fowley-Doyle.
pages cm
Summary: "Every October Cara and her family become
mysteriously and dangerously accident-prone, but this year, the year Cara,
her ex-stepbrother, and her best friend are 17, is when Cara will begin
to unravel the accident season's dark origins"—Provided by publisher.
ISBN 9780525429487 (hardcover)
[1. Families—Fiction. 2. Accidents—Fiction. 3. Supernatural—Fiction.]
I. Title.
PZ7.1.F68Ac 2015 [Fic]—dc23 2014047858

Speak ISBN 9780147517326

Printed in the United States of America

1 3 5 7 9 10 8 6 4 2

To my family—
Most Especially Claire

THE
ACCIDENT
SEASON

***

So let's raise our glasses to the accident season,
To the river beneath us where we sink our souls,
To the bruises and secrets, to the ghosts in the ceiling,
One more drink for the watery road.

When I heard Bea chant the words, it was as if little insects were crawling in under my spine, ready to change it. I was going to crack and bend, become something other. Our temples were sweating under our masks, but we didn't take them off. It felt like they had become part of our skins.

The fire broke and moaned in the middle of the room and the arches above the doors whispered. I don't know how I knew that Sam's eyes were closed or that Alice had a cramp in her side. I only knew that I was everyone. I was Alice with her mouth half open, maybe in excitement or fear; I was Sam with his hands in fists; I was Bea swaying in front of us all, her red dress soaked with sweat; and I was me, Cara, feeling like I was coming out of my skin. Bea's feet struck drum beats on the wooden floor. Her words grew louder. Soon we were all moving and the floorboards were shaking the ceiling downstairs. Wine flew from our glasses and dropped on the floor like blood.

When we stamped around the fire in the remains of the master bedroom, we woke something up. Maybe it was something inside us; the mysterious something that connects every bone of our spines, or that keeps our teeth stuck to the insides of our mouths. Maybe it was something between us; something in the air or in the flames that wound around us. Or maybe it was the house itself; the ghosts between the walls or the memories clicked inside every lock, the stories between the cracks in the floorboards. We were going to break into pieces, we were going to be sawn in two and reappear whole again, we were going to dodge the magician's knife and swing on the highest ride. In the ghost house in the last days of the accident season, we were never going to die.

1

Elsie is in all my pictures. I know this because I have looked through all the pictures of me and my family taken in the last seventeen years and she is in them all.

I only noticed this last night, clearing six months' worth of pictures off my phone. She is in the locker room at lunchtime. She hovers at the corner of the frame on school tours. She is in every school play. I thought: *What a coincidence, Elsie's in all my photos.* Then, on a hunch, I looked through the rest of the photos on my computer. And the ones glued into my diaries. And in my family photo albums. Elsie is in them all.

She turns her back to the camera at birthday parties. She is on family holidays and walks along the coast. A hint of her even appears in windows and mirrors in the zoomed-in background of pictures taken at home: an elbow here, an ankle there, a lock of her hair.

Is there really such a thing as coincidence? *This* much of a coincidence?

Elsie is not my friend. Elsie is nobody's friend, really. She's just that girl who talks too softly and stands too close, who you used to be sort of friends with when you were eight and your father'd just died but who mostly got left behind with the rag dolls and tea sets and other relics of childhood.

I've put a representative sample of seventy-two pictures taken in the last few years onto my phone to show to Bea before class. I want to ask her if she thinks there's something really strange going on or if the world really *is* so small that someone can turn up in all of another person's photographs.

I haven't shown the photos to Sam yet. I don't know why.

In the older pictures, my house looks like a cartoon house: no cars in the driveway, colored curtains framing the windows in hourglass shapes, a cloud of smoke attached to the chimney like white cotton candy. A seven-year-old me playing Steal the Bacon with Alice on the road in front of it. And there, at the side of the frame, a leg, the hem of a tartan skirt, and the heel of the type of sensible brown shoe that Elsie always wears.

Those pictures were taken a decade ago; this morning there is no cotton candy smoke coming from the chimney, and the hourglass curtains of the sitting room frame the image of my mother hopping on one leg as she tries to wrestle a boot onto her other foot. Alice, outside, stamps her own feet impatiently. She stalks up to the window and raps on the glass, telling our mother to get a move on. Sam laughs from the hallway, invisible in the morning sun that casts everything past the front door in shadow. I push my fists deeper into my pockets and look up at the sky. There are a few wisps of cloud just hanging there mirroring me leaning against the side of the car.

Alice is my sister. She is one year older and a million years wiser than me, or so she'd like to believe (and she may be right; how should I know? I am hardly wise). Sam is my ex-stepbrother, which is a mouthful to say, but as our parents are divorced, he isn't technically my brother anymore. His father was married to my mother until he disappeared four years ago. He ran off with a biological anthropologist and spends his time studying gibbons in the rainforests of Borneo. Sam has been living with us for seven years now, so I suppose to all intents and purposes he is my brother, but mostly he's just Sam, standing tall in the shade of the hallway, dark hair falling in his eyes.

Knowing that getting everyone into the car will take some time, I take my hands out of my pockets and pull out my phone again. I flip through the photos for the third time this morning, playing Spot-the-Elsie like in those *Where's Waldo?* books.

I'd never realized that Elsie always looks worried. Frown

lines crease her forehead, and her mouth makes a little pout. Even her hair looks worried, somehow, when her head is turned. That's quite an accomplishment. I wonder what my hair looks like when my head is turned. The back of my head is not something I see very often; unlike Elsie, I pose when a photo is being taken, and smile.

When Alice's head is turned (when, for example, she is banging on the front room window for the twentieth time to hurry my mother, who has forgotten something—her phone, her bag, her head—and has gone back upstairs to fetch it), her hair looks severe. It is dyed two shades lighter than her natural blond, always right to the roots, perfectly straightened, tightly wound into one of those make-a-bun hair donuts and stuck with two sticks. Alice has don't-mess-with-me hair.

My mother's hair is purple. It tumbles down her shoulders in unbrushed waves as she drives, and swings when she shakes her head. Strands of it stick to her lip gloss; she spits them out as she speaks. Today, she has painted her nails the same color. If it were any other time of year on this drive to school, she'd be reaching across to Alice in the passenger seat or fixing her hair, licking the tip of her finger to smooth the edges of her eye makeup or drinking from a flask of coffee like some people drag on a cigarette, but it's coming up to the end of October and Alice fell down the stairs last night, so my mother grips the steering wheel with white-knuckled, purple-nailed hands and doesn't take her eyes off the road.

8

She wouldn't have driven us, but she's convinced walking is more dangerous.

"How's your head feeling, honey?" she asks Alice. It's the thirty-second time she's asked that this morning (the eighty-ninth since coming home from the hospital last night). Sam marks another line on his hand in red pen. Every time my mother asks this question, Alice's mouth gets smaller and smaller.

Sam leans over and whispers in my ear. "Bet you a ten Alice screams before a hundred." I hold my hand out to be shaken. Sam's grip is firm and warm. I silently urge Alice to hold on until we get to school.

"You all have your gloves, right?" my mother is saying. "And, Sam, I'll write you a note for chemistry. Are you all warm enough? You did take your vitamins this morning, didn't you?"

"Sure, Melanie," Sam says to my mother. He grins at me. Alice will never last under this onslaught. My mother chances the tiniest peek at her before hurriedly looking back at the road. Alice is carefully tying a silk scarf to hide the bandage around her head. She has darkened her eyes with kohl so the bruise on the side of her face seems less severe. She looks like a storybook Gypsy in a school uniform.

We come to the intersection before the school. My mother's hair whips around as she frantically tries to look every way at once before crossing the light traffic. We crawl past at a snail's pace. The other drivers sound their horns.

When she has parked, my mother cracks her knuckles and shakes out her hands. She takes off her sunglasses and gives us each a packed lunch. "Now, you will be careful, won't you?" She squeezes Alice's shoulder affectionately. "How's your head feeling, honey?"

Alice's lips disappear. She gives a short, wordless scream without looking at our mother, and storms out of the car and into the main school building. I slump back in my seat.

"Cough it up, sister," Sam cackles.

When we've gotten out of the car, I reluctantly hand over a ten. We wave my mother good-bye and she drives carefully away. "I'm not your sister," I remind him.

Sam drapes an arm over my shoulders. "If you say so, *petite soeur*," he says.

I sigh and shake my head. "I know that means *sister*, Sam. We're in the same French class."

When Sam heads for his locker to get the books for his first class, I go find my best friend in the main school building.

Bea is sitting at the back of the library, her tarot cards spread out on the desk in front of her. She likes to read the cards every morning, so she can know what kind of day she's getting into. Bea doesn't like surprises. It wouldn't surprise her to know that the small group of eighth graders sitting a few desks away from her are snickering and whispering behind her back, so I don't draw her attention to them. Anyway, I'm half convinced Bea can give the evil eye to anyone who insults her.

I take one of my two pairs of gloves off my uncomfortably warm hands (it's not the weather for hats and gloves, but my mother wouldn't let us out of the house without them) and pull up the chair behind me to face Bea across the little desk. I rest my chin on the chair back in front of me.

"Elsie is in all my pictures," I tell her.

Bea and I automatically look across the library toward the window. Usually by this time in the morning Elsie will have opened up her secrets booth for the day. The youngest are always the first to come to her, before the bell rings for assembly, before the janitor opens the locker rooms and the librarian comes out of her office to tell us to get to class. They come one at a time, type up their secrets on Elsie's antique typewriter, and shuffle out of the library, heads bowed, pretending to be engrossed in the contents of their school bags. Elsie's box gets fuller and fuller with the things that can't be said. She isn't here this morning, though. Maybe she's running late.

Bea turns back to me. "What do you mean?"

I take out my phone and show it to her. I point out the mousy hair, the sensible shoes, the worry lines on the brows of every Elsie in every photograph.

Bea takes a long time over the photos. Finally she looks

up. Her eyebrows are drawn together and her mouth's a thin line. "Cara, this is . . ." She shakes her head slightly.

"A little weirder than usual?" I rest the tips of my fingers against my forehead and close my eyes. Bea reads tarot cards and lights candles for ghosts. She talks about magic being all around us and laughs when our classmates call her a witch. But this is different.

Bea goes through the photos again, scrolling, stopping, tapping the screen and peering close.

"Do you think it's real?" I say to her from behind my hands. "Or do you think I'm crazy? Please don't say both."

Bea doesn't say anything. Instead, she shuffles her cards and lays them out slowly one by one on the desk between us. She looks down at the cards, and up at me, and back at the cards again. When she finally looks back at me, she's wearing an expression I haven't seen in a long time.

She takes in my woolly hat, my remaining pair of gloves under the pair I just took off, the thick leggings I'm wearing as well as tights under my uniform skirt, the Band-Aid on my finger, the ACE bandage around my wrist, the vague aroma of echinacea and anxiety following me around like a strange sad cloud.

Bea sighs and nods; she understands.

It's the accident season, the same time every year. Bones break, skin tears, bruises bloom. Years ago my mother tried to lock us all up, pad the hard edges of things with foam and gauze, cover us in layers of sweaters and gloves, ban sharp objects and open flames. We camped out together in the living room for eight days, until the carefully ordered takeout food—delivered on the doorstep and furtively retrieved by my mother, who hadn't thought how she would cook meals without the help of our gas oven—gave us all food poisoning and we spent the next twenty-four hours in the hospital. Now every autumn we stock up on bandages and painkillers; we buckle up, we batten down. We never leave the house without at least three protective layers. We're afraid of the accident season. We're afraid of how easily accidents turn into tragedies. We have had too many of those already.

"Alice fell down the stairs last night," I tell her. "All the way from the top. Her head cracked on the banister rail on the way down. She said it sounded like a gunshot in a film, only duller."

"Oh God."

"There was no one in the house. They said at the hospital that she had a concussion, so we had to keep her awake, walk her around and around."

Bea's eyes are wide. "Is she okay?"

"She's fine now. Mom didn't want us to come to school today, but Alice insisted." I take off my hat and shake out my hair, then try to smooth it down. Unlike Alice, I don't dye my hair (also unlike Alice, I'm not blond), and it's too short to straighten, so my perpetually-growing-out pixie cut sticks up in fluffy brown spikes whenever I wear hats.

Bea covers my hands with hers. The pinkie of her right hand loops through the wool of the hat I'm holding. "Why didn't you call me?" she asks; then, as if to answer her own question, she looks back down at the cards. She clears her throat, as if she's hesitating before she speaks. Then she says it. "I think . . . It's going to be a bad one, Cara." She tries to look me in the eye, but I stare down at her cards instead. It takes a minute for me to answer.

"How bad?"

Bea touches my gloved hand gently. She says it softly. "One of the worst." She turns one of the cards to face me. On it there is a figure on a bed being pierced by swords. I shiver. My knee knocks into one of the desk legs and I feel a sharp pain. When I look down, I see that my leggings and tights have been ripped by a huge nail sticking out of the wood. A few drops of blood collect around the edges of the tear. I can feel my eyes start to fill.

Bea gets up and wraps her arms around me. She smells like cigarettes and incense. "It'll be okay," she whispers into my ear. "We'll make sure nothing happens to you. I promise. We can change this. And I don't think you're going crazy. We'll talk to Elsie. It doesn't look like she's in school today, but we'll talk to her together tomorrow. It'll be okay."

I squash down the panicky feeling rising in my throat and take a packet of pirate-print tissues out of my schoolbag.

I blot the blood off my leggings, trying to move my wrist as little as possible. I don't remind Bea that something's already happened to me, even if it's just cut skin from a nail and a sprained wrist getting out of the car last night. It's always like this: Things happen and things keep happening, and things get worse and worse. I look back across the library at where Elsie's secrets booth usually is. The empty desk is like a missing tooth.

2

For the rest of the morning I am careful, holding tight to banister rails, watching where I put my feet, avoiding corners and sharp edges. At lunchtime Alice follows me, Bea, and Sam down past the soccer fields to the train tracks behind the school. We like to come here and smoke sometimes (the teachers rarely walk by, and if we sit close to the tracks, we are hidden from the school's windows), but Alice, who is in the year above the three of us, usually spends her lunch hour in the cafeteria with her friends.

"I just can't take any more questions," Alice says when I ask why she has joined us today. "Or staring." I look away from her bruised face. Sam and I like to invent elaborate, non-sensical backstories for our injuries at this time of year. Nobody believes us, of course: The teachers wearily tell us to stop exaggerating and some of our classmates call us crazy under their breaths, but at least nobody asks us too many questions.

Alice prefers never to talk about the accidents, even with her friends. It bothers her a lot more than it does us when people in school whisper about us behind our backs. A lot of things bother Alice.

"Also," she says as an afterthought, "I could use a smoke."

Bea doesn't mention the fact that Alice doesn't smoke. She also doesn't mention Alice's bruises or the bandage peeking out from underneath her scarf. Instead, she sits down on the edge of the ditch with the train tracks at her feet and takes out her ukulele and a pack of cigarettes. She takes a drag on one and hands it to Alice. She exhales as she strums her ukulele, and her face is wreathed in smoke. With her bright-dyed halo of curly red hair, it looks like she's on fire. Beside her, blond, pale Alice looks like Snow White to Bea's Rose Red. Although Alice would never describe herself as a fairy-tale girl.

Bea likes to say that Alice is like a looking-glass version of us: practical rather than poetic. I've always thought Alice's namesake would make more sense for Bea, but then, we don't get to choose our names. Bea was named for a Shakespearean heroine, Alice for a children's book. They could never swap now. Sam doesn't know why his mother chose his name, because she died just after he was born. As for me, my mother's always sworn that my full name is Caramel. Sometimes I don't even think she's joking.

Alice hands the cigarette back to Bea, who takes a couple of drags. Her lipstick leaves bright red stains on the filter.

"Some people say that sharing a cigarette is like sharing a kiss," Bea tells us as she hands me the cigarette. I grin and close my lips around the filter.

"What people?" Alice asks. Alice questions Bea more than the rest of us do. Maybe because Alice's life is anchored in the real world a little more than ours are, or so she likes to think. She tells herself (and she tells us, loudly and often) that she doesn't believe in the accident season or in tarot cards, but sometimes I wonder if she's telling the truth. She ignores my mother's pleas to dress in protective layers, but I often think that's just so the kids in school won't stare.

"All kinds of people." Bea is used to Alice's cynicism. Sometimes I think she says even more outrageous things around her because she enjoys the challenge. "There's something so intimate about putting your lips where someone else's were just a moment before, inhaling the same air."

Sam reaches across me and takes the cigarette. His fingers brush against mine.

"It's not air." Alice pulls up tufts of grass. She has one eyebrow raised as if in disapproval, but she is smiling. "It's tobacco and tar."

"Same difference," Bea says. "You inhale it anyway."

I take out my book and look across the train tracks. The day is still bright, but fading, like it's tired of holding on to the sun and the birdsong and the green smells of the fields just outside town. Like this weird warm October weather is finally tired of pretending it's still summer and is just waiting for the rains and winds of autumn to start, to make it feel real again.

Sam leans against me and we swing our legs out over the tracks. My feet dangle over the iron and weeds: big red Docs over thick socks over small feet that could break too easily. I try to concentrate on my dog-eared copy of *Wuthering Heights,* but I keep having visions of the train arriving suddenly and crushing our fragile limbs. I try to convince myself I don't believe that for one month of every year a family can become suddenly and inexplicably accident-prone. I try to pretend I don't remember the accidents of the past—the bad ones, the big ones, the tragedies.

Involuntarily, I look over at Alice. Bea's cards said this would be one of the worst. When the worst ones happen, people die.

My heart jumps into my mouth and beats there instead of in my chest. There are too many things I'm trying not to remember and sometimes there's just no use pretending. I fold my legs underneath me and pull Sam and Alice up onto the bank of the ditch, away from the tracks. They don't ask why, only sit with me, cross-legged in the middle of the dirty grass, and Bea joins us, strumming her ukulele softly.

I put my book back in my bag and we all take out our

lunches and the cardboard cups of tea we got at the cafeteria. The tea has gone cold, but at least that means we won't scald ourselves.

Sam takes a sip of his and makes a face. "Tepid," he says. "Delicious." He looks over at Alice with a crooked smile. "So, how's your head feeling, honey?" he says in a passable imitation of my mother's voice.

"Ugh, don't." Alice tilts her head back and rolls her eyes. "She really needs to learn that sometimes *I'm fine* means *I'm fine.*"

I watch Alice tear her sandwich into tiny pieces and eat them slowly, the butt of the cigarette she just smoked smoldering at her feet. I'm not sure I believe her *I'm fine* any more than my mother did.

"She's just worried about you," Bea says.

Alice brushes sandwich crumbs off her skirt. "My friends' parents worry about them applying to the right college and not getting too drunk on nights out," she says. "My mother worries when I'm not wearing more than one pair of gloves. That's not worry, that's pathological."

"No, you're right," Sam says to her with mock sincerity. "It's not like you have a serious head injury and were in the hospital last night or anything."

Alice opens her mouth to retort, but before she can, I jump in quick and change the subject. "So what kind of schools *are* your friends applying to?" I ask.

Alice is one of those people who has a fairly large group of casual friends. She usually hangs out with the popular crowd at school, without being particularly close to any of them. They have lunch together and she gets invited to all their parties, but after class she mostly spends time with her boyfriend, Nick, who is more popular than any of them.

Nick is a musician with wicked finger-picking skills and a voice like a fiery god's. His talent comes off him like a scent that every girl can smell half a mile away. I suppose that when your boyfriend writes epic love songs to you at three in the morning and pulls you up on stage after every show, you don't really need too many more close friends.

I, on the other hand, am one of those people who has a small group of very close friends. Those friends are Bea and Sam. It is, I have to admit, a rather tiny group.

Alice pops a little piece of sandwich into her mouth. "Kim wants to do nursing," she says. "And Niamh's first choice is business and French. So if I don't get into computer science in Trinity, I'll be in DCU with her. It's, like, fourth on my list, though."

Alice will end up being the only person in our family not doing something arty or literary, but I think for her that's part of the appeal. "I'm sure you'll get your first choice," I tell her.

"If I don't die of overwork first," Alice says. "Do you know Mr. Murray has us doing two hours of study a night? As well as homework?"

"It's only October," says Sam. "No wonder you're so crabby."

Alice reaches out and shoves his shoulder.

"What you need," Bea muses, taking an apple out of her bag, "is a big, crazy party to get everybody's priorities straight."

"You're right," Alice laughs. "Homework should never be a priority."

"Homework!" Sam suddenly exclaims with dismay. He starts to root through his bag for his schedule. "Please tell me that essay on the First World War wasn't due today."

"I would," Bea says, amused, taking a bite out of her apple, "but I'd be lying."

"*Shit.*" Sam pulls his history book out of his bag and opens it on his lap. "Have you done this?" he asks me and Bea.

"We won't be able to copy each other's homework next year, you know," I say sadly. "Not if we want to do well in the exams. And we'll probably have to hand it in on time too."

"Never," Bea says solemnly.

"Well, I can tell you that most of my class definitely *doesn't* give their homework in on time," Alice says as Bea takes her history folder out of her bag and hands it to Sam. "Except for Toby Healy, of course."

Toby is one of the most popular boys in school. He has sandy blond hair and an inexplicable tan and small dimples when he smiles. He's one of the best players on the soccer team and top of his year, and still spends almost every evening in supervised study. Not that I've noticed.

Bea gives me a mischievous look. "Cara thinks Toby's cute."

"Everybody thinks Toby's cute," I say.

"I don't," says Sam.

"Everybody except Sam thinks Toby's cute."

"You don't actually, though, do you?" Sam asks me.

Alice's phone buzzes. She checks her messages but puts her phone down without replying.

"Cute or not, it would never work out," Bea says blithely. I am about to protest—despite only being very vaguely interested in Toby Healy, I feel I should stand up for myself—but Bea goes on: "For one thing, there's only room for three in our Parisian loft apartment."

Sam, Bea, and I have a carefully constructed and oft-daydreamed-about plan for when we leave school. We will move to Dublin together to study literature and philosophy, which will give us the education we need to run away to Paris, where Sam will direct French art house films, I will spend my days in dusty bookshops, and Bea will pay the rent by working as an artist's model (nude, of course).

I give Bea a playful smack and correct a few lines of Sam's history essay from the notes in my own notebook. Alice's phone buzzes again.

"Doesn't that boyfriend of yours know you're in school

right now?" Bea asks as the phone starts to ring in earnest.

"Back in a sec," Alice says, getting to her feet and moving a few feet away from us to answer. Nick finished high school four years ago; who knows what you forget when you've been away that long.

Bea starts picking out a tune on her ukulele. I recognize it as one of the particularly depressing folksongs she likes to play. Ms. O'Shaughnessy, the Irish teacher, had Bea play the song in the original Irish a few weeks ago in class. Since then she and the music teacher, Mr. Duffy, won't stop raving about Bea's "new spin on traditional music," but no one in the school folk group wants a ukulele in the band. Or maybe they just don't want a Bea.

Alice returns to us with a smile on her face. "He sent me flowers," she says, sitting down to gather her things into her bag. "To the school cafeteria. He thought I'd be there now. Kim says there are a dozen roses in a big glass vase. Everybody's talking about it."

I'm about to ask Alice what the occasion is or if Nick is just being romantic and spontaneous, when the ground beneath us begins to shake. The tracks sing. We turn to face the train. It flies past us like a snaky bird, screeching and screaming. There are faces in the windows all streaming by. The station is just down the road from the school, and the train slows to let another train by, and in one of the cars I think I see a reflection of the four of us, but different, distorted by the light and sky on the other side of the window.

They look like they are dressed up for a costume party. The redhead who looks like Bea could be dressed as a mermaid, scaly skin and all. I imagine there is a starfish stuck to her face and that her sequined dress ends in fins. Another girl with light brown hair as short as mine is sitting with her legs up on the table between her and the mermaid. She almost looks like she's wearing a strange, fluid dress the color of oil puddles, and silver Converse, with blue-green fairy wings attached to her shoulders. They are squashed up against the seat back behind her. The girl sitting beside the mermaid—in the same position as Alice, who's beside Bea on the grass—seems to be dressed as a forest, with leaves stuck to her face and to her mossy dress, and twigs and little flowers twined through her long blond hair. The boy of the group, sitting beside the fairy girl, looks like he's just walked out of a silent film. His skin is gray and he could be wearing a sort of vaudeville-circus-ringmaster top hat on his black hair. I'm a little disappointed when the train pulls away, because he's really quite beautiful.

"I wonder where they're off to," I say to Bea, who is also watching the train move away.

Alice, texting one-handed, stands up, slings her bag onto one shoulder, and hurries back toward the main school building.

"Where who are off to?" Bea asks distractedly, turning to

25

look after Alice. She starts to retune her ukulele with a series of loud twangs.

"The kids in the car right there," I say. She and Sam look after the departing train, but of course the car with the dressed-up kids in it has moved away.

"What kids?" says Sam.

Bea shrugs. "I didn't realize there was anyone in the window." She strums a couple of chords experimentally. "I just saw the four of us reflected in the glass."

I snap my head back up to look after the train, but by now it's gone. Maybe I'm just hallucinating from lack of sleep. I think of the hospital last night; the nurses who know us by name at this point, the way we had to walk Alice around and around, ask her questions, keep her awake. My knee itches around the little cut from earlier where the blood has stuck the tights to my skin.

All the rest of the day I find it hard to concentrate. When the three-o'clock bell rings, I follow Sam and Bea to the doors of the PE hall, but instead of going inside to get changed, I plead with Mrs. Smith, the PE teacher, to let me off class because of my sprained wrist until she agrees to allow me to go home. Bea, who would clearly rather not have to halfheartedly run laps in the sweaty, smelly hall, waves morosely at me as I leave to walk home alone slowly in the afternoon light.

Our house is a couple of miles outside town, down the

main road past shops and houses and housing developments, past fields and farms, and farther, down a smaller country road lined with hedges and whitewashed houses. Mostly, though, to get home from town, we follow the river. A little way off the main road, there is the river walk, which is sometimes no more than a rough track and sometimes a proper area with picnic benches and bridges to take you to the woods on the other side.

The place I like to sit is close to the smallest of the bridges—really just a wooden placeholder across the water waiting for the council to build a proper bridge of stone. Instead of going straight home, I climb down and sit on the riverbank and take out a cigarette. The ground is hard and gritty beneath me. Across the river everything is yellow and red, the fallen leaves dry and crackly and inviting. There's something about autumn leaves that just begs to be stepped on. I can hear them whispering in the breeze. I take off both pairs of gloves so the cigarette won't singe them and I sit there for a while, a splash of color on the duller bank, smoking and trying not to think about Bea's cards.

Since I was little, since long before Elsie started with the secrets booth, I've come down here when there's no one else around, to tell my secrets to the river. Sometimes I almost think I can hear it whispering them back at me.

I open my mouth to talk about what Bea said and how I'm afraid this really will be a bad one; the worst one, if that's even possible—although I can hardly imagine what could ever be worse than the one four years ago we so often try to forget—when suddenly I think I see a shape between the trees. When I squint my eyes against the sun to look closer, it's gone. I stand up and come right down to the river, the toes of my Docs almost touching the water. I could have sworn I saw a flash of mousy brown hair moving between the trees.

I take a last drag of my cigarette, put the end in the bin by the bench, and hurry over to the bridge. I'm halfway across when it begins to creak. I stop. I've crossed this bridge a thousand times. It was built before I was born, but it's sturdy; it has weathered the years. I take a careful step. Another creak, louder this time. Then, in a rush of wood and water, the bridge collapses.

I grab the hand rail and hold on for dear life as the bridge plunges toward the river. It's a short drop. The middle section of the bridge hits the water and stops, caught between two rocks. Water whooshes over my legs to my waist, but I'm still standing, leaning against the rail in the middle of the river.

I'm shaking all over, but not from the cold. *I'm okay*, I tell myself sharply. *I'm okay*. I breathe deeply until I can move again. Carefully, hand over hand, legs heavy in the water, I make my way across the rest of the fallen bridge to the other side of the river.

I climb up onto the opposite bank. Still breathless, I

edge toward the copse of trees where I thought I caught a glimpse of Elsie. Moss and bits of twig stick to my boots. They squelch as I walk. I part a row of branches and peer into the little clearing behind them. Everything is dark here, shadowed by trees. The light is watery and weird, full of whispers.

"Hello?" I feel like that girl in the horror films, the one who makes you scream at the screen, telling her to turn and run away. My heart does a little flutter dance. "Elsie?"

I think I hear a tiny noise coming from a clump of bushes at the far side of the clearing. Everything else is strangely silent. I can't hear the leaves crunch or the river flow behind me.

"Hello?" I say again. I tiptoe toward the bushes. The leaves rustle as I approach.

"Elsie?" I reach forward and part the branches quickly, like ripping off a Band-Aid. There's nothing there. Nothing except a small box squirreled away to the back of the bushes. I get down on my hands and knees and stick my head in under them. The branches catch in my hair. I blow at the leaves to get them out of my way, and that's when I see the mousetrap nestled in a pile of dusty moss.

For a minute I scan the ground, worried that I've gotten too close to a rodent's nest, but then I notice what's on top of the trap and it's not (thankfully) a dead mouse, nor is it a piece of perfectly holey cheese like in *Tom and Jerry* cartoons. What it is, is a doll.

It looks like it's been made of cardboard and wire and cloth, like the Guatemalan worry dolls my mother keeps in a little pouch hanging from the rearview mirror in her car. Only this one looks exactly like Elsie. It's got mousy brown woolen hair and pale cloth-skin and it's wearing a tartan skirt that looks like our school uniform and a shapeless red sweater of the kind Elsie always seems to wear outside of school. It even has the Peter Pan collar of a tiny shirt coming up from underneath the sweater's neck. I back away and stand up slowly.

"Elsie?" I call. "Elsie!" No one answers. A little breeze whistles through the clearing and my legs break into goose bumps underneath my wet layers. Or at least I tell myself it is the cold and the wet, and not the little cardboard doll set out like the bait in a trap.

3

When I get home, Sam's and Alice's bags aren't in a pile in the hall covered with hats and gloves and autumn leaves, so I assume they're either still in school or on their way home. I dump my own bag next to the stairs and take off my still-damp boots.

In the living room, my mother is curled up on the couch like a cat, chewing on a lock of long purple hair and sketching in a notebook. She barely looks up when I come in.

"Hi, Mom." I perch on the side of the couch and knock on my mother's boots with my knuckles. They are big green walking boots that look like they've trekked through oceans.

She shuts her notebook with a snap and smiles at me. "Hi, darling." Her voice is rough. There's a strange aura of sugary sadness about her this evening. She's still wearing her coat.

"Are you okay?" I ask. It's unlike her not to insist on driving us home from school if she's not working.

"The presses broke just after lunch," she says. "Both of them, at the same time. Figures." My mother is an artist. When she's working on prints or etchings, she uses a little studio in the middle of Galway City that she rents with some of her friends because we don't have room for a press in the attic of our house, which is where she works the other half of the time. The attic is cluttered with canvases and paints and always smells strongly of turpentine.

"So," she says, waving her sketchbook in the air, "the rest of the day was a bit of a write-off, so I went for a drink with the girls instead. I just got home five minutes ago." Then she frowns, as if she's only just noticed I'm here. "Why are you all wet?"

I don't want to tell her that the bridge collapsed, so I make something up about a pipe bursting in the girls' bathroom and drenching my uniform, reassuring her that nobody got hurt in this fictional accident.

My mother nods absentmindedly. "Is your brother home too?" she asks, pushing the hair out of her face and swinging her legs to the floor. Then she says: "Christopher called this afternoon."

Suddenly I understand. Her eyeliner has smudged a little at the edges and she looks so much younger than she is. I try to make my voice light, but it comes out as kind of teasing. "So it was *that* kind of drink 'with the girls.'"

My mother makes a face. "Don't you 'with the girls' me, young lady." She's smiling, though, and she swipes the hat from my head and ruffles up my hair. She says softly, "The accident season is hard enough to handle." I nod to let her know I understand what she means, but hearing my mother talk about it makes the sinking feeling in my tummy come back.

Christopher is Sam's father. We haven't seen him since he left four years ago. He calls maybe once a year, but Sam never calls him back. My mother keeps her ex-husband informed of his son's well-being, but every time she gets off the phone with him, she goes out for "just one drink with the girls."

"Where did you say your brother was?" she asks me again.

"He's not my brother," I remind her. "He'll be home soon, I'd say. He had to suffer through PE last class, which thankfully I didn't have to do." I hold up my bandaged wrist by way of explanation.

My mother sort of laughs and says, "Well, I'd take a sprained wrist over PE any day," and I agree.

Sam is three months and twenty-four days older than me, which means we're in the same year at school, which means we take most of the same classes. Sam and I are alike in many ways, but if PE weren't compulsory, I'd never go within half a mile of the sports fields, while Sam was on our school's soccer team for almost a year—until he broke his nose during a game one accident season and my mother made him quit.

My mother flaps her arms at me to send me toward the stairs. "Go get changed," she says. "Shoo! You'll catch your death in those wet clothes."

When I come back downstairs in more suitable (and drier) attire, my mother and I go into the kitchen and put a pizza in the oven. Because it's the accident season, my mother's got padding on the edge of every counter. She installed an electric oven a few years ago, but because the burner still runs on gas, she has disabled it, so everything we cook is either oven-baked or microwaved. The floor tiles are covered in knock-off afghan rugs. Our kitchen looks like a cross between a padded cell and a nomad's tent.

My mother hands me a bottle of beer. (My mother decided when we turned sixteen that if she drank the occasional beer or glass of wine at home with us, we wouldn't feel the need to get drunk in fields and have liver damage by the time we're thirty. I think if she knew about the parties we went to over the summer, she wouldn't be so sure.)

"Let's celebrate," she says.

"What are we celebrating?"

My mother thinks for a moment, then she says, "We are celebrating because you didn't have to go to PE, and I got to take a half-day." She's smiling, but something in her voice is off.

34

"We're toasting the last week of the accident season!" she says grandly. I think she means we're celebrating that it's almost over for another year, but there's something in her toast I find unsettling. Like the accident season shouldn't be acknowledged so openly. Like if we call it by name too often, it'll become even more aware of us. Like it's actually some creature that wants to do us harm.

But my mother is sad-smiling and trying to hide it, and her eyeliner is smudged, so I raise my bottle to meet hers.

"To the accident season."

***

When Sam and Alice get home, the whole house smells of melted cheese and I'm that type of tipsy that's a little like a wineglass, where everything outside it is slightly distorted, and I'm singing the sad, lonely folksong Bea played for us by the train tracks. Sam sits up on the table in front of me and knocks his legs into mine and sings along. His voice is scratchy and deep and he knows all the harmonies.

Alice grabs a beer and disappears into her bedroom. My mother looks after her sadly, then takes her own beer into the living room.

When they've left I remember Christopher's phone call and I'm about to mention it to Sam, but just then the slice of pizza I'm holding falls apart, splattering me with tomato sauce and melted cheese. Sam laughs at me, then darts forward and licks a drop of sauce off my chin.

I move back, surprised, then make a silly little *pfft* noise at the look on his face. "Yuck, Sam," I say, rubbing my chin with the back of my hand. "That's gross."

"No, it's delicious." He grins and steals the rest of my pizza slice. Sam's smile is wide and warm and real; it's not lost like my mother's or strange and watery like Alice's and I don't want to change that, so I decide not to mention Christopher right now. Instead, we stumble upstairs to my bedroom, where I put a record on the turntable that used to be my father's, and Sam and I lie side by side on our bellies on my bed. I show him one of the old photo albums I was looking through last night and finally tell him what I've noticed about Elsie.

I turn each page carefully, like if I turn it too quickly, each little Elsie in every photograph will startle and fade off the page. I am about to tell Sam about crossing the river earlier, and the little Elsie doll I found on the mousetrap, but I change my mind at the last minute because I've sort of convinced myself that I'm overreacting; that all I saw was a piece of fabric or a stick of wood. Sam touches each picture lightly with a fingertip.

He shakes his head. "It's so weird," he says. "I don't know how this is possible." He turns the pages of the album slowly. "Do you even know anything about her?" he asks. "I never really see her around."

"She stays in the library between classes, mostly."

Sam turns another page. "The secrets booth, right."

"Right."

"I don't think I've ever actually talked to her," Sam says. He looks at me for a second. "Apart from, like, to type up a secret."

"You've left secrets?" I don't know why I'm surprised. The secrets booth is a good way to get things off your chest, when they're things you wouldn't necessarily want to say out loud. I leave secrets too, every once in a while. Type them up on Elsie's antique typewriter and post them into the big wooden box she keeps them in. At the end of the school term Ms. Byrne, the art teacher, sets up an installation through the halls of the school. She pins up all the typewritten secrets on lengths of clothesline so everyone can read them. It gets a lot of attention from the local press, but Ms. Byrne says it's all about catharsis and community. You read the secrets and you don't feel so alone. You read your secret up there, among the hundreds of other anonymous secrets, and you know you're connected, if only by a thin length of clothesline through the school halls.

I badly want to ask Sam what he's typed up on Elsie's typewriter, but I know he wouldn't tell me. I know I wouldn't say if he asked me.

"Yeah," Sam says. "Sometimes." He shrugs, as if to say it's no big deal. The question tingles my lips. Sam's hair falls in his eyes. It's thick and wavy, closer to black than dark brown, and there is a single streak of blue dye in it that he jokingly says is to make him look like more of a rebel. Not that he needs it. I'm fairly sure some of the stares he gets from girls at school aren't just because we're considered a little bit weird.

The bedsprings creak when he shifts his weight. "Do you?" Sam asks me. "Ever leave a secret?"

"Sometimes." I stare resolutely down at the pictures in front of me. I can't stop wondering what Sam has written. I can picture him at the secrets booth, hidden from Elsie and the rest of the library by the little privacy screen she puts up, his bitten fingernails clack-clacking words he'd never say to anyone, not even to me. I bring the subject back to Elsie. "And you never talk to her when you leave a secret?" I ask him.

"No," he says, frowning like he's trying to remember something. "I guess not."

"Me either," I say, thinking. "I guess there's something furtive and kind of . . . embarrassing about it, maybe."

Sam nods. "You don't really want to stick around and chat."

I think it's kind of sad that Elsie probably sees so many people every day but doesn't really speak with any of them. I wonder if she's lonely. Then I wonder why I never wondered that before. I haven't spoken to Elsie in years, not really, and she's sort of faded into the background.

We used to spend a lot of time together when we were little. When my father died, it was just me, my mother, and Alice. Bea hadn't moved to town yet and my mother hadn't met Christopher, so we didn't know Sam either. My father died during the accident season when I was eight, one of the worst ones, when we all ended up with multiple stitches and broken bones. A van hit his car coming off the highway when he was driving home from work. After that, I pretty much stopped talking, for a long time. And although most people in school understood, the longer it went on, the more of them lost interest in trying to get through to me.

Except Elsie. I remember there being something so reassuring about having someone who seemed to understand; someone who wasn't trying to make me feel better but who was happy to just let me feel.

My mother met Christopher two years later, when Sam and I were both ten and Alice was eleven. They were only married for three years. After Christopher left, Sam went through what my mother calls a rough patch. He got sad a lot, and angry. Everybody kept talking at him and bringing him places and trying to get his mind off things, but I knew even then that that doesn't always help. So he and I would shut ourselves in my room and listen to music and not say anything for hours. Sometimes days. Then we'd stand on my bed and shout every swear word we knew (and it was an impressive number for a pair of thirteen-year-olds), and we'd throw things on the floor: nail polish bottles, pencil cases, photograph albums. Sam and I were always close, but it was after this that we became best friends.

I guess I didn't need Elsie anymore, once I had Sam. Just thinking that makes me start to feel really, really bad about forgetting her.

"And now she's in all my pictures," I say to Sam. I lie on my side facing him and prop my head up on my hand. "Do you think she's following me?" I ask. "Do you think I'm crazy? Do you think I'm imagining it? Do you think I'm maybe following her?"

"Are you?" Sam asks.

"I mean, without realizing it. Maybe I'm shadowing her. Maybe it's not her that's following me. Is it possible to unintentionally follow someone?"

Sam pauses at a picture of us at the seaside with Alice, Christopher, and my mother. It was taken on vacation in the south of France a year before Christopher left, back when things were almost normal for a while. Sam and I are grinning identical grins. We are sandy-haired and sunburned and the same height, and we look like twins. I'm wearing my first two-piece bikini, but I still look like a little girl playing dress-up. My mother looks like a 1920s model. She has buried Christopher to the ankles in sand, but he still towers over her. They have their arms around each other and you can see by the pinch in the flesh of his chest how tightly she's holding him.

Alice stands a bit apart. My uncle Seth, who took the picture, kept trying to get her to come closer, but Alice has always thought that family vacations are extraordinarily uncool. She's the only one of us fully dressed, and her T-shirt and jeans seem strangely out of place in the summer beach scene. And behind her, standing at the edge of the water, is Elsie.

"Maybe her family just happened to be on vacation in the same place as us," I say. I can hear the uncertainty in my voice.

But Sam isn't listening. "I hate him," he says suddenly.

I quickly cover the picture with my hand, ignoring the little voice in my head that says I should tell Sam his father called this afternoon. "He doesn't exist," I tell him. Then I smile and poke his arm to perk him up. "You can be part of our club. The no-dads club. With me and Alice. And Bea. We can have a clubhouse and a secret handshake."

Bea's father left three years ago as unceremoniously as Christopher, except Bea knows he's living in England with his new, successful wife and new, young, adorable children who ride ponies and do ballet and won't grow up to be eccentric tarot-card-reading teenage disappointments.

"And Melanie," says Sam.

My mother's father died one accident season when I was

six. I don't remember much about him—only that the year he died was the first year I became properly aware of the accident season. I'd never seen my mother cry before that day.

"And Mom," I agree. I push the photo album away. "Let's not think about this anymore."

Sam hesitates for a moment, but then he agrees with me and we lie on our backs and listen to the record whirring beneath the music. He points up at one of the clouds on the ceiling above my bed. My father painted them for me when I was six years old so that I could see shapes in the clouds even when I couldn't see the sky. My room has been repainted several times since then, but the ceiling stays the same.

"Skull and crossbones," Sam says.

I shake my head. "Magic wand shooting sparks."

Sam points at another. "Murky pond at sunset."

I laugh out loud. He's pointing to the cloud my father specifically painted to look like a bunny rabbit. "You're right," I say. "It's definitely a murky pond at sunset."

When I look over at him, his brow is furrowed. I think of Elsie's worried face.

"Strange little elf-girl," he says to me.

"No. Warrior queen."

He laughs at that a little. "Strange little warrior elf-queen," he amends.

"Pirate with a heart of gold." I stare straight into his eyes.

"No," he says. "Lost boy." He sounds like a ghost. A shiver runs up and down my arms. I bring them close to my body and look away from Sam. His eyes are riverbanks. They'd pull you in if you aren't careful.

"Gold-hearted lost pirate boy, then," I say like I'm still joking.

"Ahoy, matey," Sam says halfheartedly.

We look up at the ceiling clouds and listen to the music for a bit. Alice is on the phone in her bedroom. Her voice murmurs through the wall between us.

I look over at Sam. He's lying with one arm over his head, staring at the ceiling. He has the lightest dusting of freckles across the bridge of his nose and a hint of stubble on his jaw. There is a small silence as the record changes song. On the other side of the wall, Alice's voice gets louder.

I look at the photograph again. I think of Seth taking it, telling us to stop messing around because his laughter was making the camera shake. My heart feels heavy. Seth died almost exactly a year after this picture was taken. The same year Christopher left. *It's going to be a bad one,* Bea said, but I can't imagine a worse one than that.

At that moment Alice yells and something crashes into the wall in her room behind me. The impact shakes loose the bookshelf above my bed on my side of the wall. The books clatter down on top of me—their spines stinging—and then the shelf itself follows, hitting me square on the shoulder. The pain explodes like fireworks. Sam swears. I groan. He starts pulling the books and the shelf off me and I wince at the pain blossoming all down the left side of my body.

"Alice, what happened?" I yell from under the pile of books. My mother runs up the stairs. She and Alice appear in the doorway at the same time. I shove the collected works of Arthur Conan Doyle off my arm and move my shoulder carefully around in its socket.

"I'm sorry, I'm so sorry," Alice is saying. "My phone just flew out of my hand."

"I'm fine," I say quickly, but the damage is done.

My mother's eyes are too bright. She mutters about getting me something for the bruising and shuffles downstairs. Sam puts the last of the books down on the floor.

I try to grin. "Who knew reading was such a dangerous hobby?" I say. "I've never regretted my collection of fancy hardbacks before. It's paperbacks all the way from here on in."

Sam isn't listening. He gives Alice a funny look. "Is your phone really heavy enough to knock a shelf off the wall?" he asks her.

"What?"

"I'm just saying," Sam says. "Maybe you shouldn't be throwing shit around during the accident season."

Alice's eyes narrow. "Oh, for God's sake, Sam," she says. "Would you give the accident thing a rest? I wasn't throwing shit around, I was on the phone to Nick and it slipped out of my hand."

Sam doesn't look convinced. He says, "Yeah, but—"

Alice sighs and cuts him off. "Whatever," she says. "I'm going to bed. I'll try not to cause any 'accidents' from there."

***

Alice wasn't the first to jump, but she was the first to fall. It started with dares. Dare you to roll down the hill. Dare you to touch a nettle. Dare you to jump across the stream.

Mom and Dad and Uncle Seth, who was Mom's brother, and Nana Morris, who was Mom's mom, were talking to their neighbor from two doors down in front of Nana and Granddad Morris's house. Granddad Morris was on his way home from work. The dogs were on leads because Mom wouldn't let Alice and Cara near them otherwise. But not always. Only in October. Alice wondered if maybe Mom was a little bit afraid of Halloween. Or of dogs. Or both. Alice would have liked to have a dog.

Because Mom was busy talking to the neighbor, Alice and Cara and Darren ran ahead. Darren was the son of Nana and Granddad Morris's next-door neighbors and he thought he was the boss and also the strongest because he was a boy and he was eight and a half and Alice was seven and a girl. Cara was six and didn't care who was the boss. She just wanted to pick flowers.

Alice told Darren she only couldn't run as fast as him be-

45

cause she had skinned her knees falling in the school yard last Friday, but then Darren pulled up the legs of his trousers to show the scabs on his knees. They were even bigger than hers.

Uncle Seth laughed at that, and said to Mom, "See, Melanie? All kids have skinned knees," but Mom just made her mouth small, which she only did when she knew you were telling fibs. Alice didn't think Uncle Seth was telling fibs.

Uncle Seth picked Mom up by the waist and swung her around until she laughed, but it was a nervous laugh. Mom didn't like being swung around. Not when it was nearly Halloween. The neighbor made a face. Alice thought it was maybe because the neighbor thought grown-ups shouldn't swing other grown-ups around, or maybe it was because Uncle Seth had tattoos on his arms and Mom's hair was bright pink.

Uncle Seth had blond hair like Alice's. Dad had brown hair like Cara's. Nobody but Mom had hair that was pink.

Nana and Granddad Morris lived right next door to a park that had a big hill with a patch of nettles at the bottom and a stream that you could walk across and only get your knee socks wet. Alice had white knee socks with holes in the shapes of little flowers all the way up. Cara's knee socks were blue and they were always around her ankles.

Darren shouted the dares: "Dare you to roll down the hill and jump across the stream."

Darren rolled down the hill first, then one of his sisters, then one of the other boys on the estate.

When it was Alice's turn, she could hear Mom shouting, "Alice, no!" and Dad saying, "It's okay, Melanie, it's just a bit of grass," and Nana Morris saying, "Oh, is that the telephone? Be right back, Imelda."

Darren's sister was the first to jump across the stream. Quickly, before Darren could show her how much braver he was, Alice ran and jumped across before him.

When she landed, her feet fell on a big clump of grass and one of her ankles twisted, and suddenly she lost her balance and fell straight into the stream. Cara ran over to help her, but she fell too, right into the patch of nettles. Cara burst into tears.

For the first time ever, nobody came. The grown-ups had all gone inside. Alice got out of the water and went over to Cara. Crying and itching and scratched and wet, they limped back to Nana and Granddad Morris's house together.

Everyone was sitting on the couches. Nana was holding the phone and Uncle Seth was reaching out to her and Mom had her face in her hands and Dad had his arms around her.

"What's so funny?" Cara asked. But Alice knew that Mom wasn't laughing. Her hands were shaking and she looked like a broken bird. Uncle Seth's broad shoulders were shaking and he looked like a big blond bear. Dad glanced up and he shook his head.

It was Dad, not Mom, who patched Alice and Cara up and dried them off. It was Dad who told them that Granddad Morris had gone to heaven instead of coming home for tea. And *it was Dad, not Mom, who put an extra sweater on each of them and told them to sit in the front room and watch the TV like good girls and not play outside because it wasn't safe.*

Cara and Alice looked at each other. Cara's legs were itchy and red, her socks around her ankles. Alice's socks were grass-stained and wet. Granddad Morris had gone to heaven and it wasn't safe to play outside.

4

My mother spends the rest of the night pulling down every shelf in the house, and none of us get much sleep. At three in the morning, when the whirring of the electric screwdriver is setting everyone's teeth on edge, Alice comes into my room.

"Are you sleeping?" she asks.

"No. Who could, with that racket?"

"I've asked her to stop, but she's got that look about her—you know the one."

I nod. I know the one.

"I'm worried about her, Cara." Alice perches on the side of my bed. I move my legs to make room for her. When she lies down, her hair tickles my bare arms. "I'm worried about all of us." Alice has the same sad smile as my mother's. It pulls down at the edges. I want to tell her I'm worried about all of us too, but for some reason I feel like I should be the one comforting her. She so rarely talks about things like this. Of course, that just makes me even more worried.

"I'm sorry about the bookshelf," she says after a pause.

"I'm fine, really." The drilling from downstairs is buzzing in my brain. "It's the accident season. I always expect a few bruises." I wonder if Alice will get annoyed at me for mentioning the accidents like she did with Sam. I also kind of wonder why the thought of them makes her so angry, but I'm afraid to ask. It's strange enough that she's talking about them to me now, however indirectly.

Alice opens her mouth to speak but then shuts it again. She shakes her head. "Still," she says finally, "I'm sorry." She sighs and rests her head on the pillow.

I give Alice an awkward sideways-lying-down hug. Then I reach over to my bedside table and pick up my phone. Quickly, so I don't have time to persuade myself not to, I show Alice my pictures.

Still lying down, she swipes through a few of them. "Nice," she says. She tucks her hair behind her ears and looks through more. She gives a little laugh. "I remember this one. And this—wow, you and Sam look so young. When was this taken? And more importantly, what's with my outfit? Are those *Crocs*? Ugh. What was I thinking?"

I frown. "Alice," I say. "Look closer. Look who's in all of them."

"Who?" Alice tilts the phone and looks closer.

50

"Elsie."

"Elsie?"

"*Elsie.*" I put more emphasis on the word. It isn't exactly a common name. "Elsie . . ." I rack my brains for her last name. "Elsie . . . Murphy? Maguire? It'll come back to me. We were friends for a while, after Dad died."

Again, I feel a quick rush of shame at how much I've forgotten about her. Her last name is on the tip of my tongue. "Elsie," I say again to Alice. "That Elsie." I point to the picture on the phone. It was taken on a school tour of Kilmainham Gaol in Dublin two years ago. Sam and I are posing in the center of the frame and Elsie (identifiable by the sleeve of her sweater) is reading a plaque by the door of the cell.

"Where?" says Alice, shaking her head. "I just see you and Sam."

I point at Elsie's elbow. "There. And she's in all of them." I scroll through the pictures, pointing out the Elsie in every one. After a few minutes of silence, Alice takes the phone from me, scrolls back, and points to the one in Kilmainham again.

"How do you know that's Elsie?" she asks.

"That's her elbow."

"How do you know it's her elbow?"

"Look." I point. "It's clearly her sweater."

Alice gives me an exasperated look. "Cara, that could be anybody's sweater."

"How many people over the age of five do you know who wear big ugly hand-knitted sweaters?" It does look hand-knitted, probably with more love than skill. It's a bland off-white color, and bobbly.

"Okay," I say, swiping to another picture. "What about this one?" It's a picture of a house party we went to this summer after having begged Alice to persuade her friends to invite us. Alice peers at the photo. "That is *definitely* Elsie's hair," I say.

Alice shakes her head. "It's frizzy brown hair. Every second girl in this country has frizzy brown hair. *You* have frizzy brown hair."

"Not like this—not this length and in this braid and this . . . mousy. My hair's not mousy."

"Okay," Alice says. "I'm sorry. I didn't mean to insult your hair. You have very un-mousy hair."

"This isn't about my hair!" I exclaim. "It's about Elsie being in all my pictures. It's about her following me—or—or—or weird coincidences—or me going a little crazy, which apparently is the option you're choosing to go with right now."

Alice smiles fondly at me. "I don't think you're crazy, Cara. I think you've always had a big imagination, and there's nothing wrong with that." I roll my eyes. Her tone is slightly patronizing for my liking. "And," she continues with a little laugh, "I think you hang around with Bea Kivlan a bit too much. But there's nothing wrong with that either."

"You're not—"

"I think," Alice goes on as if I haven't spoken, "that there's a rational explanation for everything. Elsie goes to the same school as us, and lives in the same town, which, you may have noticed, isn't exactly a bustling metropolis. It stands to reason she'd be in a bunch of your photos."

"*All* my photos," I correct her.

"She is immediately recognizable in *some* of your photos."

I flop my head back on the bed, just about ready to give up on the argument.

"But if you really think she might be following you," Alice goes on, "why don't you just ask her?"

I huff my breath out to the clouds on the ceiling. "Because she wasn't in school today."

Alice pulls herself up off my bed, wincing at the pain from her bruises. They almost match up with where I can feel mine blooming, except the one on her face. She has taken off her makeup for bed and the bruise looks like the night sky, only angrier. "So just ask her about it tomorrow." She gives a little laugh and goes back into her bedroom, as if everything in her world is as simple as that.

***

When I sleep that night, I dream about the kids I thought I saw inside the train. The girl dressed like a forest, the tall, scaly-skinned mermaid girl, the flickering ghost boy, and the tiny Converse-wearing fairy girl. But in my dream those aren't costumes, that's their skin. They are taking the train to a party in a strange old house where all the changelings go on Halloween. The littlest girl, the one with the wings, holds out the invitation. It asks guests to come as themselves, to discard their everyday disguises. So the fairy girl lets out her wings, the tree girl removes her human mask and becomes brittle as old bark, covered in leaves. The mermaid girl uncovers her gills and lets her scales catch the light, and the boy in the black-and-white suit begins to flicker like a silent-film reel.

The old house they're going to is full of people who aren't really people. There are animals with human eyes who stand on two legs, there are lizard-things as big as horses, there are flickering ghosts and tiny pixies and tall, willowy fairies and tufty-haired goblins. There are giants crouching through doorways and there are strange fish creatures come in from the sea. Rooms and rooms filled with creatures who have taken off their costumes and look inhuman but also somehow seem so much more human than any of us ever will.

***

Sam and I have made plans to go shopping in Galway the next morning. I want to ask Alice if she'll come too because I kind of like that she hung out with us yesterday, but she has already left for Nick's house when I get up. Bea, who would usually join us, is spending the weekend with her grandparents in Ballina. Sam and I take the bus into the city alone.

The city center is crowded and noisy, but these aren't three-a.m. drilling noises or falling-down-the-stairs noises or the horrible gasp-scream sounds Alice sometimes lets out in her sleep that make me feel like I've been plunged in a bathtub full of ice water. These are whole-world noises. There are people talking and children crying and dogs barking and feet clattering on cobblestones and street performers singing and market stallholders haggling, and everything's so alive it hurts, almost.

After the whispers and stares at school and the padded corners of the house, this place is a different world. Its brightness and noise make a lump rise in my throat. There are sharp edges everywhere here, and so many people; there is traffic and there are strangers, there are animals and there is uneven ground, but walking down from the bus station with Sam by my side and the whole world real around me, I feel safer than I have in weeks.

On the pedestrian cobblestone streets, people are eating under parasols outside bars as if it is still summer, preferably in a Mediterranean country. It is certainly strangely warm for October, but the tourists are all wearing their coats. The bright-colored buildings are brighter than ever in the startling light that only happens in a summery autumn when the trees are on fire and the air is too clear and the warmth makes mirrors of every smooth surface.

Sam and I spend the better part of an hour in Charlie Byrne's bookshop, where I find a used copy of *The Secret Garden* and a volume of Sylvia Plath's poetry. Sam flicks through the secondhand graphic novel section, but all the good titles have already been bought. Instead, he buys a heavily underlined copy of *On the Road* and a book about Hitchcock films that is missing its cover.

Afterward, bags of books in hand, we wind around crowds of tourists outside souvenir shops and get ice cream at the tiny little shop on the corner. My mother texts us both every half an hour to make sure we're okay. If we don't answer immediately, she calls. During the accident season, we know to answer immediately.

After answering my mother's fifth text, Sam tells me that last night he dreamed about an old farmhouse in the middle of the country and how he knew it was empty but he kept seeing all these faces in the windows. I tell him about the kids I thought I saw in our reflection in the train window, and about my dream of the changeling siblings.

"Ghost trains and changelings," he tells me. "Spooky dreams. It's coming up to Halloween."

We get separated by a large family all walking together down the middle of the road and come together again on the other side. The laces of Sam's boots are a million years too long and he has wound them around his ankles for safekeeping, but they are coming loose and trail on the ground as he walks. I keep worrying he'll trip and fall.

"I didn't realize," I say, counting the days. "It's in six days." Then, remembering my dream, and what Bea said yesterday about us getting our priorities straight, I suddenly have an idea. It lands fully formed in the palm of my hand.

"We should have a party," I say to Sam.

"A Halloween party?"

"Yeah."

"What," Sam says, "you, me, and Bea?"

"No." I narrow my eyes at him. "A *real* party. Like the ones we went to with Alice this summer. Like the ones Toby Healy and that crowd are always talking about. We should have a party like that."

Sam bites off the bottom of his cone and sucks the ice cream through it. "No one would come if we threw a party," he says. "It'd end up just being you, me, and Bea."

"Not necessarily." I think of Alice smoking with us behind the soccer field. "It's like Bea said. People need a distraction from study and mock exams and college applications. I know a couple of people in our year who'd go. And if we can get Alice to invite her friends, who'd then invite *their* friends, we could get a really good crowd."

We cross the bridge at Spanish Arch and make our way down to the pier. Sam squints at me, the sun reflected on the water blinding us both. "Not that I'm against the idea," he says, "but wouldn't most people already have parties to go to? Like you said, Halloween's six days away."

But the idea is growing in my head like a balloon. "Not if ours was better," I say, and I can hear the excitement building in my voice. "Not if we make it a story."

"A story?"

"Like in my dream," I explain. "Where everybody takes off their human masks and comes as who they really are. So, it's a costume party, but you have to come as what you feel like on the inside. All our demons, right there in the open." I point my melting ice-cream cone at him. "Now, doesn't *that* sound better than any old house party?"

Sam smiles, but I can tell he's not convinced. "It does, yeah, but—"

"And we can make fancy invitations, like for a ball. We can explain that people are invited to take off their human disguises and come as their true selves behind the human mask." I stop and grab Sam's arm. "A masquerade! We swap our human masks for masks that represent our true selves! Who'd go to some stupid Halloween party when they could come to the changelings' masquerade?"

Sam laughs and covers my hand with one of his. "Well, *I'd* definitely go to a party like that."

"Right?" I practically bounce on the spot, close enough to step on Sam's toes. "And we could do it, we *could*. If Alice can persuade her friends—"

"If we can persuade Alice . . ."

I shrug and we walk on. "I think she might like the idea." I picture Alice's bruised face at lunchtime yesterday. Alice avoiding her friends. I pause for a second to get my thoughts in order. "I think she'd be happy to have people talking about something other than our accidents for once," I say softly.

Sam has heard me; he nods thoughtfully. Then a glint comes into his eyes. "And," he says as we finish our ice creams and wipe our sticky hands with paper napkins, "maybe Nick would let us have it at his place."

"Yes!" I squeal. "Sam, you're a genius."

Nick and his four band mates rent a house in a development at the edge of town. Most of the houses in the development were never bought or lived in, so he has very few neighbors to object to them holding band practice until four in the morning or throwing wild parties on weekdays. And Halloween falls on a Friday this year. My mother would never have to know.

"I know, I know," Sam says modestly. "What can I say? I'm brilliant."

He links arms with me and we cross the road to avoid a gaggle of angry-looking swans. The sails of the ships in the mouth of the river clink softly in the breeze. When we reach the end of the pier, there are children drawing hopscotch squares on the ground in colored chalk. In the sky the seagulls swirl, and on every bench there seems to be a couple kissing. We walk out to the edge of the water and sit on the stone wall facing the wide Atlantic and Sam whistles one of Bea's sea shanties—a particularly rude drinking song—and I laugh and call him a drunken sailor.

"I should buy myself a better hat," Sam says, touching the top of his bare head as if there is a hat there already. There would be if my mother had seen us leave this morning; as it is, we are already bundled up too warmly for the unseasonable weather with our big boots, our scarves, and second sweaters. But it's hard to get my mother's voice out of my head even when she isn't there; if I don't wear enough layers, I can almost hear her saying, *Take another sweater, would you, Cara? You'll catch your death out there.*

"That's true," I say to Sam. "Any good sailor needs a proper sailor hat." I run my fingers horizontally across the chest of my yellow sweater. My hand bumps over the embroidered sunflower. "D'you like my stripy sailor T-shirt?"

"It's the stripiest T-shirt on the seven seas." Sam draws more invisible stripes on the back of my sweater. Even under all my layers I feel his fingertips tickle my shoulder blades. I find myself wanting to lean in toward his touch.

"We should find ourselves some wenches," I tell him. "No sailor worth his salt makes port without finding wenches."

Sam moves his hand from my shoulder down to the ground behind me. He says, "There's only one wench I want," and then he starts to hum another one of Bea's sea shanties, leaning back on his elbows and singing it to the sky. I stay sitting up, face to the sea.

This is the first Sam's mentioned about a girl in a long time, and I've been sort of secretly glad because I like the way our trio is at the moment and wouldn't want anything complicating that. And then my mind registers that Sam is singing one of Bea's songs. I think: *Bea? He likes Bea?* and I don't know why, but suddenly the day seems a little cold. I hug my arms to my chest.

"You cold?" Sam asks me. "Because I bet it's a lot colder down there." He points down at the water and moves as if he's about to push me in.

I make a face and bump my shoulder with his, and we mime pushing each other into the water for a while, and I try not to focus on the thought of his perfect scratchy voice singing Bea's songs. I try not to think about why I'm trying not to think about it.

When we make our way back to the bus station, the roads are more crowded. In front of a music shop, a woman is making her small dog jump and turn and even backflip in time with a raggedy old waltz. A crowd of tourists and families stand around and clap. The little dog is dressed as a Pierrot clown, black and white and tear-stained. His ruff looks uncomfortable.

Because I am still looking behind me as Sam pulls me forward through the crowd, I walk right into someone. The someone is tall and makes a hollow ringing noise when I bump into his chest. I make to stop, meaning to apologize, but Sam is pushing quickly through the crowd, his hand hooked under my elbow. I twist out of Sam's grip and turn around to look back at the man. For a few seconds I think he has disappeared, but then I see his reflection in the window of the shop beside me. He looks like one of the human statues that busk in the city, but this isn't one I've ever seen before. He is dressed a little like the Tin Man in *The Wizard of Oz*. His suit is spray-painted silver, and so are his shoes, his hat, and even his skin. I take a few steps forward toward the window, noticing the strangest details reflected in the glass. The metal man's costume is flawless. He seems to be wearing silver nail polish on his fingernails and looks like he has painted the most realistic little hinges at each of his joints. There is something about him that seems strangely familiar. I search through my handbag for a few coins to throw in the box at his feet, but when I turn from the window, there is no one there. I shiver and quickly walk away.

When we are halfway to the bus station, Sam notices the sign for a party shop down a little alley and he takes me by the elbow and pulls me away from the main road.

"Sammy, we'll miss our bus."

"There'll be another bus," he says. "Let's go find things for the party."

Neither of us has ever noticed this place before. The

shop front is grimy and plain, but the door is wide open. I follow Sam through.

Inside, it's like a little child's dream has exploded. There are clown wigs and hula hoops, bats and spiders and scrunched-up rubber witch masks; there are Santa Clauses and Easter Bunnies and April Fools' joke tricks all stacked haphazardly together so that it looks like the whole year just dumped all its holidays in the one small room.

Sam rummages around gleefully. "So what would you go as?" he asks. "To the masquerade. What would your not-disguise be? The real you under the human mask?"

I shake my head and hold up what looks eerily like a real stuffed crow. "A taxidermist?"

"Now that's a creepy costume."

There doesn't seem to be a shop owner or anyone around, but even so I come up close to Sam and whisper when I say that this is the strangest shop I've ever seen. Sam is sorting through a bucket of eyeballs. "Everything looks too real." Even the rubbery witch mask, when I take it down from its shelf, feels a little too much like human skin. I put it back quickly and wipe my hands on my sweater.

Sam thinks the shop is a treasure trove. "Here," he says, and hands me a pair of wings. It is like somebody stretched a butterfly so it was as tall as a person, and then cut off its wings. I am used to the little gauze-and-wire contraptions you buy in toy shops or discount stores; the ones with the elastic straps that cut into your armpits. But these wings attach to the back of your dress (they are the type of accessory that would only ever be worn with a dress, I imagine) and they feel soft and supple, almost leathery, and, like everything else in the shop, just a little too real for comfort.

"They're beautiful," I say to Sam, and we both stand admiring the wings. They are a strange bluish-brownish-green color that shifts when I move, as if it's reacting to the light. After a moment I realize why I recognize this: The wings are the exact color of Sam's eyes. I put them down and step away. I say to Sam, "I'm not sure I like it here."

"Don't be such a scaredy-cat," he says, and waggles a toy black cat in front of my face. "I'm getting you those wings. You can be like the fairy girl in your dream."

Only a little reluctant, I pick up the wings again. I think of the fairy girl in her silver Converse. I have a similar pair of shoes at home. "I do like them . . ." I say hesitantly. Sam has his back turned. When he faces me again, he is holding a top hat and a bow tie.

"What is this place?" I ask him. Sam shakes his head. Behind him, hanging on the wall as if it's being worn by the Invisible Man, is an old, moth-holed suit jacket, pinstripe trousers attached to black braces, and a pair of bright white spats. When I point them out to Sam, his eyes gleam.

"Vaudeville zombie?" he suggests.

I shake my head. "Flickering silent-film ghost guy."

When he understands that I mean the changeling boy in my dream, he sort of nods in wonder. "This isn't a costume shop, I don't think," he says. "It's a magic shop."

I turn around in circles, trying to find a salesperson amid the mess. "A magical shop," Sam amends.

When I spot what looks like an old-fashioned grocery-store cash register on a table at the far end of the shop, an old woman appears from behind a starry curtain. Her hair is gray and worn in braids that wind around her head like in those medieval paintings and her body is draped in multicolored scarves. Behind me, Sam mutters something that sounds like "Of course," which I think means that this lady fits in with her shop perfectly.

We make our way past the shelves and bins and baskets toward her. Beside the table with the cash register on it, there is a rack of dresses. One of them immediately catches my eye. It's green and brown and wet-looking; it seems to be made out of seaweed and fishing nets. Next to it is a dress that looks like it's been stitched together from moss and leaves. My skin prickles. I take both dresses off the rack and silently hold them out for Sam to see.

I know he can't possibly be thinking of the other changeling girls I dreamed of, but he thinks of Bea and Alice immediately.

"For Alice and Bea?" he says. "Perfect!"

Sam takes the dresses off me and hands them to the lady

along with the wings, the jacket, the pinstripe trousers, the braces, the top hat, and even the spats. The lady says nothing as she folds everything up and puts it in two big paper bags. She punches some buttons in the old cash register and writes a price on a piece of paper. As we leave the shop, she smiles and smiles. I turn around as we walk away to see the name of the shop to remember for later, but there is no sign above the door and I can't distinguish the shop from any of the other poky little buildings on the street.

I stop in the middle of the road and quickly snap a picture with my phone. On the bus, I show the picture to Sam. We zoom the image in as far as the screen will let us, until we can finally make out a mannequin in a wizard's robe in one of the windows on the street.

"There it is." Sam points at the purple starry fabric.

I am more interested in the woman with the multicolored scarves, who is standing at the window looking straight at me. Standing behind her, almost in shadow but not quite, is someone else. Wordlessly, I point the figure out to Sam. It is blurry but unmistakable. It's Elsie.

5

Before class on Monday morning, we go to the library. I have the picture of the costume shop saved on my phone and I want to see what Elsie has to say about it. I told Bea all about it over the phone yesterday, and on our way through the school she is uncharacteristically quiet.

In the library, there is a small crowd at the secrets booth. This happens sometimes, after a particularly boisterous senior party (when the booth becomes a new confessional for the heartsick and the lovelorn, the hungover and the lost) or whenever a local paper runs a piece on the booth ("Online Art Collective Influences Student-Run Secrets Project," or "Connecting Through the Unsaid: Teenagers, Secrets, and Art"). When the crowd disperses, Bea and I come forward, but just like on Friday, Elsie isn't at her seat in front of the antique typewriter.

"Where's Elsie?" I ask the girl sitting in Elsie's place. Her name is Kim Brennan and she's a friend of Alice's, with straight, shiny hair and perfectly applied eyeliner. I'm vaguely surprised to see her here; Alice's friends aren't usually the arty library types.

"Who?" Kim asks.

"Elsie. The girl who's usually at the booth?"

"Oh." Kim shrugs. "I dunno."

"But she's always here," says Bea.

"Not today," says Kim. "Clearly."

"Well, do you know where she is?"

Kim shakes her head.

"Well, did she say anything to you when she left you with the booth?"

Kim starts to twist her hair into a braid. "Ms. Byrne's the one who asked me to look after the booth today. I guess you could ask her." She ties the braid off with a frayed elastic. It slips down her hair the moment her hands leave it. "Although you mightn't get a straight answer. I don't think she knows who's supposed to be doing this." She gestures vaguely at the secrets box. "For a teacher, she's kind of a weirdo."

Bea puts her elbows on the desk in front of Kim and assumes her best scary-crone face. "Aren't we all?" she breathes. I'm constantly amazed by how Bea just does or says whatever she feels the moment requires, but Kim doesn't seem impressed. Alice's friends aren't terribly intimidated by Bea.

"Do you want to leave a secret?" Kim asks us with a hint of impatience.

Bea shakes her head; she likes to say she has no use for secrets because she tells her whole life like a story, secrets and all. She doesn't need the anonymity of the typewriter text and the little wooden box.

I sit down in front of the typewriter and Kim puts up the folders that act as privacy shields from both her and the rest of the library. I run my fingers over the keys. The space bar is dented in the middle by so many thumbs. The secrets box sits on the floor beside me. I can spy the beginnings of one of the secrets inside through the slot on the wooden box. It says: *I cheated on my girlfriend and I don't regret it.* I can just about make out another one underneath it that says something about not believing in God. I stare at the blank sheet of paper in front of me as Bea compliments Kim on her perfectly lined cat eyes. *Do you want to leave a secret?* Kim asked, but I can't think of a single secret to leave.

I look at the typewriter and my mind is a perfect blank. I write: *I am afraid that I have no secrets.* I look over at Bea and think of Sam singing her ditty on the pier. Then I backspace to the start of the line and I type: *I am afraid of my secrets.* Then I think about the accident season and Bea's cards and Elsie's worried face in all my pictures, and I backspace again, a little bit frantically, and write: *I am afraid of everybody else's secrets.* My fingers threaten to slip into the space between the keys.

When I look up, I see that I've made a mistake: I've backspaced like on a computer, but instead of erasing my words, the typewriter has written my second sentence over the first, the third over the lot. My secret is illegible. I fold it up and put it in the box anyway.

Because I still have a few minutes before the bell rings, I leave Bea with Sam outside our English classroom and go to the art room to find Ms. Byrne, who is setting up the little studio for her first class.

"Ah, Cara," she says when I manage to catch her attention. "How is your mother?" Ms. Byrne has bought several of my mother's prints, which is the only reason she knows who I am; I did a week of art in sophomore year to see if I wanted to pursue it but dropped it quickly, much to the relief of all involved. My mother may be an artist, but I can't paint so much as a stick figure.

"Same as always," I say, trying not to think about the look on my mother's face as she pulled down shelf after shelf the other night. I shake my head and ask Ms. Byrne if she knows where Elsie is and if she will be back in school tomorrow.

"Elsie, Elsie," she says distractedly, as if she isn't sure who I'm talking about. She has her head in the storage cupboard and is rummaging around for supplies. "Here it is," she mutters, pulling out a roll of tracing paper.

"Elsie? The secrets booth?" I say to jog her memory. I

wonder if it is a characteristic of all artists to be so scatty.

"Oh, someone asked me about that the other day," she says, ducking back into the cupboard. "I put a senior in charge of it. That . . . um . . . whatshername—Kate?"

"Kim?"

"Kim, of course, sorry."

"Yeah." I bend over toward the cupboard as if that'll make her hear me better. "But it's not Kim I'm looking for, it's Elsie. She's usually the one with the booth?"

Ms. Byrne's phone rings from across the room. "Dammit," she mumbles. "Sorry, Cara, I have to take that, I'm expecting a call." She pulls a box of paints out of the cupboard with her when she stands up to answer her phone.

"Sure, but do you know if Elsie's off sick or when she'll be back?"

"Elsie?" she says, her eyebrows furrowed. "Oh, well, no, I'm afraid I don't know."

"Do you know where she lives?" I ask.

Ms. Byrne reaches her desk, still looking at me with a vaguely confused air, as if she isn't quite sure what I'm asking her. "No," she says, picking up her phone. "I don't. But I'm sure one of her friends could probably give you her address. Or her phone number."

I thank Ms. Byrne without telling her that Elsie doesn't have any friends, or a cell phone. At least, I've never seen her with one, which is unusual in a school full of surreptitious under-the-desk class-time texters and loud lunchtime music-players.

I slip into English class just as the bell rings and take my usual seat beside Bea by the window. Sam sits alone at the desk behind us.

"So?" Bea says as Mr. Connolly calls the class to order.

"Nothing." I drop my books on the desk with a dull thump. "Not a thing."

Sam leans forward so that his breath tickles my neck. "Did she at least say why she's not in?" he asks.

I half turn in my seat and spread my hands palm up. "She didn't seem to remember *who* Elsie is, let alone *where* she is." A small knot of frustration has gotten caught just below my breastbone. It feels like butterfly-nerves.

Bea is chewing on her pen. "Kim's kind of right on this one, though," she says. "Ms. Byrne is particularly spacey, you have to admit."

I purse my lips glumly. "I know. I just . . . It's stupid, you know? I haven't talked to Elsie—or even really thought about her—for years, and now there's this huge big question mark about her and *this* is when she's not around?"

"Cara," Sam says calmly, "it's been three days. Seriously. She's probably just at home with a cold."

"I know." The wedge of frustration is like a lump of bread that hasn't gone down right. What he says makes me think of Alice. *I think there's a rational explanation for everything.* "I just want to talk to her."

"So we'll talk to her tomorrow."

"Yeah, but—"

At the front of the classroom, Mr. Connolly clears his throat loudly. A few of our classmates titter. "Cara?" he says, as if he's repeating himself.

"Sorry, yes?" Louder laughter comes from the back of the class. I can feel Bea twist in her seat to glare.

Mr. Connolly sighs. "I'd like you to stay with us, please," he says wearily. "Class has started, so I expect your private conversations to stop—and will you please cease that tittering in the back, Mr. Jones. I really don't see how this is funny." Beside me, Bea turns back around with a smirk.

"Okay, Cara," says Mr. Connolly heavily with an expression that is pure, unadulterated Monday morning. "As I was saying, will you please start us off on Act Four, Scene One, and let's see what this ghost child has to tell the Thane of Cawdor about his future."

When the task of reading *Macbeth* aloud has passed along the rows of desks to Stephen Jones at the back and Mr. Connolly looks like he'd easily murder one of us for a cup of coffee, I judge it safe to lean very slightly in toward Bea. She is scribbling in a notebook and is clearly not listening to the desecration of Shakespeare's words that is happening at the back of the class.

"Did you bring in the invitations?" I ask her in an undertone.

Sam and I told Bea all about my idea for the masquerade ball over the phone yesterday, and since then it's almost all we've been able to talk about. Even Alice thinks it's a great idea, especially because Nick has said he'll let us have it at his place. The dresses Sam and I bought for her and Bea fit perfectly. When Alice tried hers on last night, she actually laughed at how perfect it was.

Sam leans forward in his seat at my words.

Mr. Connolly looks over at us sharply, so we fall silent for a few minutes while Emma McNamara stumbles over her lines. Bea quietly takes out a notebook that seems to already be entirely dedicated to the party. She flicks through pages of sketches of masks and lists of songs to put on the party mix-tape. Spooky, witchy folksongs, drowning sailor ditties, black cat and whiskey moon waltzes. She takes out a stack of fancy lacy invitations she has clearly made herself.

"*You are cordially invited to the Black Cat and Whiskey Moon Masquerade Ball*," she reads reverently. "All great parties should be named."

Sam reaches forward and tussles Bea's already-messy hair. "It's perfect," he says.

The smile he gives her leaves a bitter taste in my mouth.

***

Before our last class, Sam reminds me that we've a note from my mother excusing us from chemistry experiments this month. The chemistry teacher, Mrs. Delaney, shakes her head but hands the note back to Sam and lets us go, leaving Bea sitting in front of a line of Bunsen burners emitting long pale flames.

Sam caught his finger in a locker door this morning. The nail is mottled and blue. I press the heel of my hand hard into the bruises on the side of my left arm. Pain glows like a flare. As we walk down the road toward the river, Sam complains halfheartedly about getting bad marks on our experiments this term, but I am secretly glad to be away from unstable chemicals and open flames.

When we're halfway home I lose my footing and almost slip, but Sam takes my hand and steadies me. His bandaged finger feels rougher, slightly swollen still from where the locker door caught it. Suddenly I think of the Elsie doll in the mousetrap.

"I want to show you something," I say to Sam, and I pull on his arm and we turn around and go back along the river toward the town, to the big stone bridge that people throw their fishing lines off of in summer. There is a family with two small children crossing it from the other side. The children's bags are almost as big as they are, but the kids run like they weigh nothing at all.

"Why aren't we crossing at our bridge?" Sam asks me.

"It collapsed," I say simply. Sam just stares. We cross the bridge and walk along the bank on the opposite side of the river.

"And you were nowhere near it at the time of the collapse, right?" Sam says with a pained expression.

I wince. "I was kind of on it," I admit. "Don't tell Mom."

Sam stops for a second, and closes his eyes.

"I'm fine," I tell him, and I pull on his elbow to lead him toward the woods.

Sam walks on, but his expression is strange. He says something too low for me to hear. Then he clears his throat. "So," he says at normal volume, "where are we going?"

I tell him about the mousetrap while we walk; about the doll that looked just like Elsie, which had been set like bait in the trap.

"I know it sounds crazy, but I think she put it there herself. I just don't understand why."

Sam isn't looking at me like I'm crazy, which is reassuring. He just says, "Show me," so I point through the trees to the clearing and tell him it's right up ahead.

When we come to the clearing, we both stop and stare.

"Was it like this when you came here the last time?" Sam whispers.

"No," I whisper back. I'm not sure why we're whispering, but it feels appropriate. All around the clearing, hanging from the branches of every tree, is a flock of dream catchers, the kind you can get at the Saturday market in Galway: colorful webbed circles hung with little beads and feathers. There are maybe fifty of them, all different shapes and colors, just hanging there at head height.

"What is this place?" Sam reaches up as if to touch one of the dream catchers but then drops his hand.

I feel a lump forming in my throat. I can hardly breathe past it. My heart thuds in my chest and goose bumps prick up along my arms. "Elsie did this." I turn around and around so that the trees revolve about me, and the dream catchers blur. I can feel my heart beat in my ears.

"But why?"

"I don't know." I stop spinning and close my eyes. It takes a few seconds for my balance to steady, for my breaths to slow, for my heart to beat normally again. I take Sam by the hand and lead him over to the little bush that hid the mousetrap. When I carefully part the branches, we can see it clearly: an ordinary mousetrap, wood and wire, with a tiny little doll sitting on top of it.

Sam laughs, but I recognize it as disbelief rather than humor. "Who *is* she?"

There is a strange sinking feeling in the bottom of my heart. I say it again. "I don't know."

6

Elsie has disappeared.

I don't know how I know this, but it's something I'm almost certain of, and not just because she isn't in school on Tuesday morning either. Alice says she's probably home sick or gone visiting relatives, but every time I look for her in the library and see Kim at the secrets booth, something twists inside me and tells me she's never coming back.

Halfway through Irish class, Alice texts to tell me that almost all her friends have said they're coming to the Black Cat and Whiskey Moon Ball. *They loved the invitations,* she says. *Stop obsessing about Elsie and concentrate on the party.*

Alice thinks I'm being dramatic. Maybe before last week Sam would have thought so too, but something about looking through my pictures and seeing the dream catchers in the clearing has made him thoughtful. He believes me.

There was never any question of Bea not believing me. In French we sit at the very back of the classroom and Bea takes out her cards. Mrs. McCarthy has handed out written comprehension worksheets and is correcting last night's homework at her desk. All around us people whisper, pages turn, pens scratch on the worksheets or on notes that'll pass from hand to hand like a chain letter across the room to the person they're intended for, music hums from earphones hidden behind hair, feet tap against desks, chairs are swung back on, their legs squeaking across the floor.

"*Quietly,* please," Mrs. McCarthy says without looking up from her desk. The volume in the room lowers a fraction.

Bea spreads her cards out on the table. We are asking them about Elsie, pausing every few minutes to scribble down an answer in our worksheets.

"Who is she, where is she, what does she want?" Bea mutters as she places each card on the table with a soft *ffp* noise.

"And what does she have to do with us?" I add in a whisper, looking up at the teacher every once in a while to make sure she's still busy with the homework. *Philippe préfère faire du vélo que la voiture parce que cela est mauvais pour l'environnement,* I write absentmindedly.

"Where does she fit into our story?" Bea asks the cards softly. She turns them over one by one. Then she is quiet.

"What does it say?" Sam nods down at the cards.

"It says," says Bea slowly, "to trust."

"To trust Elsie?" Abandoning my worksheet, I crane my neck to see the cards the right way up from Bea's side of the table.

"To trust Elsie, to trust ourselves, to trust each other." She rests her chin in the palms of her hands, her fingers just brushing her cheeks. "She has been through something—something she can't get over. She needs us to help her find her way home."

"I said *quietly,*" Mrs. McCarthy calls suddenly from the front of the room. Bea quickly covers her cards with a folder, but Mrs. McCarthy still hasn't looked up.

"But why is she in all my pictures?" I hiss to Bea. "Is she following us?"

Bea shakes her head. "I don't know. See this card?" She's pointing to a card with ten stars shining over a castle. "Ten of coins. It's saying she's like a mirror."

"A mirror? A mirror of what?"

Bea cocks her head to one side, then shakes it so that her hair falls almost to her shoulder. "I don't know," she says again. I can tell it's hard for her to admit.

"Okay, class," says Mrs. McCarthy, getting up from her chair. "Hand your worksheets up to the front of the room when you're ready and take out your textbooks."

I've only answered every second question, probably badly, but I hand my worksheet to the girl in front of me anyway. "So where is she?" I ask Bea.

Bea taps a card with four sticks stuck in the ground in a square. "At home, or wherever she feels that home is."

Sam looks around the crowded classroom. Worksheets flutter from hand to hand to the front of the room. People whisper as they take out their books. The morning sun streaks in through the dirty windows. "Not here, that's for sure."

"So what do we do?" I ask. Mrs. McCarthy calls the class back to order and starts telling us which page to turn to, but her words hardly register.

Bea turns a card to face me. It has three stars hung above an archway. "Three of coins," she says. She points to herself, to Sam, and to me, then to the three stars on the card. She says, "We work together, we trust each other. We find her."

"And how exactly," says Sam, "do we go about doing that?"

Bea's eyes glitter like the sea. "I have an idea."

Mrs. McCarthy's voice cuts loudly through her words. "Miss Morris," she says to me. "Mr. Fagan. If Miss Kivlan is distracting you with her magic spells, you can sit up at the front of the class."

Bea quickly hides her cards, but half the class has already turned around to laugh and stare.

"Sorry, Mrs. McCarthy," we mumble.

Mrs. McCarthy turns to Bea. "Miss Kivlan," she says. "We are not in Hogwarts, we are in fifth-year French. So you can now lead the class in a chant about irregular verbs."

The entire class starts to laugh. It might be my imagination, but the laughter seems less mean today than it usually does. Maybe the idea of magic spells is more appealing when the people doing them have invited everyone to a Halloween ball along with the most popular seniors. Bea gives me a small smile as she opens her book.

***

After all our classes are over, we sit out on the steps of the main building and wait for the school to empty. Cars drive into the parking lot and drive back out (our mother's is not one of them; she is working late at the studio but calls every half hour to make sure we are all well wrapped up, protected, not jumping in rivers or running with scissors). People walk home in twos and threes. Outside, on the road, the buses chugga-chug, waiting for everybody to come aboard. Teachers' heels clatter past. Little brothers and sisters shout, dogs bark, the wind whistles. Our extended Indian summer is finally coming to a close.

While we wait, we are joined by Alice and Kim and some of Alice's friends: Niamh; her boyfriend, Joe; his brother Martin, who is in our year; and Carl Gallagher, who is Toby Healy's obnoxious best friend. Carl sits up on the top step, very obviously close to Bea, but she doesn't seem to notice. I can't help but think that nobody sits that close to me. I look over at Sam, who is on the other side of Bea. Then I look down at my hands.

Everybody is talking about the Black Cat and Whiskey Moon Masquerade Ball. It's the only reason Alice's friends are sitting with us in the first place, I think, but I like that they're sitting with us at all.

"You got some Metallica on that playlist?" Carl is asking Bea. "You need some old-school stuff for a Halloween mix. Pink Floyd? Guns N' Roses? Here, let me play a couple of songs I think you'll like."

Joe, who doesn't look particularly impressed at Carl's sudden interest in Bea, is asking Alice about liquor. "Do you think Nick could do a beer run for us before the party? I mean, I have a fake ID, but it'd be cool if he could get it for us—you never know when you'll run into a neighbor at the liquor store, you know?"

Before Alice can answer, though, her phone rings.

"Speak of the devil," Joe says.

While Alice walks away to talk with Nick on the phone, Niamh and Kim discuss costumes. "I heard Katie Donoghue's going as a bunny. Like, in a headband with ears and a fluffy tail."

Kim snorts. "A bunny. To a masquerade. Does she not get that this *isn't* just some stupid old Halloween party? That's the whole point."

"I know, right?"

Bea has taken out her ukulele and is singing softly. A train trundles by on the tracks at the far end of the school. Little by little the parking lot empties. Soon only the last few stragglers, the janitors, the principal and her office staff, and the few pupils and teachers who stay around for detention or supervised study are left on the school grounds.

"So, hey," says Carl, standing up to leave, "we're heading to this open mic thing in the bar at the university. Want to pretend to be college students for the evening?"

"It'll be great," says Martin. "We'll sit around and talk about philosophy lectures—"

"It's easy to do," Joe cuts in. "Just make shit up and sound pretentious."

"And drink a few beers, play some songs. You guys in?"

"Sounds great," Sam says. He turns to us. "Melanie's staying late at the studio, right? We can get a lift home with her."

I give Sam a look that tries to convey the sense of *Remember the plan?* but I can't fault him for wanting to go hang out with the popular guys for the evening.

"Bea and I have . . . some stuff to do," I say vaguely. Bea nods and Carl looks slightly disappointed. "Definitely next time, though."

"More spells to cast?" says Martin, who is in our French class. He waves his arms as if brandishing a magic wand, but his smile is playful.

"That's right," says Bea with a wicked grin. "Lots of dancing naked around bonfires and sacrificing virgins. Would you like to volunteer?"

Martin's expression flickers. "Next time, maybe," he

says, only slightly frostily. I give Bea a kick. She spreads her hands to me as if to say *What?*

Alice tut-tuts. "Bea, play nice with the other children," she says, and Martin and Joe laugh. Bea winks at Alice with a shake of her curls.

"Okay," Alice says, looking at her phone. "I'm meeting Nick in the city in an hour anyway, so I'll get the bus with you."

"See you two later." Sam gives me and Bea a one-armed hug good-bye and follows Alice and her friends to the bus stop.

I stare after them until Bea pulls me up. I sigh. "We had better find what we're looking for," I say. "And it had better be worth missing *that*."

Bea and I sneak back into the main building. Bea sticks her head up to see through the mottled glass window in the top of the door to one of the classrooms that is used for super-vised study. She makes a little whistling noise and quickly ducks her head back down. We giggle and run down the corridor to hide around the corner. A few minutes later, Toby Healy comes out of the classroom.

As well as being quite possibly the prettiest boy in school, Toby is also the son of the secretary. Alice has some-how managed to persuade him to steal his mother's keys to the office for us. I don't know how she did it; Toby is hardly the rule-breaking type.

When he hurries toward us, I get a butterfly-fluttery sense of nervousness and excitement that is either because we're about to break into the secretary's office, or because Toby is one of those guys who looks more like a character in a film than a real boy. And a little voice in the back of my mind wonders if maybe, just maybe, he might be helping us because he's slightly interested in me. I've certainly noticed him smiling and saying hi to me in the halls lately, although maybe that's just because I'm Alice's sister.

Toby looks back over his shoulder and turns the corner to join us. "Right," he says. "Mrs. Delaney thinks I've gone to the bathroom, so I better be quick." He fishes a set of keys out of his jacket's inside pocket. He holds them out but stops before Bea can grab them. "What do you want these for, anyway?"

"Never you mind," says Bea.

Toby gives her a look. "I could get into a shitload of trouble over this—you know that, right?"

Bea rolls her eyes. "Don't be dramatic," she says, which I think is kind of funny coming from Bea. Toby mutters something that sounds a lot like *witch*.

"We're just looking for someone's phone number, that's all," I cut in quickly.

"Does it have anything to do with the masquerade ball? I'm really looking forward to Friday."

I feel a little flustered all of a sudden. I knew Alice had invited her friends, but I didn't know that Toby Healy was actually going to come.

"Yes," says Bea emphatically. "It's very important."

Toby looks curious but he doesn't ask any more questions. "Cool," is all he says. He hands me the set of keys, pointing out the one that opens the office. "Slip it in my locker when you're finished," he says. "It's number 503 outside Mr. Connolly's class." Then he flashes us a grin, says, "See you there, then," and winks at me before he hurries away. I exchange a look with Bea, who barely suppresses a smile as I hand her the key to fit into the lock.

We try to be in and out of the office lickety-split, like lightning. The filing cabinets squeak and we muffle our laughter. Bea whispers that we're lucky our school still lives in the Stone Age, that most schools' files are on computer, password-protected, but here they're kept in cardboard files in cabinets that don't lock. This is one of the good things about living in a tiny speck of a town in Middle of Nowhere, County Mayo: We haven't all quite caught up with the twenty-first century yet.

"What's her last name again?" Bea asks, thumbing through the alphabetical files.

I open my mouth to answer, then frown. "I've been blanking on it for the last few days," I say. "I *know* I know it." I rub my forehead with exasperation. "Try under *M*?"

Bea shuffles through a few files before pulling one out triumphantly. "Got it!"

Elsie's file has a tea stain on it, straight across the last name. The cardboard is stuck together—the tea, I imagine, was milky and sugary, turned to syrup when it dried—but the information we want is on the front cover. Bea jots down an address and a phone number in her homework notebook and we hightail it out of the office like bandits, running low under the classroom windows.

Once we've sped out of the main building, through the parking lot and out of the school, we screech and whoop in triumph. We skip and jump along the grassy side of the main road, and once we hit the smaller country road out of town, we spread our arms and spin like tops. Our uniform skirts swish out like tartan bells.

When we are properly breathless we throw ourselves down by the side of the road near the river and Bea pulls out Elsie's phone number. Without saying anything, she hands it to me and I take out my phone and dial the number. Everything goes very quiet. Above us the trees rustle and the birds chirp. In the field, the sheep bleat. The air smells a little like rain. I put the phone to my ear and hold my breath. The call takes a moment to go through, then my phone makes a sad little *beep beep beep* noise and the connection dies. Bea looks at me expectantly. I shake my head. "Either her phone's turned off, or this isn't a real number." I don't know why, but it gives me a sinking feeling.

Bea looks disappointed. Then she sits up straighter. "Let's go to her house," she says.

"To her *house*?"

"Why not? If Alice is right and she's just sick at home, we can take her some cookies and a box of chamomile tea and see how she's doing."

I think about the tiny Elsie like a voodoo doll on the mousetrap and I say softly, "I don't know . . ."

"Come on, Cara," says Bea. "Let's just drop by to see if she's okay and to invite her to our party. Maybe she'll be happy to have visitors."

I look out across the river to where the trees rustle. I think about the photos I printed out and all the questions I have. I turn to Bea and grin. "Okay," I say, and she holds out her hand for the notebook with Elsie's address on it. "Let's go find Elsie."

7

When we get to the address, even Bea won't believe it.

"There must have been a mistake."

We took the river road away from town in the opposite direction to where we live, past housing developments and vacation homes, past fields filled with sheep and cows and horses, past big modern houses like Bea's and smaller cottages like the one my mother's friend Gracie bought and renovated a few years ago. The last house we passed was maybe five minutes ago, and the next is far away up ahead, around a bend in the road and hidden by trees. To either side of us there are only fields.

We stand there staring at the house from the road. It's grand, like a manor house in a period film. It has big bay windows and a porch supported by pillars. But the windows are cracked and broken and the porch sags. Ivy has grown in through the cracks in the window frames and is slowly breaking down the walls.

"I saw you take down the address."

Bea shakes her head. "I must've read it wrong."

This isn't Elsie's house. This isn't anybody's house, or at least it hasn't been for a very long time. We've followed the river all the way and we've lost it; it streams in under the garden before us and comes out the other side. The garden is enormous. The gates to the driveway are tall and wrought-iron, all curlicues like haunted houses in horror films. The whole house looks like it's haunted.

"Why would she give this as her address?"

I shrug. "Maybe her parents are gangsters and she doesn't want them to be found. Or maybe there's a house with the same number on a different road on the other side of town that looks the same. The name, I mean."

"Maybe." Bea reaches out and rattles the gates. They're padlocked shut.

I take off my gloves and touch the gates myself. The metal is startlingly cold. I try to judge the distance, then I take off my backpack and throw it over the gates. Bea shouts a laugh. She swings her satchel after my bag and we both grab hold of the gates and climb. I'm encumbered by multiple sweaters and a coat, but it's Bea's tights that get caught in the iron vines and swirls. We help each other over carefully.

"Climbing down's a lot harder," Bea observes when we've reached the ground on the other side.

I do a quick check: All my clothes—and, most importantly, my skin—are intact. "You know," I say to Bea a bit breathlessly, "for someone who's so afraid of accidents, I sure do a lot of stupid stuff." Bea laughs and hugs me, and we both jump up and down inside the hug for a bit before pulling apart and considering the house in front of us.

It's as if Bea senses my momentary hesitation. "Well," she says, "we've come this far." She firmly takes my hand and we march up to the front door like we belong there.

We huddle in under the dilapidated porch roof until I gather my courage and grasp the heavy doorknocker. Bea holds her breath. I raise the knocker and clack it back down loudly. The sound echoes dully through the house. I move aside and give Bea a turn. Unsurprisingly, nobody comes to the door.

That's when the magic happens. Or maybe it isn't magic. Maybe it's only that the door was never closed, or that somebody else broke in before us, but it doesn't matter. I wish at the door, I wish hard; I whisper, "Please be open, please open, open," and Bea takes up the chant so that we are both repeating, "*Open open open*," and I reach out and take the door handle in my non-gloved hand and it turns as if it's inviting us in. The door swings open.

The hall is dark because of the thick layer of dust on the

windows. It filters the light from outside, which was already gray to begin with, into a shadowy gloom. The windows not coated with dust are broken and a slight wind whistles mournfully through the house, lifts up the last shreds of wallpaper, rustles the mouse droppings, the carpet hairs, the cracks in the doors, stirs up the ghosts.

"Can you feel it?" Bea whispers.

My eyes are wide. I nod my head, just once. I can feel it. We take a couple of tentative steps farther into the entrance hall and stare up and up, standing in the middle and gazing through the staircase to the ceiling upstairs. I tilt my head back and close my eyes, and I can hear a faint whispering all around me. Bea moves forward, through the hall and down some steps into what used to be the kitchen, and she drops onto her hands and knees and presses her ear to the floor.

"It's the river," she tells me. I kneel down beside her and listen, and the whispering gets louder. The river runs here, right under the floor of the kitchen.

"This is a witch's house," says Bea. "It's full of ghosts."

I think about what Toby whispered in the school corridor. "It's your house, then," I tell her. "You're more witch than anyone I know."

Bea's teeth glow in the gloom of the kitchen when she grins. "Let me show you around, then." She gets up off the floor and holds out her hand. Her palms are black with dirt.

Her skirt is no longer blue-green tartan—it's dusty gray and flecked with rust from the iron gate, her tights are in tatters and her hair is wild and she's never looked more beautiful. I think about Sam singing her ditties on the pier and feel the familiar pang of wishing I were—or maybe even just looked—a little more like Bea. But I quickly shake off the feeling and take my best friend's hand and we explore the witchy house.

"Here's the back kitchen," says Bea in the pantry. "The river flows underneath us. We witches eat it for breakfast, because that's where all the lost souls go to drown, and lost souls are the witches' favorite meal."

There are still cans and boxes stacked around the kitchen, food well past its expiration date, wall outlets oozing green metallic liquid from not having been used for so long. We walk through rooms like little girls lost in the woods.

"This is the ballroom," Bea says when we reach the entrance hall again. "This is where the witches dance. Where we fly to the ceiling." She points up at the roof above. "Where we waltz with the ghosts."

The staircase is old and rotting. Wood gives slightly under our boots. We climb anyway.

"Once upon a time," Bea says, "when the witches lived here, they enticed young virgins into their house with the promise of truths and stories." Her hand is hot in mine. "And because the witches were so beautiful, in a fiery, midnight way, the pretty virgins would always follow them."

We climb and climb. The staircase creaks.

"The witches would lead them upstairs and let them choose objects from their witchy bedrooms, and they told them stories about those charms. And when the stories were done, the witches would take as payment three hairs from the virgins' heads, because every witch knows there's nothing more potent for powerful spells."

My hand leaves a trail in the dust of the banister.

"But every once in a while," Bea continues, "the prettiest virgins would find an object they weren't supposed to touch, and that was the witch's kiss. All witches keep their kisses in everyday objects, so that their hearts won't break too often."

I look across at her, only slightly afraid I'll miss my step. Bea is focused on the stairs below us, slowly picking out a path around the rotten steps. "What happens when somebody finds the object?" I ask her.

We reach the landing.

"I don't know," Bea says. Her lips are red and wide. "I'm just telling you a story."

Upstairs, there is a long landing lined with doors. We count five bedrooms, a small closet, and a huge bathroom. The bathroom is beautiful but covered in grime. Bea and I write our names with our fingers in the dirt of the claw-footed tub. Except for one, all the bedroom doors are open. The mess inside reminds me of Sam's room. We ghost through the four open rooms and consciously leave the closed double doors halfway down the landing for last. They are pale, once blue maybe, with paint peeling like lolling tongues to the carpet. They are intricately carved with the same vines and swirls and curlicues as the gates into the garden. Bea and I take a door handle each and swing into the master bedroom.

It's empty. The other rooms were full and cluttered with the remnants of life: books and papers tattered and torn to dust, moth-eaten clothes, ripped sheets and feather-coughing pillows on the bed, knickknacks on the shelves. In one Bea whispered that dust is really made up of the skin of the dead. This room, though, is the deadest room of all.

Our footsteps echo despite the dust. The ceiling is high and the plaster around the light fixtures is carved with the same pattern as the bedroom doors. There is no bed. There are no wardrobes or bookshelves. There is only the peeling wallpaper, the wooden floorboards, the big bay windows with their heavy, half-rotted drapes shuttering out the light. I make my eyes wide, try to take everything in. When we step inside the room I notice that what I thought at first might be a pile of dirt in the middle is actually the remains of a fire pit, hollow and soot-blackened.

Bea's face mirrors mine. We shuffle forward, trying to mute our steps by sliding across the floor. Ours are the only footprints on the carpet of dust.

"Whoever lit this fire did it a long time ago," I say to Bea. All that's left is the charred remains of logs and a huge scorch stain.

Bea is grinning, her teeth gleaming in the dim light. "What is this place?" She says it like an exclamation. "What happened here? Why have we never heard about this?" She laughs, and the music of it bounces around the walls.

I laugh along with her. "What a find."

"What a find!"

That's when I see the button. It's big and red and nestled in amongst the blackened remains of the fire. I reach across the pile of old wood and pick it up. I rub it between two gloved fingers to make it shine. I show it to Bea. It's the brightest thing in the room.

Bea touches the button with the tip of her finger. "Look," she says. "It's the witch's kiss."

And then her lips are on mine. She tastes like black-cat nights and chimney smoke and forever, and something sweet and redder, like a cherry inside of a flame. I've kissed Bea before, that soft lip-to-lip in spin the bottle when we've had too much red wine, but this is different, this is wilder. She's kissing me like there's something to prove, like there's somebody watching, like she's testing herself or maybe testing me. I break away from her, confused. The whole house sighs.

"Hear that?" Bea says breathlessly. "The house liked that."

Then an idea lands in the palm of my hand like a big red button. "We should have the party here."

Bea's eyebrows disappear into her bangs. She grabs me by the shoulders and kisses me again, quickly and lightly, the way she usually does. "You're brilliant! The ghost house presents the Black Cat and Whiskey Moon Masquerade Ball. It's so perfect I could cry."

I clap my hands and we both bounce on the balls of our feet. "I love it, I love it!" We chant it like we chanted to open the door, and the house creaks and groans around us.

"Oho," Bea whistles. "Listen to that. This house is just aching for a bit of excitement. Some sexual energy." She winks at me. "I get the feeling this house wants our party as much as we do."

***

When I get home, Sam is in the kitchen eating Chinese take-out from a foil box while my mother makes tea for her and Alice.

"I got it on the way home," Sam says. "Want some?"

The smell of curry sauce makes my mouth water. I sit up on the padded kitchen counter and steal Sam's fork.

"Did you see Melanie's hand?" Sam asks me. "How many accidents is that this season? We should be keeping count." Alice huffs out her breath, but for once she doesn't argue.

My mother holds out her heavily bandaged left hand. "I

feel like Sleeping Beauty," she says. "I thought I'd banished all the X-Acto blades from the studio."

I peek in under her bandage to see the stitches. What a strange way to force skin to heal, I think: You staple it together and wait until it knits itself whole.

"The others must think I'm the clumsiest woman on the planet," my mother says. None of the other artists at her studio know about the accident season. Only Gracie, her best friend, has ever noticed the layers and padding that appear around us every October. But Gracie is a fairly no-nonsense type of person, so my mother never talks about it to her. She says she doesn't think Gracie would believe her if she did. We have all become very good at hiding things from other people. We have all become a little too good at keeping secrets from friends.

My mother takes her hand back from me and I finish off the last of Sam's curry.

"Did you not eat at Bea's?" my mother asks. I texted after school to tell her I was going to Bea's house. During the accident season she likes to know where we are at all times, and something tells me she wouldn't be keen on the idea of me breaking into an abandoned house by the river.

"I did," I lie. "But Sam offered, so it'd be rude to refuse."

"Did you get through to Elsie?" Sam asks.

"Elsie?" my mother asks, turning around. "Who's Elsie?"

"Just a girl from school."

"She and Cara used to be friends," Alice explains. "Just for a while, after Dad died."

"We're not really friends," I say, as if to explain why my mother's never heard of her. "Bea just wanted to call her." I glance over at Sam, who shakes his head at me, ever so slightly. "To tell her what our English homework was for this week," I lie easily.

"So did you tell her about the homework in the end?" Sam asks.

I glance up at my mother. She's standing at the sink, rinsing out the teacups. Because her back is turned, I feel confident I can give Sam a significant look without her noticing. Sometimes it feels as though she has eyes in her sides. "No," I say out loud. The memory of Bea's kiss is like a ghost on my lips. "She wasn't answering her phone. Bea and I just hung out and went for a walk by the river." Technically, I think, that's not even a lie.

My mother turns around and regards me wryly. "Sometimes I think you're more in love with that river than you've ever been with a boy."

I stare resolutely at the empty takeout box in front of me.

Sam punches me playfully on the arm. My bruises have faded, but it hurts a bit. "I didn't think that river was your type," he says.

"Well, he's no sad-eyed guitarist or brooding Victorian rogue," says my mother, who likes to tease me about my taste in music and books. I tell her that the river makes better music than any musician and that brooding rogues are totally making a literary comeback.

"And what's your type?" I say to Sam. "Dreamy-eyed witch-girls?" My words sit uncomfortably in my throat.

"Something like that."

It's funny how quickly the ghost of a kiss can turn sour. Too-sweet incense and stale cigarette smoke. *He's your brother,* I tell myself angrily. *Why shouldn't he like your best friend?*

"And Alice's type is too ordinary for a wild child like her," says my mother, handing Alice her tea. Alice raises an eyebrow. My mother is joking; Nick is anything but ordinary.

When my mother goes upstairs to finish up some sketches, I tell Sam and Alice about the ghost house. When I get to the part about holding our Black Cat and Whiskey Moon Masquerade Ball there, their eyes light up in exactly the same way so that they look like they really *are* brother and sister. I take out my phone to show them some of the pictures Bea and I took of the dusty rooms. Sam and Alice crowd close. I show them the pantry with the river running invisibly under it, I show them the view of the staircase from the hall, I show them the cluttered, abandoned bedrooms, and when I get to the picture of the master bedroom, all the breath whooshes out of me at once.

I took the picture from the farthest corner of the room, the one by the double doors. In the frame we can see the peeling walls and the dusty floorboards with the shuffle tracks made by our booted feet. We can see the fire pit in the middle of the empty room, but that's not what's making my skin crawl. I tap the image to zoom in. There are the dirt-streaked glass panes of the bay windows, there are the heavy, moth-eaten drapes, and there, half hidden by the curtains, pointed face peeking out with that familiar worried look, is Elsie.

8

I keep expecting Elsie to reappear. I glance around every corner on my way to class the next morning. I jump when I hear footsteps and turn around quick, but it's only some eighth graders trekking mud in from the soccer field, or older girls in heels. Still, I can't shake the feeling that I'm being followed.

After roll call, Bea and I go to see Mr. Duffy, who is the seniors' class advisor. He is barreling past a flock of first years on his way down the corridor to the music room. I shoulder a couple of tussling boys aside to catch up with him.

"Mr. Duffy?" I say loudly.

Bea waves her arms to get his attention. "Sir?"

He stops in front of his classroom door and looks at us over his glasses. "Ah. Miss Kivlan. And Miss . . . Morris, isn't it?" he says. "Alice Morris's sister?"

"That's right." Alice and Bea both do music, but Sam and I wanted to take German, and because of the way the timetables worked out, we couldn't do both. "Sir," I say, "we're looking for a senior called Elsie. She's the one who does the secrets booth, you know?"

Mr. Duffy shakes his head. "Doesn't ring a bell," he says. As if on cue, the bell for the beginning of our first class rings. "Your sister would be a better person to ask." He turns to unlock his classroom door. A group of ninth graders is beginning to form in the corridor behind us.

"She doesn't know her," I say quickly. "I just need her phone number. Or an address? It's just . . . she hasn't been in for a few days and I really need to find her."

"It's about the secrets booth," Bea adds. "We wanted to do an interview with her for the school website."

Mr. Duffy unlocks the door and the third years all file into the music room. "Who's her homeroom teacher?" he asks me. "They would have all that information. Although, to be honest, it's probably against school policy to give it out."

"I don't know who her homeroom teacher is," I tell him. "But I thought you might . . ."

"I'm afraid I don't know the girl. But I'm sure she'll be back before midterm, and if not, you can interview her after the break."

Mr. Duffy makes to follow his form into the classroom,

but Bea subtly squeezes her foot into the doorjamb so that he has to stay and answer. Mr. Duffy looks at her foot and sighs. He says to me, "You know, when you've been teaching as long as I have, Clara—"

"Cara."

"Cara—you can get a little muddled. I've had a couple of Ellies—"

"Elsie."

"Elsies. And a couple of Ellas and Essies too. You see what I mean?"

"Yeah, but . . ." I say, trying very hard not to sound impatient or rude. "But she's in your year. I don't know if she does music, but she'd be at assemblies and—"

Mr. Duffy looks at me shrewdly. "Not all students are as . . . vocal in class as others," he says, looking pointedly at Bea, who stares back, unabashed. "And I'm sorry to say that not all students are equally memorable either. I have a lot of students like that in my classes. They work hard, they keep their heads down, they give me no reason to complain about them. Now I suggest that you two take a leaf out of her book and do the same." And he closes the classroom door.

We get similar answers from every teacher we approach; nobody seems to know where Elsie is, and most people think we're being silly worrying about her not being in school.

"Well, even if it's just that she's off sick," Bea says, "I wish someone would actually talk to us about her."

We are standing by the wall of the gym in PE, where Mrs. Smith (who refused to excuse me from class two weeks in a row) has stretched a moldy-looking net across the middle of the hall and is trying to teach us to play tennis. Bea and I hang back as far away from the action as possible, vaguely swinging our rackets whenever the teacher looks our way. Sam, on the other hand, seems to be engaged in a deadly battle with Stephen Jones; both of them are hitting the tennis ball toward the other with vicious underarm swings that send Mrs. Smith into paroxysms of glee. Mr. Breslin, the boys' PE teacher, is out sick, so Mrs. Smith is supervising both classes. Thankfully, this means that she is sufficiently distracted to allow me and Bea to continue our conversation uninterrupted.

"I just don't know who else to ask," I say over the *toc-toc* of tennis balls being hit, the squeaking of sneakers on the gym floor, the huffs and puffs of our classmates, who are far more engaged in the games than we are. "It just seems like nobody knows anything about her at all."

Bea taps her racket on the floor thoughtfully. "I'd suggest looking online, but without a last name, we're not going to get anywhere fast."

"She doesn't really seem like the social media type."

"And Mrs. Healy wouldn't tell you anything?"

I shake my head. I went to the secretary's office between classes, but it was as fruitless an exercise as when Bea and I broke in. "She said that none of the sixth years' attendance records are cause for concern right now, and basically just told me to mind my own business."

Bea sighs. "Adults are useless."

We watch Sam and Stephen run up and down the net for a while. Sam swings hard and the ball almost hits Stephen in the face.

"No fouls now, boys," Mrs. Smith shouts merrily. "Forty–fifteen to Mr. Fagan over here." Sam brushes his hair out of his eyes with a shake of his head. Martin high-fives him as he takes his turn at the net. A couple of the more popular girls watching them cheer. I frown at them without really meaning to.

Bea's voice cuts through my thoughts. "So, random question," she says. "What do you think of Carl?"

"Carl Gallagher?"

"Yeah. What do you think of him?"

"Honestly?"

"Honestly."

"He's kind of pretentious and has shit taste in music."

Bea laughs out loud. One of the girls waiting for her turn at the net turns around with a frown, but Bea stretches her mouth out into a demon snarl and she quickly looks away. "I suppose you're right," Bea says. "Still, at least he's interesting."

I mutter that I don't think he's all that interesting actually, and Bea laughs again. "Since when did you get so honest, Cara?" she says, which I don't think is fair because I'm nothing if not honest. It's just that sometimes I prefer to keep my honesty to myself. I tell Bea as much and she laughs even louder and bumps her hip against mine.

"I know that," she says, more seriously. "I'm sorry."

"Why?" I ask her. "What do *you* think of Carl?"

Bea screws up her mouth, as if she's thinking hard. "Same as you, mostly," she says. "But I think every witch needs someone to kiss on Halloween."

I raise my eyebrows. "You kiss a lot of people."

"I do. Kissing's important."

I don't disagree on that particular point, but I can't stop there. "You kissed me."

Bea smiles. "That was just part of the story."

"Part of what story?"

Bea waves an arm vaguely. "Part of the story of the ghost house," she says. "It needed a kiss to wake it up, to ready it for the party."

I know Bea well enough to understand that this isn't the reason she kissed me at all, but I decide to let the subject drop. "Well, it's certainly awake now," I say. Bea grins and winks suggestively, but behind it all she looks a little relieved.

"So you think Carl will find the witch's kiss there?" I ask her, with another bump of a hip.

We've told everyone about the party's change of venue,

and the fact that it will be held in an abandoned house has made everyone even more excited than before. We've also been very careful not to talk about the party around my mother, who thinks we're just spending a quiet Halloween night at Bea's house watching horror films and handing out candy to trick-or-treaters.

Bea grins and shakes her head. "Not a chance. But I'll probably kiss him anyway."

We both giggle a bit as the rest of the class takes turns serving.

"So who are *you* going to kiss at the ball, then?" Bea wants to know. Across the gym hall, Sam is splashing his face with water from a plastic bottle. The ends of his hair drip onto the collar of his T-shirt.

I turn away from him and punch Bea's arm lightly. "No one," I say. "Your kiss has ruined me forever."

Bea ruffles my hair. "Nonsense," she says.

But I am hardly listening. By the tennis net, Sarah Keogh, who has long brown hair and perfect eyebrows, has come up to Sam, who is talking to Martin. It would appear that Martin's popularity is rubbing off. When Sarah smiles, her teeth are very straight. I force myself to look away and think of something else. I think about Toby Healy winking at me when we broke into the office yesterday. He has pretty lips, and his eyelashes are long like a girl's. I say this to Bea.

"Another sad-eyed guitarist," she says.

"He plays the guitar? Be still my heart."

We both laugh. "He does seem interested in you all of a sudden, though," she says. "I think there's potential there."

"All of a sudden? Excuse me," I reply haughtily. "How do you know he hasn't been secretly in love with me since first year and was just waiting for an excuse to let me know?" Then I snort a laugh. "Seriously, though, I'm sure it's only that he's just noticed I exist, not that he is interested in me in any way."

"We'll see," says Bea with her eyebrows raised.

Suddenly there is a lot of noise and movement by the tennis net. A shout, gasps, a volley of curse words and calls for the teacher. It's hard to see what has happened with all the people crowding around. Bea and I drop our rackets and run; this time of year, we always assume the worst.

At the center of the crowd Sam is hunched over, almost bent double. His hands are on his face and there is blood dripping from between his fingers.

"Sam!" I practically scream. Everyone makes room for me to rush up to him.

"Miss, it wasn't me, miss, it wasn't my fault," Stephen Jones starts shouting as Mrs. Smith hurries over from the other side of the hall.

"It was *your* ball that hit him." Sarah Keogh arches her perfect eyebrows. I put my arm around Sam.

"Yeah, but it was an accident. I didn't do it on purpose."

"I'm fine," Sam says thickly. When he takes his hands away from his face, I can see that his mouth is full of blood. "I'm fine," he says again, to reassure the teacher. "He's right, it wasn't his fault. I'm okay, it's just my lip." Blood drips steadily into his cupped hands.

"Let's get you to the nurse," says Mrs. Smith wearily; this is not the first accident Sam has had in PE class. She holds out an arm to help him to the nurse's office, but he waves her away.

"It's fine, Mrs. Smith," he says, walking easily to the door with the air of someone who has suffered worse injuries than a busted lip. He shakes his hair out of his face with a bloodstained grin. "I know the way."

***

Having a stepbrother should have made a lot of things easier, Alice thought. For one thing, it meant that she and Cara could have a referee when they played Steal the Bacon. Cara always tried to cheat when she'd gotten hold of the ball—or the shoe, or the rolled-up sweater, or whatever they had to hand to be the bacon. But it turned out that Sam couldn't be trusted to tell on Cara, even if she cheated.

Normally, in October, Alice and Cara weren't allowed to play outside unless Mom or Uncle Seth or someone was watching, but since Mom had married Christopher last summer, lots of little things had changed.

"You did not touch the edge of the driveway that time,

111

Cara," Alice shouted after Cara got to the ball before she did.

"Yes I did!"

"You didn't! Sam. Tell her she didn't touch the edge."

Sam shuffled his feet a bit on the concrete. "I dunno, Alice," he said in a voice that Alice knew meant he totally did know. "I think she did touch it."

Alice threw her hat down on the driveway in annoyance. "She did not and you both bloody well know it."

Sometimes having a stepbrother just meant having one more person to gang up on you.

Mom and Christopher came into the garden, Christopher with a spade and trowel and gardening gloves. Mom never usually gardened during the accident season.

She shaded her eyes and looked over at them. "Why don't you three play on the grass instead?" she said. "I don't want you falling on the driveway."

"You can't run as fast on the grass," said Cara. "Also, it's way too long."

Christopher kissed the top of Mom's bright-orange-dyed hair. He was so tall he didn't even have to raise his head. "I'll get to that next," he said.

Mom gave a small shudder. Alice knew she didn't like having the lawnmower out at this time of year. There were a lot of things Mom hid away in October.

"So," Christopher said to them, struggling to put Mom's gardening gloves onto his big hands. "Who's winning?"

"Me," Alice and Cara said at the same time.

"Cara," said Sam.

Alice gave Sam the evil eye. "Fine, then," she said. "Your turn." Let's see who wins when he's playing against her, *she thought.*

Sam and Cara played five rounds of Steal the Bacon while Alice refereed and Christopher weeded the flowerbeds and Mom watched nervously from a safe distance. Sam let Cara win every round.

By the time Cara's new friend Bea rode up on her bicycle (Alice and Cara weren't allowed to have bicycles even though Cara was ten and Alice was eleven and it wasn't the accident season all the time), Mom had relaxed and was chatting and laughing with Christopher over the rosebushes. Alice and Cara and Sam and Bea decided to play relay races across the empty field next door. They got Christopher to count down THREE TWO ONE GO, and all four of them raced from the fence at the side of the garden to the other end of the field.

Alice and Sam were the fastest, but because they both had to swerve around a whole heap of cow patties right in their path, they ended up tied with Bea and Cara just before the finish line at the opposite fence.

Slightly frustrated, but still laughing, Alice ran the last few meters to the fence at the same time as the others. The problem, Alice thought afterward, was that they hadn't realized a new fence had been put in. If they had, they would've seen that the

113

grass sloped steeply downward just before it. If they'd known that, they wouldn't have fallen those last few meters, right into the new electric fence.

Alice shot backward so fast that she landed on her back in the grass. The impact knocked all the air out of her lungs and for several long, long seconds she couldn't breathe. When she turned her head she saw that Cara's eyes were closed. As if from very far away, she could hear Bea screaming for Mom and Christopher. Bea, who hadn't slipped down the slope. Bea, who hadn't run into an electric fence. Bea, who wasn't affected by the accident season.

Alice pushed herself up on her elbows. Cara was opening her eyes. On Alice's other side, Sam was lying on the grass like she was, his face pale, clutching his ankle with both hands.

Alice could see the panic in Mom's face as she ran up. When she saw that Sam was hurt too her hands flew to her mouth and she looked horrified. Christopher bent down and picked Sam up like he weighed nothing at all. Mom hurried over to Alice and Cara, but she kept looking back over at Sam, and Alice knew they were both thinking the same thing.

Sometimes having a stepbrother meant having one more person to be afraid for during the accident season.

***

At lunchtime Kim closes up the secrets booth early, but before she does, I sit behind the privacy screen and type up another secret to slip into the box. I write it quickly, and some of the letters stick and some of them don't come out at all, so that what ends up typed on the piece of paper is this: *It's neever theones i kiss that I'm inlove wth.* I don't expect it to get put up at the end-of-term installation, and that's partly why I decide to put it in the box.

Kim follows me back to the cafeteria. She tells me that this year Ms. Byrne wants to do something different with the secrets booth installation; she wants students to illustrate the secrets, make up a whole secrets room in one of the classrooms, with the secrets typed out and hung up but also with paintings and sculptures made up to represent them. I tell her I'm not sure about this. I kind of like the secrets installation every term, the way they're all hung up on clotheslines throughout the school hallways, just above our heads, like they're the words we're silently saying. Like little thought bubbles that we can read but can't reach. It's equal parts eerie and reassuring.

Kim looks at me appraisingly. "Your mother's the artist, isn't she?" The Artist, as if my mother's the only artist in the world.

"Yeah. One of them, anyway."

"Figures." Kim pushes open the cafeteria door and lets me through. The sound inside is like a fog. "Hey." She stops, and holds me back. "Why don't you take it?"

"Take what?"

"The secrets booth." I open my mouth to say no immediately but Kim cuts me off. "I only did it because Ms. Byrne asked me to, but I'm thinking of dropping art anyway—I'm doing eight subjects as it is." I shake my head and try to speak, but she cuts me off again.

"You *get* it," she says, and that stops me. "That stuff about the pages being the stuff we're saying, like thought bubbles? I'd never have thought that up."

I glance over at a group of fourth years in the cafeteria. Two of them are soldered together at the lips, their tongues working with grim determination. Beside me, the heels of Kim's shoes click on the floor. "I'll think about it," I tell her.

At a table by the window, Sam and Bea are sitting with Niamh, Joe, and, to my great surprise, Toby. Sam's mouth is no longer bleeding. After spending the rest of PE as well as our Irish class in the nurse's office with a bag of ice held to his face, he looks positively cheerful. Possibly because Ms. O'Shaughnessy now has no idea he didn't do his Irish homework last night.

Alice is just outside the window, talking on the phone. Her face is stormy. Toby makes room for me to sit up on a table with him. Bea gives me a not-very-subtle wink as I climb up beside him. She has been writing lines of a poem out on a sheet of paper. When I sit down, she folds the paper over her words and hands it to Kim.

"Exquisite corpse," says Bea.

"I'm sorry, *what* corpse?" Kim asks with one eyebrow

raised. Sam laughs at Kim's perplexed look. I'm guessing Kim and her friends don't usually spend their break times writing poetry together. I chance a glance at Toby beside me, wondering what he'll make of this. He grins at me.

"Exquisite," says Bea.

"That doesn't really answer her question, Bea," I say. Kim tries to unfold the paper, but Bea snatches it back off her.

"An exquisite corpse is a type of poem," she says.

"As well as being a type of dead body," says Sam.

Bea smacks his leg. "A type of poem," she continues, "that's written by more than one person." She takes a notepad out of her bag and tears out another page.

"The first person writes three lines, then folds the paper over the first two lines and passes it to the next person, who takes the first person's last line as reference for their own three lines," Bea says. "Et cetera."

"It's mostly used with drawings," I try to explain, noticing Kim and Niamh giving each other loaded looks. "One person draws a head, folds the paper, someone else draws the torso and so on, so that the finished drawing usually looks like some kind of Frankenstein's monster." Kim and Niamh still look bemused. "Hence the term exquisite corpse?" I kind of mumble, running out of steam. Maybe there is no hope for us; maybe we will always be too weird for the popular crowd.

Bea hands the sheet of paper back to Kim, who takes

it with some reluctance. She looks toward Alice, who is still on the phone outside, gesticulating angrily. Niamh giggles nervously.

"Go on, then," Joe goads. "Write us a poem."

Kim scowls, but for some reason decides to humor us. She bends her hair over the paper. Beside me, Toby drapes an arm over my shoulders. I blush at having him so near, but I don't move away. I don't know what I did to make him notice me, but I'm kind of glad he has. I am also glad he seems less fazed by the exquisite corpse than Kim and Niamh. I am pretty sure that the girls and Joe are only sitting with us because Alice was; I don't know what Toby is doing here at all.

"So, Cara," he says. "Bea was telling us all about the abandoned house you guys found."

"Yeah," I say. "It's amazing. It's spooky and beautiful."

"It's the perfect place for our masquerade," Bea agrees.

"So what's your costume, then?" Toby asks me. "How will I recognize you under your mask?"

"I'll be a fairy. And you'll recognize me because I'll look like me, but with a fairy costume." Toby's arm is casual and warm around me, and a little reassuring sitting on the fake-wood cafeteria table that's probably thirty-five years old and wobbly on its legs. Outside, Alice looks like she's shouting. "But not a little buzzy kid's-toy fairy. Not a fairy like . . ." I struggle to think of a fairy.

"Tinker Bell?" Niamh suggests.

"Actually no." I think about it for a second. "Tinker Bell's kind of like the type of fairy I'm thinking of. She tries to kill Wendy—she's got this mean streak, this vindictiveness. She doesn't quite follow human rules, and that makes her unpredictable, and a little dangerous."

"Like the mermaids in Peter Pan too," says Bea. "They try to drown Wendy."

"Poor Wendy—all these mythical creatures trying to do away with her," says Sam, and we all laugh.

"I'm going as the type of fairy who's a little bit dangerous," I say. "Who you wouldn't want to lower your guard in front of 'cause you'd never be too sure what she'd do."

"I like that," says Toby. He leans in even closer to me, conspiratorially. "Sounds . . . unpredictable." I don't know why, but I blush again. I know that his sudden interest in me is fleeting; that he has probably already been out with all the pretty, popular girls and I am what's left over, now that he has noticed I exist. But he has noticed I exist. And maybe that's enough for now.

"How about you?" I say quickly, noticing Sam and Bea stare. "What will you be?"

"You'll just have to wait and see."

"But then how will we recognize you?" I say, teasing.

Toby raises an eyebrow. "Maybe I'll let you peek in under my mask."

Niamh splutters. Joe pats her on the back. My face

flushes (again), but thankfully Bea distracts everybody from me by shaking her head sagely and saying, "No no no, you don't want to do that." Toby looks up at her.

"The masks are important," Bea says. "So the ghosts won't recognize us and try to follow us home. Because if any one of us slips up, you know that's what they'll do. All the ghosts hanging out on the ceiling, watching us dancing beneath them, just waiting for one of us to take off our mask."

Toby is giving Bea that look that a lot of people give her when she spins her stories. Sam, who seems to have noticed, is frowning at Toby. He turns and tugs on Bea's hair playfully.

"We'll just have to make sure to tie the masks on tight," he says.

Bea purses her lips and pats Sam's cheek. "At least you understand me, Sammy," she says. I don't know why, but my heart gives a little jump. It might be my imagination, but when Sam looks over at Toby's arm around me, I think I notice a mean glint in his eyes that is as blue as the streak in his hair. Heart beating ever so slightly faster, I lean more comfortably against Toby.

Kim hands me the sheet of paper with a line written on it about a midnight masquerade. Alice is finally coming inside again and I'm thinking about my own mask—swirls and sequins the same color as my wings—but in the back of my mind, there is still that pointed, worried face staring out from behind the curtains in the ghost house. It occurs to me that

Kim asking me to take on the secrets booth earlier suggests that she doesn't think Elsie's coming back to school at all.

"Hey, Kim," I say after the bell rings and Toby takes his arm (and the rest of his body) away from me with an inexplicable peck on the cheek that I quickly file away to think about later. Kim fastens her bag closed. "Why do you want me to take on the secrets booth? I mean, instead of Elsie."

"Elsie?"

"Yeah, Elsie." I walk out of the cafeteria with her, holding back slightly from the others. "It's always been her project, ever since second year. I think she's even the one who invented it. Pioneered it. Whatever."

Kim makes a puzzled little pout. "Well," she says, "I don't really know about that."

"But"—I take hold of Kim's elbow and pull her closer toward me—"did Ms. Byrne say something to you about Elsie not coming back?"

"No, nothing like that," Kim says, but she still seems puzzled.

"Did Ms. Byrne say anything about Elsie to you at all?"

"You know, I don't think she did." Kim just sort of shrugs and leaves me out in the crowded corridor with a sinking feeling in my heart.

***

By the end of the day, this is what I've learned about Elsie: She doesn't have any friends, she stays at the secrets booth

121

between classes, nobody really knows her. None of the teachers or students I've asked know where she is or where she lives or even what subjects she's doing. She keeps quiet in class; nobody notices her. It seems like she lives her life just at the corner of the frame. She is forgotten once you've turned the page.

9

We want to go to Bea's house to make our masks for the
Halloween ball, but when we come out of our last class, Nick
is standing by the doors to the main building. He is wearing
a brown leather jacket and skinny jeans and his hair is perfectly tousled and he's too gorgeous to possibly belong by the
big glass doors of an ugly building that gives onto a school
parking lot. A small group of girls walking behind us slow
down and whisper to each other as they walk by. A bunch of
boys in Alice's year throw back their shoulders and stand a
little straighter when they see him. Alice herself stands on her
tiptoes to kiss him.

"To what do I owe the surprise?" she says in a voice that
is not entirely her own. It's lower, like it's trying to be more
grown-up, huskier, like she's not really Alice at all. It makes
me feel strange to hear it.

Sam and Bea and I don't see Nick all that much; he doesn't really hang out with Alice's friends (which I suppose makes sense because he's twenty-two and therefore both older and wiser, and he's a musician, which makes him infinitely cooler). He and Alice mostly just spend time alone together or with his band mates. If I were Alice, I wouldn't be too happy—hanging out with Nick's band also means hanging out with the flocks of girls who stick around after his shows—but Alice says that is all part of the lifestyle and if Nick is going to make it as a musician, she has to get used to these kinds of things. She sometimes jokes that he hardly has time for her with all his hordes of adoring fans, and when she says it, it's like there are two Alices looking out at me: the one who is laughing but a little bit jealous that her boyfriend's so popular, and the one who is almost relieved.

Dating a musician sounds like a lot of work to me, but what do I know? I've never properly dated anyone. And when I see the way Nick looks at Alice like she's the only person on the planet he can see in full color, I think the work must be worth it.

Nick places his hand gently on the small of Alice's back and he nods at the three of us in greeting. He bends to whisper in her ear, but the sound carries. He says, "I have rehearsal in a half hour, so I can't stay long." He kisses her hair. "But I had to see you." Alice's face softens.

I think about her shouting on the phone this afternoon

and wonder if she and Nick were arguing earlier and making up now. I try to pull Sam and Bea away to give them some privacy, but Bea is standing like stone with her arms crossed and won't budge. I raise my eyebrows at her in question.

"Are you coming, Alice?" Bea asks.

"Two seconds," Alice says, and she leads Nick away across the parking lot so that they can speak in private. I can't help but watch them. It can't have been Nick she was arguing with on the phone, I think, because of the way they stand so close to each other, and the way Nick makes sure he's touching her every second. I wonder if I'll ever find someone who touches me that way. Sam clears his throat beside me. I drop my eyes and fuss with my hair under my hat to hide the blush I can feel creeping over my cheeks.

After about ten minutes, Nick leaves (but not before kissing Alice so deeply that most of the kids in the parking lot stop and stare) and Alice, looking a little dazed, comes back to us.

"Everything okay with lover boy?" I ask her playfully.

"Why wouldn't it be?" she says lightly, and we cross the parking lot to start walking to Bea's.

After a few steps we stop, though, because my mother's car is parked by the school gates. For a fleeting moment we consider evading her—doubling back over the soccer field and around the school so she won't see us leave—but the fact that she is here at all when she should still be at the studio already doesn't bode well for us, so we all slowly walk over to the car.

My mother is not in the driver's seat. We all clamber into the back, my hips bumping with Bea's and Sam's, Alice pressed against the other window like a squashed fly. Gracie waves backward at us from the driver's seat and pulls away. In the passenger seat, my mother is sitting cradling one arm—wrapped in a cast and a sling, clearly broken—in the other. She and Gracie explain together as Gracie drives.

We're coming up to the last days of the accident season. Things almost always get worse now, before it ends. Last year at this point, Alice broke two fingers; they got caught in a car door when Nick was driving her home from a party. Two years before that was when Sam broke his nose playing soccer. (The bone set almost right; you can only see the slightest deviation to the line of his profile when he looks at you a certain way. I tell him it makes him look daring, like a pirate.) A few years before that, I broke my leg and Alice put her arm through a glass door. One year my mother fractured her collarbone; another I ran barefoot into the base of the sink and lost an entire toenail to the bathroom floor.

And that's not counting the hundreds of cuts and scrapes and bruises, the knocks and frights for our lives. The could-have-beens, the almosts, the heads that didn't quite crack on the marble tiles at that particular angle, the jagged glass that didn't quite hit that particular vein, the water that didn't quite fill the lungs before being expelled again. But we never talk about those.

Today my mother got hit by a car. She is shaken up and bruised and her arm is broken in two places, but, Gracie says, she is lucky to be alive. Every time she says it (and she's said it three times already), my mother winces. We pretend not to notice. At home, we all fuss over her and she tries to shoo us away.

"I'm all right," she says. "I'm fine—just leave me alone with a glass of wine and a shitty film."

We bring her pillows and more pillows, painkillers, chocolate; we bring her and Gracie wine and we sneak another bottle upstairs for us for later. We pick out shitty films where no one ever gets hurt, except maybe their feelings, but only because of a misunderstanding that turns out all right in the end. We leave her and Gracie in the front room and go out into the back garden, where the trees are swaying but we can't feel the breeze from the grass.

The sky is getting dark already; autumn light always catches me by surprise—the evening seems later than the time tells me it is. We huddle together in a protective circle and Bea rolls a joint with some of the weed Martin's dad grows in his shed. It takes her a long time, even though she often smokes her own rolled-tobacco cigarettes. While we wait, shoulder to shoulder to keep out the wind that is picking up and skipping around the garden, gathering the darkish clouds around above us, threatening rain, I take out the sheet of paper from lunchtime and we finish the exquisite corpse.

I can identify everyone's lines immediately. Bea's are the brutal ones, the ones that'll stay with you. Sam's are spitquick and playful. Kim's are simple, like song lyrics. Niamh's make references to other poems we're studying in class. Alice's must be the metaphor-laden ones that never really say what they mean. Mine are just mine; just there, hiding in among everyone else's.

The poem is a chimera, multi-headed, multi-tongued. It's all over the place and confusing, and all the more beautiful for that. Bea says she'll scan it and print us all a copy to keep.

"Typing it out wouldn't be the same," she says. "The different handwritings are part of the poem."

I think about the typed-up secrets and Elsie's disappearance and I ask Alice if there's anyone in her year Elsie actually talks to. "I mean, outside the secrets booth," I say. Bea licks the rolling papers one last time to seal everything together and sparks the joint to life with an old Zippo lighter that used to be her dad's.

Alice thinks about it for a while. "No," she says. "I guess she's never really had any friends."

"Not since you, anyway," Sam says to me.

In the gloom of the garden lit by papery embers and the

glow of the kitchen behind the apple tree, I think about how Elsie and I just drifted apart as children; or rather, I drifted and Elsie just stayed exactly the same. The thought makes me strangely sad. I wonder why I'd never really thought of Elsie until that day last week when I noticed her in the first photo.

Sam is saying, "But there must be someone she at least talks to more than, I don't know, nothing?"

We all think about it for a bit. "Not in my year," Alice says finally. "But Elsie's in your year anyway—you guys would know more than me."

"No," I say slowly. On either side of me, Sam and Bea shake their heads. "I always thought Elsie was in your year."

"She's not in my year, Cara."

"But she's been here ever since we were . . ." Bea says slowly. Smoke swirls around our faces. The ground is very firm beneath my palms. I lick my lips.

"Yeah, but she was with us the whole time in elementary school too." Sam leans forward and pulls up some grass in the middle of our little circle. "Like, she was around when we were in fifth grade."

I rub my arms. "I guess she must be in our year and we just didn't notice," I say. My voice sounds a little wobbly. I wonder how it's possible to so completely overlook someone you once considered your friend. I feel horrible.

Sam takes a long drag of the joint. When he exhales, he makes the smoke into circles. Bea giggles softly and pokes her tongue into one. Then we all crack up. We roll around on the grass with laughter, and I pretend that I've forgotten about forgetting Elsie. Sam puffs out some more circles and we all join in tonguing them. He tries to teach us to breathe them out like that, but only Alice even comes close, and her smoke signals are more like fat snakes. When I say this, we all laugh some more.

"But there are no snakes in Ireland!" Bea giggles, spreading her arms wide. She loses her balance and knocks into Alice. Now we are mostly laughing at her. Slightly cowed, Bea stays propped up by Alice's shoulder and unfolds our exquisite corpse again and reads it out loud.

It is like a ghost story written in verse form. Stanzas. Meter and rhyme, although none of it rhymes. Just meter, then. She takes one line from each of us and strings them together to make a sort of chorus that she repeats throughout the poem like a song: *So let's raise our glasses to the accident season,/ To the river beneath us where we sink our souls,/ To the bruises and secrets, to the ghosts in the ceiling,/ One more drink for the watery road.*

In the dusky light of the garden the world does look watery. Beside me, Sam slips in and out of sight, black and white, and Alice's skin has taken on a greenish hue from the bushes beside her. Bea's hair—curls tangled by the wind—sticks out from her head like she's in water. My own head feels light and airy and strange.

When it gets too cold and there are no more smoke circles to blow, we go inside. My mother is still in the living room with Gracie; they are laughing about something and their voices from down the hall sound very far away. We tiptoe up the stairs anyway.

We decide to all sleep in the same room. Since Alice's is the biggest, we haul my mattress and then Sam's mattress across the landing and (not without some difficulty) through the door to her bedroom. We are trying to be quiet so my mother won't suspect anything, but it's probably a lot more likely that she just doesn't care what we're up to, if we aren't splitting skin or breaking bones. Which really leaves room for a good bit of mischief.

Finally, when our mattresses and duvets and pillows are in Alice's room, we take Alice's mattress down from her bedframe too, so that the floor is carpeted in mattresses. We all put on our pajamas and sit bunched up in duvets and propped up by pillows and we stay up most of the night talking and drinking, gossiping and giggling, and hiding from half-remembered things.

When we finally fall asleep we are like puppies in a litter. I dream about the changelings again. In my dream they are weak; they have been in the human world for far too long. The woodsprite, the girl who looks like a forest, was once able to make trees grow and flowers bloom. She was in love with a boy she thought was human, but he was really a wolf in disguise. Now her leafy heart is broken and she is forgetting the language of the trees.

The mermaid, the girl who looks like the sea, used to be able to make the rain come, to call up water from the ground, to stop tears. But now her eyes are dried up and her throat is like a desert. The ghost boy, the boy who flickers like a silent-film reel, used to be able to fade in and out of sight, in and out of reality. He was able to slip seamlessly into stories, music, dreams. But now it's his heart that feels like it is fading away. The fairy girl, the girl with wings growing out of her back, used to be able to fly. But now she is stuck to the ground, dancing in her silver Converse and wishing for the sky.

I wake up thinking I've fallen after trying to fly. I have ended up in the crack between two mattresses. Alice and Bea are sharing the same duvet, and when I look over at Sam, he is awake beside me.

"I can't sleep," he whispers. "Come for a walk with me?" He puts a finger to his lips and motions toward the door.

We put our boots and coats on over our pajamas and go outside. I stop in the hall for a moment and open the door to the living room just a crack. My mother and Gracie are both fast asleep, my mother lying on the couch and Gracie curled up in an armchair. There are several empty bottles of wine on the coffee table and discarded chocolate wrappers all over the floor. I smile and quietly shut the door.

Sam and I walk down to the river. We don't really say anything, and halfway down the road, when the light of our front porch has been hidden by trees, Sam takes my hand. We haven't brought a flashlight and the sky is full of clouds, but we can still somehow see where we are going. The night is so warm it seems like summer, but there are clouds gathering overhead, threatening to bring us all back to autumn. Still, there's something eerie about the weather this October, but it's dry and mild and the leaves crinkle underfoot, and in this dreamlike state I think it's kind of perfect.

When we reach the river, we take off our boots before the grass steeps downward to the bank, and we carry them in our hands and clamber down barefoot. Across the water the trees are whispering leafy secrets to each other, or maybe to us, but we don't have the right language to understand. Even the wind is warm.

Sam stops us right before the riverbank, and when I notice what's wrong, we both just stand there and stare at the water.

The river is frozen. The current is still. The occasional rock pokes through the ice like a broken tooth, but the rest of the river is a shelf of frosted glass. Sam drops his boots and reaches for my hand.

This can't be possible, I think. *This is a dream.*

And it does feel dreamlike, all of it: Sam's hand in mine, the warm air on my cheeks, the warm grass beneath my bare feet, the bright sheen to the cloudy sky, the river that has frozen on a strange mild night. This couldn't be anything but a dream.

That's why I hardly hesitate when dream-Sam's hand tightens on my dream hand and we walk out onto the ice. The cold numbs our feet. Our skin sticks to the frost like it would to a Band-Aid, but we walk out anyway. When we reach the middle of the river, we start to laugh. We face each other and hold hands, and we laugh and laugh as if we are the river, as if we're making the sounds it makes when it isn't still. We stare down at our bare feet on the frozen-over water, and when we look back at each other, our eyes are wide and we are so close, and for just the tiniest moment I think that Sam might bridge the distance between our mouths and kiss me, and for an even tinier moment I kind of wish he would.

I freeze like the water beneath us. Sam is like my brother. Where are these thoughts coming from? I try to blink them out of my head, but all I can see are the freckles on his skin.

A crazy thought comes into my head: *This isn't a dream. This isn't a dream and I just thought about kissing Sam. This isn't a dream and I'm out on the ice of a frozen river in the middle of the accident season.*

That's when the ice cracks.

I give a little scream. Our grip on each other's hands tightens. For a few heartbeats we stay still as statues, as ice sculptures, but when the ice cracks again we start to slide carefully toward the riverbank. We try to spread our weight. We tread carefully. The ice cracks. We move faster. It cracks again. Soon we are running, our hands still gripped together, our feet freezing and slipping, and the cracks are multiplying like music notes and Sam is falling but I'm pulling him along until we finally reach the grass of the riverbank, where we collapse, panting, hands still held.

We lie on our backs and look up at the clear night sky. Our feet are still touching the ice. We don't ask *Is this happening?*; we don't look at each other reassuringly and say *It's always happening*; we don't say anything and Sam doesn't move to kiss me again. If that's even what he was doing.

We realize it immediately when we sit up: We're on the opposite side of the river. Somehow we must've got turned around. On this side, the trees look down at us like the ridiculous children that we are. From the other side, our boots wave their laces. The wind is picking up.

"No way I'm crossing that again," Sam says. His voice is husky, as if from sleep.

"We can go the long way and cross at the main bridge," I tell him. "But without our boots . . ."

"It's either that or drowning."

"I've never been the biggest fan of drowning."

Sam kisses the knuckles of my hand he's holding. "Come on, then, little sister," he says. "Let's go home, out of this weird night."

"I'm not your sister," I remind him, and I lead him into the forest, where it's easier to follow the path than to navigate the rocks on this side of the river.

The path brings us to Elsie's clearing. The dream catchers are still there. They spin in the wind like exotic birds dancing. Their feathers are weather-tattered now, though, and they are missing strings and beads. But there's something else tacked on the trees; something new. A lot of somethings. I walk up to one of the trees to look closer. Sam follows, naturally, as our hands are still joined. "Paper?" he says, with uncertainty.

They look like sheets of brown paper, hundreds of them, stapled to every tree. "More like sandpaper, actually," I say to Sam, noticing their texture. He holds out a hand and touches one. His fingers come away sticky.

"Flypaper." One summer when we were little and my mother'd had a particularly successful run of painting sales, we all went on vacation to the Pyrenees. We rented a little house outside a village and spent our days hiking and our evenings using sugar to bait flies into our hands. My mother hated the flies; she hung flypapers on the ceiling and above every door, and Christopher, who is taller than any of us, kept getting his hair caught in the stuff with the flies. I look quickly at Sam, wondering if he's remembering the same thing, but he's still staring at the flypaper, deep in thought.

"I just don't get it," he says finally.

"I know what you mean." We walk away and leave the

clearing behind. The flypapers gleam wetly on the trees and the dream catchers shake in the wind. Twigs stick into the soles of my feet, the flesh too soft from always wearing shoes. "I just wish I knew where she was."

"We have to find her, Cara," Sam says. "Seriously."

"I know," I whisper. I am so glad he agrees with me. I feel the need to speak to Elsie like an urgency; my blood beats with it. "We have to find her soon."

10

Gracie is too hungover to drive us to school the next morning, and my mother can't drive with a broken arm, so the four of us walk all the way, our own heads tight and pounding from last night. We squint in the weak morning light. Alice and Bea, who seem to be in a slightly better state than me and Sam, walk a little way in front of us, heads inclined toward each other, deep in conversation. Sam and I walk silently, farther apart.

We don't talk about leaving the house last night, but I think it is more so that we don't persuade each other it wasn't real than to pretend it didn't happen. It would be too easy to let logic tell us that the river couldn't be frozen on a warm night, that there couldn't possibly be a spooky clearing in the woods filled with dream catchers and flypapers and a tiny doll version of a possibly missing girl set like the bait in a mousetrap. But maybe we also don't talk about it because of our hands held, our bodies close, Sam's eyes aligned with mine as we stood on the ice.

We woke up with our hands side by side but not touching, and this morning it's like we're being careful not to get too close. My thoughts tangle between the words *brother* and *ex-stepbrother,* first focusing on the difference between the two and then rejecting it. *It's the same thing,* I tell myself firmly. *Sam is my brother. It's beyond wrong to be thinking like this.* My brain ends up tangled with so much shame and confusion that I just try to leave it be, ignore any thoughts that flash through it and just concentrate on the straps of my school bag on the bruise on my shoulder, on the taste of cold toast in my mouth as I walk, on the feel of the road under my Converse. (Sam and I silently pick up our Docs from the riverbank on the way to school but they are waterlogged with morning dew and entirely unwearable, so we are both stuck with thin-soled footwear for the day.)

Elsie's invitation to the party sits in the front pocket of my school bag. I touch it throughout the day like a talisman. The need to find her haunts me, taunts me with how easy it should be and how difficult it actually is. And I don't know why, but I feel as though we are running out of time.

I tell Bea about the flypaper trees during math class, but she doesn't seem to be listening. She keeps texting under the table and won't tell me who she's talking to.

"Ugh. Please don't tell me you're ignoring me to text Carl Gallagher," I say with a grimace.

Bea smiles mysteriously. "Every good witch needs a couple of secrets."

I am about to remind Bea that she never keeps secrets, when it hits me. "The secrets booth!"

Sam turns around from his seat in front of us. "What about it?"

"Of course," I say, mostly to myself. "There are always articles and local news stories about it, right? Elsie's bound to be mentioned in them."

"Of course!" Sam smacks the desk with the palm of his hand. "It's a good thing one of us has a few brain cells left," he says, before quickly turning back to his math book when the teacher looks our way.

Sam and I spend our lunch break in the library, looking up articles about the secrets booth and printing them out to read after class. We also photocopy every school newsletter from the past five years and spend a frustrating fifteen minutes quizzing the extremely unhelpful librarian about Elsie.

"She's here every day," I exclaim, waving my arms at Kim, who is sitting at the secrets booth by the window. "Right there! Every day!"

"I don't know the girl," says the librarian for the seventh time. "I can't help you. Now, that'll be five-fifty for the photocopies."

When we get home after school, Bea calls me because she is having a fight with her mother. This happens fairly often: Bea and her mother have similarly dramatic personalities that can't seem to help but clash. While I talk to her in a soothing voice, Sam sits up on the newly bubble-wrapped kitchen table (Alice crashed into it earlier, slipping on a bump in one of the mock-Afghan rugs) and eats slices of plastic-looking cheese straight from the packet.

My mother, who is in a surprisingly good mood, is playing a bunch of 1950s rock 'n' roll songs. She turns the volume up so that the whole house is jitterbugging under its felt and plastic wrapping. She has spent the day hiking in the mountains with Gracie. She tells us how good it feels to just let go for the first time in weeks, to not worry where you put your feet, to know someone's there to hold you if you fall. Gracie has written a haiku about the walk on the cast on her arm. It is silly and sweet.

Suddenly, over all the 1950s rock, I can hear Alice's raised voice from the stairs. It sounds like she's shouting over the phone. When I go into the hall to ask her what's wrong, she is putting on her coat.

"Be back later, Mom," she calls into the kitchen.

"Where are you going?" I ask her.

"Just over to Bea's." Alice shrugs on her coat and frees her hair from underneath her scarf.

"Bea's?"

Alice slings her bag over one shoulder. "Yeah, Bea. Tall girl, red hair, hippy skirts. You know the one."

"She had a fight with her mom," I blurt out.

Alice opens the door. "Yeah, I know." She stops just long enough to stamp her heel properly into her boot and she is gone. "I'll tell her you were asking after her," she calls back over her shoulder. I stand in the hallway, stunned.

When I go back into the kitchen, my mother is singing along to something that sounds like it belongs in *Grease* and Sam is laughing at something she's said and is trying to persuade her that he didn't eat all the sliced cheese. I stand in the doorway and look at them like they're on television or in a picture. I half expect to see Elsie's foot hiding in the corner of the frame.

"Everything okay?" my mother asks, pouring milk into her tea. "Where's your sister off to in such a hurry?"

"To Bea's," I say, and my mouth is kind of twisted.

"Bea's?" Sam looks as surprised as I feel, only probably a lot less upset.

"Very good," my mother says distractedly. When she bends to put the milk back in the fridge—one-handed, her other arm useless in its sling—her hair falls like a tangled purple curtain in front of her face.

Sam just sort of shrugs. Straightening up from the fridge, my mother bumps her head on the edge of the padded counter. She makes a face and rubs it.

"But," I say, because I can't let this go just yet, "I just talked to her. Bea, I mean. She'd had a fight with her mother. She didn't want to come over."

My mother takes a bottle of arnica pills from the cupboard and pops a couple under her tongue. "Maybe she wanted someone to come to her," she says, lisping because of the little pills.

I start to feel guilty. "But she would've asked."

Sam helps my mother peel a banana and carefully pours his own tea. (We stopped my mother from hiding the electric kettle two weeks ago. We are content to live without sharp knives and the gas burner, but living without tea is just impossible.) "I think it's a good thing for Alice to be spending more time with Bea," she says. "She spends so much time with Nick and his posse, and female friendships are so important."

"But she's *my* best friend," I say, and then I feel silly and childish. My mother is right: Nick takes up so much of Alice's time outside school.

"I know you feel left out," says my mother, echoing my thoughts exactly. She comes over and puts her good arm around my shoulders. "But you've got your brother to keep you company. And me."

"He's not my brother," I mutter, and my mother laughs.

"If you say so, *petite soeur*," Sam says, and my mother laughs louder.

When she goes up to the attic to work, Sam and I sit in the living room and look through the newsletters and articles, searching for any mention of Elsie. She is almost as elusive in text as she is in person; we find mention of "a fourth-year girl" here, "a student" there, like glimpses of an ugly cardigan or a hint of mousy hair. I wonder if Alice is right about all this; I wonder again if there is such a thing as coincidence.

"I can't believe Bea asked her over and not us," I say to Sam after a while, as if I were talking to him in my head about Alice all along.

"I don't think it was like that." Sam flicks through the music library on his laptop while trying to find more articles online. "Alice probably asked Bea. Maybe she needed someone to talk to. And Bea's good at that sort of thing."

"Aren't we?"

Sam looks at me. "Not always," he says with aching honesty.

I look around the living room, wrapped up like a fragile package, and I think about all the secrets hiding in the sharp edges of things. "I guess," I say. "I guess Bea doesn't really do secrets." I think Bea could set up her own secrets booth, sell all the unsaid things for ten cents a pound. How many secrets would fit into a pound? I wonder.

"She kissed me," I find myself saying. From the laptop a woman's voice sings softly. The guitar notes accompanying her song are like plucked heartstrings.

Sam is very still. "Bea?" he asks.

I nod. "In the ghost house."

Sam sort of shrugs it off. "You guys have kissed before," he says. "At parties, in spin the bottle."

"I guess." I want to tell him about the way she kissed me—like she wanted to prove something, like it wasn't really me she was kissing, and how she hasn't talked about it since that one time in PE class (not that I have either), but instead I ask, "Did you ever kiss her?"

"In spin the—?"

"Outside of that."

Sam's fingernails drum on the keyboard. "Once."

"Oh." I realize the second he says it that I don't want to know, but he tells me anyway. I try not to listen without actually blocking my ears.

"It was at that party in Joe and Martin's house this summer. You and Alice'd gone to the liquor store and the others were in the kitchen getting ice cream."

I remember the night. Alice had taken us to the party Joe was having because his parents were out of town. It was one of the first times we'd properly hung out with her friends, and it was mostly because Martin had invited some people in our year too. We'd been sitting out on the veranda and Bea'd read the cards for us in the light-hearted way she does sometimes, when all the questions are about love and sex, and none are about anything serious. (But is there anything

145

more serious, I wonder now, than love and sex? Not hardly.)

"Anyway," Sam says. "Everyone else left and she still hadn't read my cards, so she did, and then I kissed her."

I make a choked sound in my throat. "*You* kissed *her*?"

Sam doesn't look at me. "Yeah. I just wanted to . . ." He sighs. "Her cards'd said something that I didn't want to believe, so I kissed her to prove them wrong."

Now I really want to cover my ears. I reach up and brush my hair away from my face instead. "How does that even—?"

Sam speaks louder over me. "I didn't feel anything." He is staring resolutely at the newsletter pamphlets in front of him.

My hands drop into my lap. I want to say a hundred things, but I end up with a sarcastic "Yeah, right."

"Yeah," Sam says simply.

"But . . ." I look up at the ceiling as if it'll give me answers. It's unresponsive, however, blank and white. It's the only part of the house that doesn't look bandaged. "But you like her."

"So do you."

"No, I mean you *like* her like her." I feel like I'm twelve again. "You kissed her."

"Yeah, but it was just a kiss. It was just to see . . ." Sam sort of laughs. "I'm not in love with Bea, Cara."

I look down at my hands. "I thought you were."

"Well, I'm not." A new song comes on. "Never have been."

146

All of a sudden my heart feels funny. Sam isn't in love with Bea. *Not that it matters if he was,* I tell myself. *He's my ex-stepbrother. He's like my brother. He's my brother.* Sam is still talking, but I almost can't listen to him. *Never have been,* he said. *There's only one wench I want.*

"*Cara,*" Sam says, and I quickly realize that it's not the first time he's tried to get my attention in the last few minutes. He is holding up one of the school newsletters from several years ago. The original pamphlet we photocopied was slightly torn. All that's missing is part of a paragraph about the bridge the council has been saying it'll build across the river for the last twenty years.

I scan the page quickly, looking for a mention of the secrets booth. I shake my head. "What?" I hand the pamphlet back to Sam, who turns it toward me again and points at the torn-off piece about the bridge.

"I bet they won't even build the actual bridge now," I say, thinking of the way the wooden one crashed into the water. "They'll probably just repair the old one."

"*Cara,*" Sam says again. "*Look.*"

"At what?" I read the torn article quickly, muttering the key points out loud to let Sam know I'm paying attention. "*Construction of bridge halted yet again . . . years since original bridge collapsed . . . town mayor putting pressure on county council . . . says it's a travesty it hasn't been rebuilt yet . . . local girl Elsie—* Wait, what?"

The article stops there. It's the line immediately below the quote from the mayor, but the rest of the article has been torn away.

I look up at Sam. "Do you think it's our Elsie?"

"It's worth a shot. It's not a very common name."

I twist my mouth, trying not to look doubtful. "It doesn't tell us much."

"Right now it's all we have to go on," Sam says. "If we can find the rest of the article, we can see if it is our Elsie."

I look back down at the pamphlet doubtfully. It looks like a newspaper article pasted into the school newsletter. "It could be from the *Telegraph,*" I say with uncertainty. "Or *Western People*. But their offices are in Castlebar and Ballina. We won't be able to get out there before they close. It's almost half past four."

Sam shakes his head. "There's this magical place," he says with mock solemnity, "called a library—I don't know if you've ever heard of it, but they have books, and also newspapers, and back issues of newspapers . . ."

I give his arm a playful thump, but I can feel the beginnings of excitement fluttering in my chest. "Okay," I say, taking out my phone to tell Bea and Alice to meet us in town. "Let's go."

***

Our small town is more crowded than usual today: The buses from Dublin and Galway seem to be full of college students who have taken Friday off and are home early on the Thursday afternoon bus for the midterm break, and parents and local schoolchildren are hurrying around before the shops close, buying Halloween decorations and trick-or-treat sweets for tomorrow. Some of them are dressed up already, and in a couple of the pubs, loud work parties of costumed people spill onto the street.

Bea and Alice are waiting for us across the road from the library as we walk up. I weave around the costumed people outside the pub, ducking under elbows to dodge their drinks. That's how I bump into the man. His chest makes a hollow clang where my hands hit him.

I say, "Oh, I'm sorry!" as another man steadies me, but the man I bumped into has slipped into the pub. When I peer through the window beside the open door I see that it's the metal man statue I walked into on the day Sam and I found the magic shop in Galway. Sam stops behind me. I stare through the window into the man's eyes. They are as gray as the rest of him. Something about the shine of his skin is unnatural, which is to say more unnatural than silver body paint. Or perhaps a lot more natural; it looks like metal-made skin. The man smiles mechanically and I shudder. He moves across the window as I walk and his strange eyes find Sam, and then Alice ahead of us. His smile gets wider. Even the corners of his mouth are little hinges.

"Come on, let's go," I say slowly, and I take Sam's hand

and hurry onward to Alice and Bea. I take Bea's hand as well and lead them quickly across the road toward the library. The metal man stares through the window. Alice crosses after us more slowly. When she's just stepped off the curb, she turns around and looks at the statue man one last time. She frowns and starts to say something as if she wants to call across to him. Sam's face falls.

A car speeds around the corner ahead of us. The driver only sees Alice at the last minute. I can see what's about to happen, but I don't even have time to move before the screech of brakes rips across the road. The driver tries to stop the car, but it's too close to Alice. The front of it crashes into her and she is flung over the hood and onto the road. The car skids to a stop.

I think Bea screams, or it could be me. We all run to Alice. The only thing I can register is that she is moving, and just as we reach her I have a moment of swooping relief because it looks like she is trying to get up. But then her face turns ghostly white, her eyes roll back into her head, and she collapses. With incredible speed (and a presence of mind that I don't have) Bea catches Alice before her head can hit the ground.

I vaguely feel my knees sting as I drop onto the road beside Alice. Her eyelids are flickering and Bea's arms around her are shaking. Sam and a woman who must be the driver of the car are there beside me, and a small group of people has gathered at the side of the road, calling out questions and suggestions.

I reach over and tap Alice's cheek. "Alice." My voice is hoarse. "Alice!" I give her a little smack and she opens her eyes. The driver breathes a sigh of relief. Alice looks confused for a second, but then she gasps and lets out the tiniest whimper that quickly turns into a sob. When I look down at her, I can see why. She is covered in blood. Her tights are ripped and the skin of her knees has split open. Her hands and elbows are bleeding badly too, and there is a long, jagged gash in her right arm that shows through the tear in her sweater. Bits of dirt and gravel are embedded in her skin.

But it's Alice's left arm that makes me stop trying to pull her up. Her shoulder is out of its socket. It's a small difference, but it looks so wrong—a bump where there should be sharp lines. I swallow down a wave of nausea.

Alice's breathing is shallow and quick.

"It's okay," Sam says from beside me. "It's okay—here, give me your arm."

A woman emerges from the crowd at the side of the road. "I'm a certified EMT," she says. "Can I help?"

"So are we," Sam says without looking at the woman. My mother has had us all take first-aid courses every year from the age of eight. We can dress wounds, improvise slings, and set bones in minutes. Alice blanches, but she hands Sam her arm.

He grips her hand and I brace her arm just under

the shoulder. Gently, with Alice wincing beneath us, Sam straightens her elbow and pulls her arm slowly toward him until the joint slips back into place with a pop.

Alice bites back a scream, then shudders.

"Better?" I whisper. She nods, but her eyes look haunted. I glance across the road at the people still milling about outside the pub and wonder if the metal man is still watching from the window. Suddenly my face stings as if it's been slapped. I frown and shake my head, put my cold hand against it to cool it down.

Sam, Bea, and the EMT lady carefully help Alice to the side of the road, while the driver of the car wrings her hands and apologizes over and over. Alice keeps saying, "It's fine, it's fine," but when she stands up, she swoons again, and leans heavily against Bea.

"We need to get you to the hospital," says Bea, and Alice nods again. The owner of the corner store across the road, Mary Daly, ushers us inside and we sit Alice down on the chair behind the counter. Then she hands Alice some chocolate and a soda. "For the shock," she says.

"Will I call an ambulance?" the EMT woman asks.

Alice answers, her voice suddenly strong. "No, it's fine, my boyfriend lives just down the road. He can—" She stops then, breathless with pain. "He can drive me there."

I unwind my scarf from around my neck and make a sling for Alice's arm.

"Don't you think we should ask Gracie?" Sam says.

"No," Alice replies quickly. "I don't want to worry Mom. I'll get Nick to pick me up."

"Alice, I think we should call an ambulance," says Bea. Mary Daly and the EMT lady nod their heads.

"*No,*" Alice says again. She sits up straighter and tosses her long hair behind her back, as if to prove she can. "I'm fine."

"Alice—"

"I've had worse." Alice gives a dry little laugh. "We all have."

Maybe it's because she has mentioned the accident season, however indirectly, but Bea doesn't push the point. Instead, she takes out Alice's phone, dials Nick's number, and holds the phone up to Alice's ear.

While she talks to him, Sam and I do our best to clean and disinfect her cuts. The crowd disperses, until we are alone behind the counter. Because we are so close to Alice, we can all hear both sides of her phone conversation.

"Where were you last night?" is the first thing Nick says when he answers the call.

"Hey, Nick," Alice says in a falsely casual voice. "I've just had a bit of an accident and I don't want to bother my mom. Are you free now? Could you drive me to the hospital?"

It's as if Nick hasn't heard her. "Where were you last night, Alice?"

Alice makes a curtain of her hair and hunches over, as if

153

that'll stop us from hearing. "I was with Cara and Bea. We just hung out at home."

Nick's voice gets lower, but I think I can make out the words. "You were supposed to be hanging out with me."

"Nick, I'm sorry. My mom broke her wrist, so I had to stay home." Alice lowers her voice to match his, but hers is soft where his is all knives. Beside me, Bea crosses her arms and makes an angry, impatient noise.

Alice seems to go through this a lot, with Nick. My mother says he's awfully insecure for someone so popular, but Alice says it isn't insecurity, just jealousy. Just love. I don't know anything about that kind of love, but I imagine that if you feel that strongly for someone, you do end up getting a little possessive. My mother calls theirs a firecracker romance.

Alice winces as Sam sticks some butterfly bandages over the cut on her arm that won't stop bleeding. "There must have been broken glass on the road," he says in an undertone.

Nick must have heard what Sam just said, because when he speaks again, his voice is completely different. "Are you okay, love?" he says through the phone to Alice.

"A car crashed into her," Bea says, very loudly, next to the phone.

Alice winces again. "I'm fine," she says over Nick's sounds of concern. "I just need a lift to the hospital. I'm in the corner store across from the library."

"I'm on my way."

When Alice hangs up, she looks even paler, but she turns to Bea with her head high. "Don't make a fuss," she says.

Nick drives up five minutes later. Alice stands once he comes inside.

Every time I see him, I'm surprised by how beautiful Nick is. His hair is dark and falls in waves to his jaw and his eyes are kind of intense. He is tall and broad and he crackles energy.

"Okay," Bea says in a tight voice. "Let's go."

Nick glances at Bea, who seems to be looking anywhere but at him. "I'll take her," he says. "You don't have to wait with us." He turns back to Alice and strokes her cheek softly. "Come on, then, love," he says to her. "Let's get you patched up."

Sam says, "I'll come with you too. I'm supposed to be meeting up with Martin in the city later anyway."

Nick doesn't look too happy about having a third wheel, but he says, "Okay, man, I'll drop you off outside the hospital. But I'm going in with Alice."

Bea scowls, but Alice gives a tight little smile. She thanks Nick with a kiss and turns to me and Bea. "Don't make a fuss," she says again. "And don't tell Mom. I'll spend the night at Nick's so she won't worry. You guys go home," she says. "Nick will take care of me."

"Yeah, I'm sure he will," Bea mutters darkly. I look over at her sharply. She frowns as she watches them drive away.

When Nick's car is out of sight, I run across the road (looking both ways carefully before crossing) and up to the library just as the librarian locks the door.

"No no no," I say, standing in front of her to block her path. "I really need to find a newspaper article," I say, very quickly. "It isn't online and it's really important and I know the library's closed tomorrow and I can't go in to Ballina or Castlebar because I've got school and then it's Halloween and anyway I don't know exactly what newspaper the article's in, so I'd have to go to both and I really can't wait until Monday, please can you give me just five minutes?"

The librarian raises her eyebrows. "Library's closed, love," she says. "You should have done your homework earlier if it was that important."

Bea appears behind me. "It's not for homework," she says. "But it really *is* important. It's for a friend. It was an article from a couple of years ago about the bridge that collapsed and the council was supposed to rebuild. Do you think we could just take a few minutes to see if we can find it?"

"I'm afraid not," the librarian says. "I have to pick up my son from training at a quarter past." She pockets the keys and starts to cross the parking lot. "But if it's information about the bridge you want, you might catch someone at the council offices if you hurry. They'd have copies of certain articles on file."

Bea and I practically run to the council offices. We get

to the front door, breathless, just in time for the man in the gray suit inside to flip the sign from OPEN to CLOSED. Bea knocks on the glass and I try to plead with the man to talk to us, but he just shakes his head, points at the CLOSED sign, and disappears back into the building.

"Dammit!" I stamp my foot in frustration. I turn to Bea, but she is engrossed in her phone.

She looks up and says, "They're still on the road."

I sigh and walk away from the offices. "Alice'll be fine," I try to reassure Bea. "Like she said, we've all had worse. And she has Nick to take care of her."

Bea just scowls. All the way home, her face is a storm. We stop at the river, where the wooden bridge is being rebuilt. I lean against the picnic table and look out at the water. I wish we'd been able to talk to someone about Elsie. I feel like I need someone to remind me that she's real.

Bea is muttering things about asshole musicians under her breath. When I ask her why she suddenly hates Nick so much, she reminds me about his and Alice's fights and his three-a.m. calls, about Alice stamping up the stairs after she's been with him and all the times she says he's not talking to her for some reason or another, and as Bea speaks, it feels kind of like a blurry picture's suddenly becoming clear.

"A big part of Nick's appeal is sex," Bea says. She lights up a cigarette and passes me another one. Her mouth is hard and thin when she smokes. "He's good at it, and he's good at making Alice feel good."

I kind of squirm back when she says this, not really comfortable with knowing the details of my sister's sex life. "Well, that's . . ." I don't really know what that is.

"But something he's *really* good at is emotional manipulation." Bea's mouth puckers around the sounds. I nod slowly and say I can see that. The huffs he goes into, the way he wears his popularity like a bright tie that'd choke any other person. Bea lowers her voice and talks to the strangled grass underneath the bench.

"Alice told me something earlier," she says. "About Nick." She kicks at the tufts of grass. "Just before the summer, Alice went to one of the senior parties and they got drunk and played truth or dare, right, and she and Kim were dared to run out onto the road in their underwear." Bea's foot taps restlessly against the bench. "So, the next morning," she goes on, "Alice went to Nick's place and told him all about the party and how he should come along next time, but he didn't like that she was drinking without him and that people'd seen her in her underwear."

My cigarette's hanging in my hand by my side. I flick away the column of ash and take a drag. Bea keeps going. "So they had a fight about it, and then they made up and had sex." She says the next part a little bit faster. "So, he likes to tie her up." Another squirm from me. "And she's fine with that, except for that morning he tied her to a chair in his bedroom and left her there."

I breathe in too sharply and the smoke scratches the back of my throat. "Hold on—*what?*"

"He went out to buy smokes," she says. "He went out to buy smokes and he left her tied up so tightly that she couldn't get free no matter how hard she tried." My mouth is open. "Three hours later—she could tell by the alarm clock sitting on his chest of drawers—he came back." I blink hard a few times to get the image out of my head.

"He said *Oh,* and he was smiling. He said *I forgot.*"

"But how—?" I say. "Why didn't—? How long has he—? Why is she still with him? She's with him right now. Why did we let her—?" I have to stop and catch my breath. "Why didn't she tell me?" My voice comes out louder and more pleading than I'd meant.

Bea doesn't answer. Instead, she takes out her cards. She spreads them out on the picnic table in front of us.

"She's attracted to trouble," Bea says. "Because at least that way she knows it's right in front of her and not hidden away. Not like you."

"Like me?"

"That's what this means, here." She points to one of the cards. "You only let yourself see the good things, but that's . . . You only see what's safe, what you want to see."

"What do you mean?" Her words are like a smack. "No I

159

don't," I say faintly. I can't tell if I feel ashamed or indignant. "That's not true. Bea. Why would you even say that?"

"It's not me." Bea shakes her head. "It's the cards."

"Right." I can feel my mouth pucker up like I've tasted something bad, or like I'm going to cry. I don't know when Bea suddenly became best friends with Alice and knew all her secrets. I don't know why that's bothering me after what Bea's just said about my sister. There's a lump in my throat that doesn't budge no matter how hard I swallow. We both drop our cigarette butts on the ground and I stamp them out with the toes of my boots. Bea's lipstick stains the grass like blood.

11

When I get home, my mother is sitting in the dark in the kitchen (Bea is not the only person in my life with a penchant for the dramatic). I flick the light on and she looks surprised to see me back. She tries to act normal, but I can see that she's added an extra rug to the kitchen floor, and when I go to boil some water for tea, I see that the kettle's gone. I also notice the date on the calendar that hangs on the back of the garden door.

Between the weirdness of last night, and finding out that Sam kissed Bea this summer, and Alice's accident, and what Bea told me about Alice and Nick, I had completely forgotten what day it is. I stop in the middle of the kitchen and turn to face my mother.

"Are you okay?" I ask. It's a stupid question; I know she's not okay.

My mother tries to smile, but it looks like a grimace. "I just have a headache," she says. "I'm going to go to bed. Don't forget to unplug everything before you go upstairs, okay? And be careful opening that cupboard—I think its hinges are loose. And don't go near the window in the bathroom."

I just nod my head sadly and let her go upstairs, and I wonder where the person who was so excited about a walk in the mountains this morning has gone, but I suppose I know the answer. She's gone back in time, in her mind, to another unseasonably warm October four years ago, and to the last of the tragedies.

My eyes fill with tears suddenly, and my heart tries to jump at my teeth and my throat closes before it can leap from my chest. I take a few deep breaths like my mother always tells me helps when you're in crisis—in through the nose, all the way from the diaphragm, as if you're about to sing opera. Not that I've ever sung opera. I wonder who is telling my mother to breathe deep tonight.

I call Gracie. She is eating when she answers, and the chewing sounds are loud and distorted. Her earrings clack against the side of the phone.

"It's the thirtieth," I tell her. She doesn't say *Cara?* because she already knows it's me, and she doesn't say *What?* because she knows what I mean.

"Oh God," she says instead. "I completely forgot. She was acting so normal earlier. She seemed happy."

"Maybe she forgot too, for a while." Maybe she feels like forgetting makes it worse. I know I do.

My father died in the first week of the accident season when I was eight years old. Like us, my mother broke down and slowly got back up and mourned, and many years later she stopped hiding from the world that one day in early October, and instead every year she takes us to our father's grave and tells us stories about him so we'll never forget. My uncle Seth died four years ago today and my mother still hides from the world on that day. But we don't talk about that. We talk about Seth when he was alive but we never mention how he died. It's like my mother still refuses to believe he's gone.

Gracie sighs over the line. "I'll give her a call," she says. "Talk to you soon, Cara." When I hang up, I feel a little better. That's what best friends are for, I think. Then I think about everything Bea said about me earlier (*It's not me, it's the cards*) and I don't feel so much better again.

Alice comes home before Sam. It's close to midnight, but I wasn't expecting her home at all; she's supposed to be staying at Nick's. I am in the sitting room in my pajamas with one of Bea's mixes on for company, trying to lose myself in my book. Then Alice comes through the door and my mouth drops open and my heart hits the floor.

Her lip is cut and her eyes are red. One of her cheeks is turning the dark pink of a new bruise. I jump up from the couch and run to her, and she drops her bag where she stands and just sort of sways on the spot as I hug her tightly. Something tells me these new bruises weren't accidents, but I don't know how to ask.

Alice isn't saying anything and I don't really know what to do, so I sit her on the couch and go into the kitchen and microwave a mug of water because I don't know where my mother's hidden the kettle. I make up two improvised hot whiskeys with my mother's Scotch and generous hunks of lemon studded with cloves. I make them very sweet, and the sugar looks like glitter at the bottom of the glass.

We sit on the couch in silence and drink, and when we're finished I know I've waited long enough to say something, so I say, "Alice, did Nick . . . ?" but suddenly I find that I can't finish the sentence. I'm not sure what I'm trying to ask. I can't even really look at Alice after everything Bea told me. Instead I go into the kitchen and make another couple of hot whiskeys.

When I come back into the living room I try saying it in a different way. "Bea told me something, after you left for the hospital." I put the tall glasses down on coasters on the wrapped-up table. Alice takes hers immediately. "About Nick." I pick my glass up more slowly and sip, savoring the warmth.

Alice is shaking her head, her hair making curtains over her face, shutting her off from me.

My throat is trying to close, but I have to ask her anyway. "Nick," I say again. It's the closest I can get to the question.

"I should probably finish with him."

I open and close my mouth a few times before I can speak. "What happened tonight?"

"They said the shoulder was relocated properly, although apparently you're not supposed to fix it yourself. Or get your little brother to fix it for you." She sort of laughs. Before I can interrupt, she goes on. "Also, ten stitches . . ." She points at her right arm, the one that had the cut all down it. "Five here." She shows me the thick padding on her right knee. "I feel like a rag doll, all sewn up." She smiles crookedly.

"What about that?" I point at the cut on her lip. Alice sighs.

I whisper so low I'm not sure she hears: "Was it Nick?"

Alice is quiet for so long I'm almost sure she didn't hear me. "I don't know what Bea told you," she says finally, "but it's not like . . ." She pauses for a few beats. "We just fight sometimes. I mean, I hit him back. Sometimes I hit him first. I wanted to come home after the hospital, he wanted me to stay with him—he blocked the door, so I hit him. I started it."

Now I can't stay silent. "Because he wouldn't let you leave. And whatever about hitting him first, he clearly hits you harder. Alice"—I say her name like a plea—"he *hit* you. Alice, this is serious. This is so, so serious."

"It's not like that. He's not . . . It's not like that. It was a mistake," she says. "We have a . . . tempestuous relationship." She smiles wryly. It's another term my mother uses for their shouting matches over the phone.

"But why do you let him treat you like that? Do you love him?" I don't know where that second question came from, but suddenly I need to know.

Alice takes a while before answering, and when she does, it isn't the answer I was expecting. "I think so," she says slowly.

Frustration builds up with the lump in my throat. "But why—? How—?" I want to ask how she could possibly even think she loves him after all this, but instead I ask a slightly easier question. "What does that even mean, *I think so*? How can you not know?"

"It's complicated, Cara." She touches my hair like she's the one who's comforting me. "I probably should just break up with him. But we have all this history, you know? And he gets me. Maybe that's why we fight so much. I get him too, more than anyone. He has this fascinating soul. His darkness is part of that." Then she sort of laughs at herself. "I sound like Bea." She leans away from me and tilts her head slightly to one side. "You want to know a secret?"

I'm not sure how many more secrets I can take, but I nod my head anyway.

"There's someone else." Alice's smile plays at the corners of her mouth. We are maybe a little bit drunk. The darkness is close around us and it's almost like it's listening. This house is taking lessons from the ghosts. "Someone new. Or rather," she corrects herself, "someone old. Someone who's always been there and I think I've always known is just right for me, but I've never let myself believe it, or even think it."

The darkness shivers over my skin like little needles. I think about a warm hand in mine as I walked barefoot across a river that couldn't possibly have been frozen. I think about riverbed eyes. Without really realizing that I'm thinking out loud, I say: "I know exactly what you mean." I say it faintly, and my breath mists before me. I can see the words exit my body. I can see them right in front of me.

Alice hasn't noticed. "But I'm scared," she's saying. "Isn't that crazy? I'm scared to admit things. To admit that I was wrong." She puts her empty glass down and twists her hair forward over her shoulders and fans out the ends on her sling. "I'm scared of being happy."

That's when I realize that Alice has never been happy, not for a very long time. The knowledge shakes me. She must have told me, shown me in a million ways for years, but I never really realized. I lean forward and take her good hand in mine. I whisper, "I'm sorry," because there's nothing else I can think of to say.

Alice turns her hand so she's the one holding me. "It's okay, little sister," she says. "It's going to be okay." But it doesn't feel like it'll ever be okay.

I can't hear my mother upstairs anymore. I wonder if Gracie's phone call made her feel better or if that's even possible. Not for the first time, I think about what it must be like to lose a sibling. I cling to Alice like I'm drowning, or like she is, and I don't want to let go. *The worst one yet.* Bea's words buzz in my brain.

"It's the thirtieth," I whisper into Alice's hair.

Alice pulls away and looks at me. She nods. "I know. How is she?"

"Bad." I pick at some fluff on one of the couch's cushions. "I'd forgotten," I say quietly. "Is that really selfish and horrible?"

Alice rubs my arm. "Not at all," she says. "It's normal. Life goes on."

Not for everyone, I think. "I miss Seth more than I miss Dad," I tell Alice. If I were at school I'd type it up on Elsie's typewriter and it'd be put up with the other secrets on the clotheslines through the halls, but I'm not at school, and telling secrets to a sister-friend is almost as good.

Alice's voice is a whisper. "Me too." Secrets are even better when they're shared. I look down at Alice's bandaged legs. I want to tell her what Bea's cards said, warn her to be careful, but I am too afraid.

"The accident season leaves its marks," I say instead. I think about my father, I think about Seth. I think about all the near misses, about the car driver slamming on the brakes today, about how fast she would have been going if she hadn't seen Alice at the last minute. I think about Alice hitting her head on the banister rail as she fell down the stairs the other night. No one in the house. She might not have woken up from her concussion or been able to call the ambulance. Sometimes it seems like more than luck when we survive the accidents.

"I didn't fall down the stairs," Alice says suddenly, as if she has read my mind. I look up at her face. "I wasn't even here. In the house, I mean." I remember getting my mother's call that night, taking a bus to the hospital and walking a concussed Alice around and around.

"But you hit your head—"

"On Nick's mantelpiece."

My heart drops down into my stomach. "Alice," I say, because it's the only thing I can think of to say.

"We were having a fight. He pushed me, I fell—he didn't mean it, it was nobody's fault. It was an accident," she says, "but it wasn't because of the accident season. It isn't always about that."

I wince. It feels like my whole body is wincing. "I think it is." Alice tries to cross her legs, but the padding on her knees won't let her. Her tights are still stained with blood. She grimaces. "I can't believe I didn't see that car coming," she says.

"None of us did." I shake my head. Then, remembering,

I say, "You said something, before the car hit you. When I bumped into that street performer statue guy."

Alice shrugs and drags herself backward so she's sitting more comfortably against the back of the couch. "The guy in the Tin Man costume? I just thought he looked like somebody," she says. "That's all."

I pull some fluff away from the cushions. "I thought I heard you say *Christopher*," I say, remembering Sam's expression, wondering if he heard what I heard.

"I was wrong," Alice says, and she gets up off the couch. "Obviously." She picks up our empty whiskey glasses one-handed to take them back to the kitchen. "It was one of those weird resemblances that disappears with a trick of the light." She turns at the door to the hall and hitches a little sigh. "I'm going to go check on Mom."

The padding on every surface feels oppressive, like there isn't enough room to breathe. It feels like there's a lot not being said. I think my whole family is like that: We bite back the things we can't say and we cushion every surface for the inevitable moment when they all come fighting out.

***

Sam comes home some time later. Alice and I are back in the living room together with the television on low in the background. The sound of it is muffled in the over-padded room. My mother is upstairs with the tea we brought her. We suspect she won't sleep much tonight.

The first thing Sam does when he comes in is ask what happened to Alice's face and she tells him the same thing she told our mother: It was an accident. I avoid Sam's eyes. He stares at Alice for a long time.

"Okay," he says, but it doesn't sound like he believes her. "How's Melanie?" he asks, sitting down on the coffee table beside us. "Today's—"

"The thirtieth, yeah," says Alice. "She's upstairs. She's okay, I guess. As okay as she can be." She gazes up at the ceiling like she can see through it to our mother's room. She has a funny look on her face. "She's keeping her secrets," she says.

I frown. Alice's cheek is turning purple. Her lip has stopped bleeding, but it's swollen and looks sore. I glance over at Sam and think that Alice is hardly one to talk about keeping secrets.

Sam seems to think so too. His face gets cloudy. "Yeah, that's how we do things," he says. "Isn't it?" His voice is sharp. He stands up and then sits down again. "I *hate* this!" he says loudly. I look up at the ceiling like Alice just did and hug my arms to my chest.

Sam says, "In this house we never really know what's wrong, only that something's wrong. It's fucked up." His foot taps on the ground like he's nervous, or angry. He points an accusing finger at Alice. "And what the hell happened to you after I left you at the hospital? Or are you keeping your secrets too?"

171

"Sam," I say like a warning.

"No, he's right," Alice tells me, and she suddenly sounds just as angry as Sam. "You're right," she says to him. "You want us to share our secrets? Okay, I'll tell you what I think— I'll tell you a secret." Her voice is dangerous, like the edge of a cliff. She says, "I think this accident season thing is bullshit."

I put up my hands to stop her, as if her words are physical things that can reach out and hurt us. "Alice, come on."

"It is."

I look anxiously toward the living room door. Sam didn't close it when he came in, and I'm worried my mother will hear.

"What about all the falls and bumps and bruises?" I say it in a whisper that comes out as a hiss. "What about the car that just hit you? Mom's hand, her broken arm? The bookshelf that fell on me? Sam in PE?"

"Coincidence," says Alice. "For the most part. The rest? They're not accidents. You think my phone just slipped out of my hand that night? I was angry." She says it with passion. "I threw my lamp at the wall."

Sam opens his mouth to say something, but I cut him off. "But it was still an accident that my shelf fell down," I say. My hiss gets louder. "And what about all the cuts and stitches? What about the broken bones of every other year?" My voice is at normal volume now and it feels too loud to my ears. "What about the narrow escapes, Alice? Like the time Sam cracked his head on the kitchen tiles? Or when that glass

172

broke and nearly severed the vein in your wrist? Or the time I almost drowned?"

Alice's eyes are like someone else's. "You really think all those were accidents?"

Later I'll let myself look back on that sentence and figure out what's wrong with it, like in a children's picture puzzle, but for now I just raise my voice even louder and say, "What about the tragedies, Alice? What about Dad, and Granddad? What about Seth?"

"Oh yeah?" Alice shouts. "What about Seth? What about how he died was an accident?"

"Alice," Sam says softly.

"Look," she says, "I know you don't want to believe it. I know you never have, but that wasn't an accident. He didn't hit his head on that rock by accident."

And maybe her words are physical, maybe they do grab us and take us away from the wrapped-up doll's house to the evening after one of my mother's gallery openings in Westport four years ago. They bring us right there—I can see by his pale face that Sam's there with me: We're not in the living room anymore, we're down past the pier, by the rocks, we're daring each other to jump into the water fully clothed, but my mother won't let us. Not during the accident season, she says.

"He didn't know that there were rocks there," Sam says in a strange voice. "None of us did."

"Yeah," says Alice. "None of *us*"—she gestures around

at the three of us—"pushed him in. That part, that wasn't an accident." She shakes her head and talks over us when we try to speak. "Seth was pushed into the water, he hit his head. That's not an accident. And I know you don't like to think about it because Christopher's your father, but—"

"It was an accident," Sam says again. His face is too pale and his cheeks are flushed. They stand out; they remind me that there's blood beating under there, a network of veins.

I put my hands on his. "It was a game," I say to Alice. "Christopher just did it as a joke. We've done the same thing in summer. I can't count how many times I've pushed Sam into the river." Sam's hands reach around and squeeze mine.

Alice's face is unreadable. "If that's what you tell yourself," she says. "But I don't think it's what Mom tells herself. I don't think that's what keeps her awake at night."

Sam's face is furious, but his eyes are filled with tears. Alice gets up and storms out of the living room, and when she has gone, the whole house feels more breakable than ever, and unsafe even under all its layers.

***

When we go to bed, I lie awake for a long time. My head swims from the whiskey I drank with Alice and from everything she has said. I feel that strange stinging sensation against my cheek again. It lingers like pins and needles. The wind whistles by my window, and suddenly I want to be outside. I open my bedroom door to go downstairs and Sam is standing there, right in front of me, his eyes hooded and his hair messed like he's been tossing and turning in bed. One of his hands is raised like he was about to knock.

"Hi," I say.

"Hi."

I feel silly and tipsy in my pink fleecy pajamas. Sam inclines his head toward the stairs. "I heard you moving around in your room," he says, "and I just wondered if you wanted to go for a quick smoke before bed." He is wearing a rumpled hoodie over his pajamas and his feet are bare. "I couldn't sleep," he adds.

"Me either," I say. I realize that my chest is tight. Maybe a smoke would help.

I follow Sam downstairs and out through the kitchen door. The rain is torrential against the windows, but we shelter between the back door and the shed and the wind doesn't even ruffle our hair. It slants through the garden and needles through the trees. The world looks like it's melting. I light a cigarette with shaking hands and pass the lighter to Sam. I don't know what to say.

"Do you remember that street performer in Galway the day we found the magic shop?" I say after a long smoky silence. I reach up and touch the shed roof. It's rusted and slick with rain.

"A street performer?" Sam hugs his arms to his chest, his cigarette perilously close to his clothes. The wind finds its way in through our pajamas.

"The metal man. The human statue guy."

"You mean the guy in the Halloween costume earlier?"

"I don't know if it was a Halloween costume. I bumped into him last week in Galway too." I take my hand down from the shed roof too quickly and the side of a corrugated-iron sheet cuts me, slices into my palm like a lifeline. Blood beads through the seam. I close my fist so Sam won't notice. I'm not ready to go inside just yet. "I just thought that's why you seemed to recognize him."

"I never saw him before," says Sam.

I back away from the shed and lean against the cold wall of the house. "Alice thought he was someone else," I say. "That's why she stopped. That's why the car hit her."

Sam shrugs. "I guess he looked like the Tin Man from *The Wizard of Oz*."

I don't know why, but I keep going. "You didn't think he looked like Christopher?"

Sam sort of smiles. It looks more like a grimace. "I guess," he says. "Maybe. If he were ten years younger and made of metal. It was just a passing resemblance, but I'm sure Melanie knows that guy. She knows most of the street artists around here." He takes a sharp drag of his cigarette. "I wouldn't even know what Christopher looks like anymore." He tosses his hair out of his eyes. "He could look completely different. I know I do. If he saw me now he'd never recognize me."

I think of Sam at thirteen, his hair shoulder-length and tangled, his body scrawny, his eyes cheeky and confident, his voice pitching like a ship at sea, and I smile. Then I look at Sam at seventeen. I stand out in the yellow light of the kitchen window in front of my ex-stepbrother and really look at him. I see the blue streak in his dark hair, the freckles on his cheekbones, his fingernails bitten to the quick. I see his broad shoulders and big, square hands. I see his smile that flickers like a silent-film ghost. I look into his riverbed eyes and they look straight back into mine and my heart gives a little lurch.

"And you know what?" Sam says. "I'm glad. I don't know what I'd do if I looked like him."

I'm taken aback by his tone. "But he's your dad, Sam."

"Yeah," says Sam. "And what good does that do me? He left." He finishes his cigarette and buries his hands deep into the pockets of his hoodie. "He doesn't love me, he doesn't care. He never cared. I kept trying not to believe it for years, but there's nothing I can do about it, so . . ." He shakes his head with one eyebrow quirked like it doesn't even matter, like it's no big deal. "So I hate him." There's something underneath the raised eyebrow and the feigned nonchalance, though—I can feel it. It simmers like a storm.

Then he says it, softly but fast, like something he needs to get out but doesn't want to say. "I think maybe Alice is onto something."

I'm sure the shock registers on my face. "What?"

"I've been thinking about this," he says. "So much. I've

been going over and over everything: how he left, why he didn't take anything with him, why he only calls once a year, why he never comes back, not even for a vacation. Don't you think there's something that doesn't add up?" His eyes on mine are almost pleading. I don't know if they're pleading with me to agree or to prove him wrong.

"I don't know, Sam," I say finally. "I think it just sounds like a shit person who doesn't care about anyone else."

Sam's eyes are dark in the cold night. River-after-sunset eyes. "I guess you're right." He seems relieved. I try not to think about what Alice said earlier. *It was an accident,* I think. *It was the accident season. That's all there is to it.* I'm not sure I believe myself.

Sam leans back against the shed wall and lights another cigarette. I check the cut on my palm and see that it has stopped bleeding. I crack my knuckles loudly in the careful quiet our words have left behind. Beside me, Sam blows out three perfect smoke circles. I stretch after one of them before it wafts into nothingness and I stick my tongue through it like we all did last night out here in the garden before Sam and I went down to the river and it was frozen. It seems like a long time ago now.

Breaking the smoke circle is like breaking a spell. Sam grins at me and it's as if the last few hours have been forgotten. I giggle. The air is cold and dries my tongue. I taste smoke and rain and mushy autumn leaves. Sam takes another puff, and soon there are three more smoke circles floating around our heads. Like a little kid trying to pop all the soap bubbles, I tongue every one of the circles. Sam puffs out some more and curls up his tongue in that way that's supposed to be genetic and pokes at the smoke circles with me. We laugh low so as not to wake anyone up. The house is silent and seems far away behind us.

I go after one of the smoke circles that has drifted away. It is deformed and oblong, and when I lean forward to catch it with my tongue I overbalance and almost fall down the back step into the stormy garden, but Sam grabs my waist and pulls me back into the shelter of the shed and we both laugh some more.

We are very close. I notice it suddenly. Sam's arms are still around my waist. He smells nice. His hair is completely black in the darkness and I can hardly see his eyes.

"When you kissed Bea," I say to him slowly in the circle of his arms, "you said it was to prove the cards wrong." Sam nods slightly. "Did it work?" I ask.

Sam stares straight at me. "No," he says.

I know he won't tell me, but I ask anyway. "What did they say to you?"

Sam just sort of smiles. I duck my head awkwardly. I uncross my arms and let my hands rest lightly on Sam's shoulders. "You're warm."

Sam laughs a little. I clear my throat.

"So, um," I say awkwardly, keenly aware of his arms around me, "did you have a good time in the city with Martin?"

"We just hung out at the arcade, played some games. But then I told him about the shop where we got our costumes and he wanted to go, but we couldn't find it."

"What do you mean you couldn't find it? It was just off Shop Street."

Sam shrugs. His arms are still around me. I'm finding it a little difficult to concentrate on what he's saying. "It wasn't there."

"Like it'd closed down?"

"Like it'd never existed."

Little goose pimples prickle my skin.

"I mean, those costumes are almost too perfect, you know?" he says. "You already sometimes look like you have wings."

He brings his hands up behind my back to my shoulder blades. His hold brings him closer to me. His face is only inches away. He lowers his head and rests his forehead against mine. We lick our lips like a mirror image.

Sam kisses me. It starts with the lightest touch of lips on lips, tilted heads, short of breath. We hover as if on a threshold. My heart beats hard. Then our mouths press together. Our eyes close and our lips open and Sam very slowly slips his tongue into my mouth, and when I touch it with my own, he deepens the kiss, wrapping his arms around my waist and pulling me tight toward him. Our mouths become my whole world. Warm lips, gentle tongues, quiet breath, wild hunger. My hands curl in his hair. We are connected lips to lips, chest to chest, knee to knee like we're just one person. I can feel the kiss in my mouth and in my mind, as a crazy wanting in my heart, as butterflies in my tummy and as a great ache stretching lower, all the way to my toes. I can feel it in my heartbeat and in every bruise. I've never been kissed like this.

Then the house phone rings. It is three o'clock in the morning and it rings like the end of the world. Sam and I spring apart like the opposite poles of two magnets. I turn and run into the kitchen to answer.

It's Nick.

"Cara?" he says. "Can I talk to Alice?"

I don't even think. I say, "No."

"She's not answering her phone," he says like he didn't hear me. "But I thought she'd be up."

My heart is still pounding. I can hear someone coming down the stairs. Footsteps and heartbeats. Sam stands shadowy in the doorway to the kitchen. The back door is still open, spills cold air all through the house. Sam's hands are at his mouth.

Alice comes into the kitchen and makes to take the phone out of my hand. My fingers tighten automatically around it. She pulls at it, but I won't let go.

"Call my cell," she says into the phone, bending her head to my hand so he will hear her. Immediately her phone starts to ring.

I shake my head. "Alice, no."

The look she gives me is sad but fierce. She turns and goes back upstairs, talking softly on the phone to Nick. I just stare after her because I can't move. Sam is behind me, but he isn't moving either. Numbly, I walk upstairs to my bedroom without turning around. When I get into bed, I notice that I am still holding the phone.

12

Sam is asleep when the rest of us are ready for school the next morning. Alice thumps on his door, but he doesn't come out. My mother passes by and says, "He is like a sleeping bear—don't open the door to his grotto!" and Alice laughs.

I can't laugh. All I can think about is last night. I try not to think about it, but of course that never works. It's like that saying about elephants. *There's nothing I can do,* I tell myself, *but pretend it never happened.* A little lost thought comes up and says, *Yes, it turns out you're really very good at that.* I squash the thought like an insect on my leg. I bang on Sam's bedroom door.

"Sammy," I yell like it's any other morning. "Get your lazy ass out of bed." The groan from inside really does sound like a bear. "Sam!" I shout louder.

Sam opens the door. His eyes are squinty and his hair is tousled and he leans on the door frame, his face in the tiny open gap onto the landing. I imagine questions in his eyes, but I also imagine excuses. I imagine regret. The rain, the whiskey, the cigarette smoke like a shared kiss. I stop myself on the word *kiss*. *He's my brother,* I remind myself for the hundredth time.

"We're going," I say. I make my voice impatient.

Sam's eyes are sad like the deepest water. "Yep," he says. His voice is whiskey-hoarse. He clears his throat. Alice hurries across the landing and down the stairs and Sam waits until she's out of sight before saying, "Can I talk to you for a sec?"

He opens his door slightly wider and I can see in the thin gap that he is halfway through getting dressed; he is barefoot and topless, his trousers low on his hips. My face burns.

"We're late," I say, and my voice sounds strangled.

Alice calls from the kitchen and my mother hurries up the stairs to fetch something she's forgotten in her room.

"You know Melanie will be another twenty minutes," Sam says. "Cara, please."

"We're *going!*" Alice shouts from the hall.

My mother emerges from her bedroom holding a pair of socks in one hand, her wallet and phone tucked into her sling for safekeeping, and her sunglasses dangling from her mouth. "Sam, aren't you dressed yet?" she says, lisping through the earpiece of the glasses between her teeth. I take the glasses from her mouth so she won't break them, or her teeth. "Hurry up—you three are walking to school. Gracie'll be here any minute to drive me to work."

"Hey!" Alice shouts louder. "Guys! I've a test first period, so you'd better not make me late."

My mother smiles and shakes her head. "You heard the woman," she says, pointing her wallet at Sam. "Hop to it."

Sam retreats into his room without a word. I stare at his closed door for maybe a fraction of a second too long, because my mother gives me a funny look as I trudge down the stairs.

Alice hasn't told our mother about her accident yesterday. She isn't wearing her sling, and has put on uniform trousers instead of a skirt so there's no way my mother would know she was at the hospital last night with a dislocated shoulder and butchered knees, needing multiple stitches. All my mother knows—or thinks she knows—is that Alice got hit in the face by a soccer ball crossing the field after school.

Alice spends most of the walk to school complaining about her sadistic economics teacher who has sprung a surprise test on them on the last day before the midterm break. She doesn't mention her accident, or Nick, or anything we talked about last night. She and Sam act completely normal around each other. I can't tell if Sam and I do the same; I've forgotten what normal feels like.

To me the school day drags by, but Bea is practically bouncing through every class. People keep coming up to us in the halls or the cafeteria to talk about the party. Some of Alice's friends organize to meet us at the ghost house later tonight to set up, and it's easier than I expect to get swept up in party preparations so that everything else is almost forgotten. Even finding Elsie seems to have faded into the background. I'm not sure I can take any more surprises after everything that happened last night.

Finally the bell rings for the end of our last class. Bea, Alice, Sam, and I change out of our uniforms in the school bathrooms. Then we walk to the ghost house, armed with bags of costumes and decorations, candles and flashlights that Bea has been keeping at her place so our mother won't know about our plans, as well as three bottles of wine that Sam's had hidden in his cupboard since my mother's last dinner party. We send my mother cheerful texts about decorating Bea's garden for trick-or-treaters so she won't suspect a thing.

A few days ago we agreed to come early to the ghost house, to have some time there by ourselves before the party starts. I tell myself I'm glad about this; that showing Sam and Alice around and drinking wine before the ball will make everything seem normal again.

By the time we've reached the ghost house, the sky is all dark clouds and the afternoon is murky. The temperature's down by several degrees today and the wind is fierce. It whips my scarf around my neck, threatening to strangle me. I look up at the big bay windows of the master bedroom, and for just a moment I think I see a face behind the net curtains. I blink and the face is gone.

Bea and Alice climb over the gates first, and when they're both in the garden, I pass the bottles of wine through the bars to Alice and throw the bag over to Bea. When I start to climb over ahead of Sam, I notice that it's easier to climb without gloves on my hands, and with the canvas Converse I usually never wear during the accident season on my feet. I realize that, apart from the night before last, on the ice, this is the fewest layers I've worn in any accident season since what happened to Seth. And here I am scaling gates to break into abandoned houses. If only my mother could see me now.

At the top of the gates I wobble. I'm trying to shake the image of Seth out of my head, but I shake a little too violently for the ancient gates and the blowing wind. When I bring my left leg over—my right already wedged between the bars on the ghost house side—I lose my balance. My left leg kicks out into thin air and the force of it makes the right one slip. I hardly have time to gasp. Suddenly both my legs are kicking out more than two meters above the ground. Alice screams. My hands grip the gates like vises and I try to scrape my feet back over the iron curlicues until they've found new footholds. My heart hammers in my mouth and my hands begin to sweat. My grip slips.

"Cara!" Bea shouts. She holds her arms out toward me, as if that'll help.

It feels like my feet don't belong to me. I can't make them do what I want them to do; my shoes slide across the bars of the gate and I can't find any of the metal swirls to brace myself on. All I can see are my white knuckles gripping the rusted bars in front of me. The gates shake.

"Sam, stay where you are!" Alice shouts from below. "If you try to climb, you'll shake the gates."

I can feel Sam let go of the gates. I try not to panic. I pedal my feet uselessly, until finally my flailing legs find a foothold. I wedge my feet into the bars and press myself tight against the gate. The muscles in my arms scream.

I stay folded over the top of the gates just long enough to steady my breath before making my careful way down. I'm glad when my feet find solid ground. Between the top of the gates and the ice on the river, I think there isn't nearly enough solid ground in my life right now. When Sam lands on our side of the garden, he puts his arm around me.

"You okay, little sister?" he says softly, sounding like the Sam I've always known. My heart tries to skip a beat, but I ignore it. *Everything is back to normal,* I tell myself. *It was wrong, he regrets it, we're not going to talk about it. This is for the best.*

I am concentrating so hard on this that I forget to remind him I'm not his sister. Because for all intents and purposes, I am. *Back to normal,* I remind myself again. *For the best.*

When we get onto the porch, Bea holds out her hand to push the handle, but the door just opens by itself, like it has felt our bodies in front of it, like it knows we want to come in. Alice gives an uncertain laugh.

Inside, the house feels different. Maybe it's because of the darkness—the hall is lit by shadows and flashlight beams—or maybe it's the wind crying in through every crack, but today the ghost house feels more haunted than it did before (and it already felt haunted enough). Alice and Sam are mesmerized. Bea gives them the grand tour. When we get to the double doors to the master bedroom, we all fall silent.

I set my shoulders. "Okay." I gesture to Bea to take one of the handles. I take the other. Together, we push open the doors into the master bedroom and let Sam and Alice step inside.

Nothing has changed. It's like the picture I took. The walls are peeling and I can almost make out faces in the faded paper. The dirt is thick over everything, except the trails our feet left last time. They are the only tracks in the room.

We train the beams of light over the floorboards to the fire pit. Sam mutters a quiet "Wow."

Bea marches straight to the bay windows and pulls the curtains. The dust makes clouds around her head. There is no one there. There is no Elsie. There are no ghosts; only the dust in the light, our breath and the wind in the quiet, and the feeling that something, or a lot of somethings, are watching us. So maybe there are ghosts after all.

Alice kneels down on the dirty floor and opens the backpack I hadn't noticed she was carrying. Inside, along with the battery-charged music docks she borrowed from Nick for the party, she has packed away what looks like hundreds of candles wrapped in paper. She takes them out one by one and calls for us to help. Her voice echoes around the bare room. I shiver.

Bea and Sam set out the candles; little tea lights, colored candles from gift shops, big church candles that remind me of Christmas. In the gleam of the flashlight they look like bones. Alice follows behind us with one of those long tapered lighters you use for barbecues, and forms a hundred flames. The flickering lights make me anxious. Everything in the room is just so flammable, and we are most of all.

Bea takes four more paper packets out of her bag. They're clearly not candles. She hands one to each of us, and when we open them, we see the masks.

"We made them yesterday," says Alice. "We needed to

use wire and pliers and knives, so we didn't want to do it at our house, and Bea's mom had loads of stuff we could use, so we decided to make them a surprise."

I hold up my mask in the moving light. It's delicate and sparkly and the sequins look like a statue's tears. In the darkness it's the same blue-brown-green as the river in sunlight. When I put it on, it fits as if it's been molded from my bones. Beside me in his black mask, Sam looks like a bandit, like the pirate in *The Princess Bride*; he looks like half his face has been erased. Like a censor bar's sitting over his cheeks, hiding his eyes. It's creepy. Across the room Alice's face is made of tree bark and autumn leaves. Bea's skin is scales.

I touch my cheeks, my glitter tears. "You really made these?"

Alice nods.

"They're kind of creepy," Sam says, echoing my feelings exactly. "They feel like they've been cut off someone else rather than made."

Alice looks proud, but I feel uncomfortable and unlike myself. I want to take the mask off, but the others keep theirs on, so I don't touch it. Something about the way it wraps around my face makes me hear my breath much louder than usual. I keep jumping and wanting to turn, thinking my breath is the breath of someone else behind me.

Sam turns off his flashlight and we're surrounded by candlelight. We sit down between the window and the door (almost as if we are ready to run away at any minute) and pass around the jam jars that Bea's brought with her to use as glasses. We open one of the bottles of wine and fill them to the brim.

"This really is the perfect place for our party," Bea says. Beside her, Alice smiles under her tree-bark mask. I wonder if she is imagining her friends' reactions to the place or if the ghost house really is working its spell on her. Outside, the wind rattles the windowpanes and downstairs it sounds like a wolf's been let into the house.

We sip from our jam-jar wineglasses and listen to the howling, and Bea tells us about the wolves of Ireland; how, not so long ago, forests covered all the land, and the wolves roamed free. How they'd wander from coast to coast and sometimes turn into beautiful, tall humans and come up to the villages to seduce the sons of millers and the daughters of smiths. The sons and daughters'd spend one night with the wolves and fall in love forever, and when the wolf left the next morning—padding silently and four-legged back into the trees—the son of the miller or the daughter of the smith would spend three years searching the forests, barefoot and trembling, until they died from exhaustion at the foot of a tree. And then the wolf would come back and feast on their flesh.

Beside me, Sam laughs, maybe a little nervously. "You have a morbid mind," he says to Bea.

Alice, who usually scoffs at Bea's stories, starts asking Bea questions about the wolves. She sounds more curious than sarcastic, but then with Alice it's sometimes hard to tell. "Is there a way of telling," she asks, "that they're a wolf and not a human?"

Bea takes a pack of cigarettes out of her pocket and lights one. The candles all jump at the new piece of fire in the room. "Traditionally, they have more hair than humans. Male werewolves'll have hairy chests, and both will have long matted locks and wild thickets between their legs."

Sam chokes on his jar of wine. I pat him on the back until he stops coughing. Alice holds out her hand for Bea's cigarette.

"Wolves also make excellent lovers," says Bea. "Or so I've heard."

"From who?" I want to know. Bea just smiles mysteriously.

"Humans also make excellent lovers," says Alice, who knows far more about these things than I.

"Oh, but not like a human wolf." The walls seem to bend forward to listen, and even the heavy curtains creep toward the sound of Bea's voice. "When they look at you, it's like they can see clear through your clothes and right in under your skin. Like they can smell on you what it is you desire and just how hard you want to be held. They'll pin you to the floor until you almost die with pleasure; their hands on your hips will raise bruises, and their kisses are like bites that'll devour you whole. You'll never get out alive."

The wind picks up outside and the house shudders. Sam huffs out his breath in a rush. "Well," he says, and he sounds a little dazed. I don't know if it's the hundred burning candles or the wine setting my throat on fire, but underneath my mask my face is flushed. I can't seem to get the picture of Sam standing topless in the doorway to his room out of my head. I am careful not to look at him.

"And once you've spent a night with them, you're theirs forever?" Alice says.

"Forever."

"And there's no way to break the spell?"

Bea laughs. "It's not a spell, Alice. It's something worse."

"Something worse." Alice's eyes are little flames. Bea refills her jar with wine and Alice drinks like it's water.

"Alice, hold on," says Sam, and I put out my arm as if to stop her. She has a wild look to her that has very little to do with the tree-bark skin of her mask (although, masked and wine-drunk in the candlelight, we are all a little wild tonight). When the bottle gets passed back to me, it is empty. My head is starting to spin and I'm beginning to believe the ghosts are drinking with us. Why else would we have finished a whole bottle so fast?

"So what if you were right?" Alice says to Bea, her voice hard but serious. "What if it was real and there were wolves

with human bodies seducing human lovers and then waiting for them to drop dead before feasting on their flesh?" She
laughs then, and even Bea looks worried. "Say it was true. How
would you stop it? If it's not a spell, then how do you stop it?"

For once Bea doesn't know what to say. She reaches over
to her bag and takes out her cards. She shuffles them and
spreads them out on the floor in front of us. I expect Alice to
roll her eyes or tell us she's only joking, but instead she stares
down at the cards with the same intense look as Bea. I glance
over at Sam. He looks at me. I wonder if I look as worried as
he does. I wonder how much he suspects about Nick.

Bea stares at the cards for a minute and then says, "You
have to kill the wolf." Then she shakes herself and says,
"Metaphorically." She looks over at Alice. "We are talking
metaphorically here, aren't we?"

"Are we?" Alice says. "You tell me, Miss Ghostwatcher,
Miss Cardreader, Miss Witch." She smacks her hands on the
floor impatiently and then cries out. The palm of her left
hand has landed on something that was caught between two
floorboards. She pulls it out. It's another big red button.

"The witch's kiss," Bea whispers.

Alice stares at the button and puts it in the pocket of her
jeans. I think about the button I found, now sitting with the
clutter on my bedside table. She reaches behind her and pulls
the second bottle of wine out of my bag. She unscrews the
cap and holds up the bottle.

"To the wolves!" she shouts, and she takes a sharp swig. She hands it to Bea, who takes it eagerly.

"To the ghosts!" Bea's lips leave red stains on the mouth of the bottle and the wine leaves red stains on her lips.

I take the bottle and raise it so that the wine sloshes over the side. "To the river underneath us!" When I hand it to Sam, he just looks at me. I gesture for him to take the bottle. When he raises it to toast, he's still staring me straight in the eye.

"To our secrets," he says. I feel like I can't breathe. Bea nods solemnly and Alice gives a hard little laugh. The room has become hot and airless. Outside, it sounds like a storm. Inside my head is pretty stormy too. The rain's a bit like music. We start to sway where we sit. My palms are sweaty. I take off my coat, and then my sweater, unwind my scarf.

"Take off your shoes," Bea says suddenly. She jumps up and kicks off her witchy boots. "Listen to the ghosts—listen to how they liked our talk of wolves." Her bare feet stamp on the floor and the whole house groans. "Listen!" Bea shouts, and she laughs out loud. Alice stands up with her and takes off her little pumps. She knocks on the floor with her feet. The house creaks like it's responding.

Sam and I take off our shoes as well because I don't think it's in our natures to disobey Bea. Not when she looks this witchy, at least. Her hair is big and tangled, and every curl sticks up at an angle under the slowly glowing scales of her mask. Her face looks like the sea and her eyes are pearls. Her dress sticks to her body with static, and she and Alice hold hands and stomp and stamp and the whole floor shakes.

"Get up, get up!" she shouts.

Sam gets up off the floor slowly. He holds out his hand to help me up and I hesitate for half a second before taking it. But I do take it. And I keep my hand in his for a second and a half longer than is necessary, just to prove to him that everything is fine and forgotten, that everything's back to normal. Whatever that means.

Bea gets us all to hold out our jam-jar glasses and she fills them to the brim with wine. We raise them for another toast.

"To the accident season," Alice says breathlessly. My own breath catches in my throat. A particularly strong gust of wind blows in under the door, and suddenly the room's filled with dancing light. Sam cries out. In the middle of the room, in the circle on the floor that's been charred and blackened, in the dusty remains of whatever once burned there, a fire flares up.

Alice lets out a wordless shout and Bea starts to laugh and laugh like she's possessed. Immediately I look for an explanation: I tell myself that some of the candles blew over and caught fire in the dust, but really I think we all know it's just magic. So when Bea dances over to the fire, we follow like the Pied Piper's children. When she starts to speak, she's like a sleepwalker.

She recites our poem as a chant—the exquisite corpse we wrote together out in the garden. She has learned it by heart. She takes the chorus she made with one line from each of us and repeats it so that it sounds like a prayer, like a spell, like she is stitching us all together with our own words.

"*So let's raise our glasses to the accident season,*" she says, and we move the way she moves and our feet clap the floor in the dust along with her. "*To the river beneath us where we sink our souls.*" Bea raises her glass and we toast the fire with her. My skin crawls like I'm being walked on by a million tickly legs. "*To the bruises and secrets.*" Alice raises her glass above her head and the wine falls on her hair like red rain. "*To the ghosts in the ceiling.*" The house screams. "*One more drink for the watery road.*"

The music is suddenly louder even though no one's touched the volume. It's playing songs I've never heard before, and I know Bea's music collection pretty well. The room is huge. We dance around it like animals. The flames make stains on our skin.

We dance hard; we collide, breathless. We slip and hit off each other, and every time our bodies touch, the electric lights spark even though there's no power in the house. We stick to each other and wind our arms around each other and we move together like that. We are all entwined limbs, but we're somehow still dancing. We're monstrous, magnificent. We are one enormous creature taking over the night. We have eight legs, four beating hearts, a thousand beads of sweat on a thousand tiny hairs spread over one giant body.

And we are chanting together and the music playing is the sound of our dancing and it is all so loud that I close my eyes to drown out the noises, but then suddenly I feel something like a kiss on my eyelids and a little voice whispers, "Wake up wake up wake up," and when I open my eyes, there's someone else, someone breathing when I breathe, moving when I move. I look up and it's Elsie.

I scream.

Alice trips over something and smacks into the ground and Bea screams too. Sam runs over to help Alice, but he lands badly; he kicks one foot over the fire and sparks hiss up. The house howls. I grab my school bag and throw it on the fire. It's just big enough to cover the flames. The wind outside reaches its crescendo and the bay windows blow open and all the candles sputter and die in the rain that comes in on the wind.

We are left in darkness. The house is quiet. I crawl over to the other side of the room and find the flashlights by touch. The light is weak after all the candles and the fire, and under our masks we all look so pale. Bea is holding Alice in her arms and Sam is limping painfully up to them, shaking his head. I switch on all four flashlights—two in each hand, bumping their beams against the walls and the ceiling—and when all of them are lit and focusing together around the bedroom I can see that we're alone. If we were ever anything else.

I don't know who starts it. It could be Bea, cradling Alice in her arms. It could be Alice, bruised from her fall. It could be Sam, collapsed by the pit where the fire was burning half a minute ago, one sock slightly singed and one toe swollen, maybe sprained. It could be me. It could be Elsie, although I can't see her and therefore must assume that she isn't here (if she ever was). Someone starts it with a little startled laugh, and then suddenly we're all laughing. Chuckling at first, or little giggles, and then the laughter grows and becomes a sort of breathless mirth. The sound of it reverberates on the ceiling, it bounces against the walls, it trips around us until Bea is rocking on the ground, holding her sides, and Alice is almost crying from it.

It takes a long time for us to catch our breaths. Sam limps around and lights the candles again, even though I tell him I don't think it's a good idea.

"It's okay, little sister," Sam says, and he comes over to me. His eyes are dark underneath the mask.

"I'm not your sister." My voice is hoarse and too quiet. Sam opens his mouth to say something but then closes it again with a shrug. My voice gets even quieter. "You're supposed to say, *If you say so, petite soeur,*" I tell him. Sam smiles. I can't tell if it's a normal smile or a sad one; the mask hides his face too well. I can't tell who any of us are anymore.

Bea gets up and herds us all out of the master bedroom. She and Alice take the flashlights and Sam and I collect an armful of candles each, and we go into the bathroom where the mirror is cracked and dusty and reflects the flashlight beams and the candlelight so that the whole room glows. Bea rummages around in her bag for the big box of her mother's stage makeup she has borrowed for the night. She sits Alice down on a stool and begins to paint her arms and legs like the bark of trees. I suggest that Sam strap his toes together so the swollen one won't move and I start to get some painkillers from my bag, but Sam holds me back.

"It's probably the wine," he says, "but I don't feel a thing."

Alice stares at her reflection in the mirror and I stare at Alice. Her sleeves are rolled up so that Bea can paint her arms. Her bruises are a patchwork of new and fading, but there are cuts on her arms that look like cat scratches, which I tell myself must be from climbing the iron gates. Although they almost look as if they're days, or maybe weeks, old. I blink. The world has become fuzzy at the edges. I strap up Sam's toes and we drink our wine and Alice picks up a makeup brush and paints Bea's legs ocean blue while Bea paints hers.

When Alice and Bea are made up, we all go back into the master bedroom to change into our costumes. Bea and Alice chat and laugh, help each other with their zips and buttons, run out into the bathroom and back to check out their dusty reflections. Alice uses eyelash glue to stick scales onto Bea's face, and Bea glues tiny leaves to Alice's. They are like earth and water. They go too well together. It makes my heart hurt.

When she is dressed, Alice is that girl in the Greek myth who turned into a tree. Her skin is bark and her branchlike arms are beginning to flower. She looks like a forest that just came to life, and she has come to life dancing. How amazing it must be to have legs after so many years as a tree. Beside her, Bea is the sea. There are gills in her neck that seem to breathe when she moves, and the scales on her face and on her mask shimmer. Her hands are webbed with silk and there is coral stuck to her skin.

Beside the two of them I feel ridiculous. A child's fantasy, all dressed up in her mother's clothes. The top of my tutu dress is made of several silk scarves stuck together and I worry that it shows too much. I keep pulling at the edges of it, trying to cover up. I think of the pictures of Alice when she was younger, fully dressed on the beach while the rest of us ran around in shorts and bikinis. I am all hard glitter and leathery wings. My tights are too sheer and my mask is too colorful and everything's so bright it's surreal. The others look almost eerie; I am only cutesy and winged.

"Everyone should be here soon," says Alice, checking the time on her phone.

Bea pulls on her good arm. "Come downstairs with me," she says to her. "Let's start decorating."

I tell myself not to take it as a snub that they don't wait for me and Sam before clattering down the rickety stairs.

Behind me, Sam clears his throat. "Can you give me a hand with this face paint?" he asks.

I turn around and let myself look at him properly. With his costume on, his skin looks flickery, like he might not be all there. He has put temporary black dye on the blue streak in his hair and he is holding out the box of Bea's mother's stage makeup. It was Bea's idea to paint his skin gray, make him completely monochrome, so that he would look like he's stepped right out of a silent film.

I dab one of Alice's makeup brushes into the face paint and he closes his eyes. I brush the paint over his eyelids; I cover the scattered freckles on his cheeks. My heart hammers against my rib cage like it's trying to get out. I follow the contours of Sam's face like I'm learning it by heart: the arch of his cheekbones, the scratchy stubble across his jaw, the almost-straight line of his once-broken nose. It makes it easier that his eyes are closed. It also makes it a little bit more like a kiss.

My hand trembles when I run the brush over his lips. When I'm finished, he licks them and makes a face at the taste of the paint. He opens his eyes and smiles.

"It's proper stage makeup," I say, and the words come out faint, "so it won't just rub off."

Sam stares into my eyes. "Okay," he whispers. "Good."

I am still standing right in front of him, the brush held in a shaky hand. Sam reaches up and takes it off me, gently, his hand meeting mine and lingering there. He licks his lips again and my face flushes with the memory of last night's kiss. And then I remember the regret I saw in his eyes this morning, the way my mother looked at me when I stared at him a moment too long; I remember *If you say so, petite soeur,* and how everything is supposed to be back to normal now. My face burns hotter, but now it is mostly with shame.

I pull my hand away from Sam's and take a couple of quick steps back, clearing my throat loudly.

"We should go help the others decorate," I say in a rush.

Sam doesn't move. His hand is still held up where mine was a moment ago. He drops it slowly. "Cara," he says.

"I'll just grab some of the stuff," I say, my voice still high-pitched and slightly frantic. I busy myself picking up our normal clothes from the floor and shoving them into our bags.

Sam takes his mask back from on top of one of the bags before I can cover it with clothes. When he puts it on, his eyes darken and he becomes a train-robbing bandit, a highway pirate, a masked avenger. He also looks a little like a ghost. I can feel him watching me even though I'm trying not to look at him. When I have gathered all our things, I hurry to the door.

"Cara," Sam calls again from behind me. "Can we just talk about this?"

My heart feels like it's falling down the stairs. I force myself to turn around and look at him. "I know it was a mistake," I say, and the words sound small. "I'm sorry. There's nothing to talk about."

13

When the sun has fully set and we are all masked and costumed with wine-stained lips, Kim and Niamh, Martin, Joe, and Toby meet us at the gates of the ghost house to help set up the party. Toby touches the edge of my mask gently after he has climbed over the gates.

"I love your costume," he says into my ear. "It's beautiful." I blush under my mask.

When we show everyone around, their mouths are like caverns. They use the word *perfect* so much, I'm not sure what it means anymore. The windows stare down on us, and behind the porch, the house seems like it's laughing.

Inside, we decorate the place to look like a nightmare carnival. We hang bats on the rafters, peering down from the broken ceiling, we wind black and red ribbons and fake spiders' webs up the dilapidated stairs, we put up signs saying

CAUTION and DANGER—and the more I think about it, the more dangerous this party seems, so I stop thinking about it for a while and let Bea's music and Alice's instructions guide me through the night. Whenever I look at Sam, I stop thinking even more.

"What about the master bedroom?" Alice asks, when we have decorated all the other rooms upstairs.

The rest of us don't answer right away. It's the one place we are reluctant to share. We haven't decorated it with bats or spiders' webs, only flowing drapes and candles. At first we consider bolting the doors to the party, but we decide that the temptation to open Bluebeard's chamber would be too great.

"And anyway," I tell the others, "it's not like it's our house. We don't own the place, we don't get to decide."

"If not us, then who?" Bea clearly also feels strongly about this particular room. "The ghosts?"

"Then let the ghosts bolt the doors," I say.

We go out into the misty garden and Bea finds a huge rock in what used to be the flowerbeds before weeds strangled everything in sight. When she holds up the rock, I take a few steps back, but Alice's eyes gleam. Niamh and Sam hold the enormous iron gates steady—the metal shrieking in the darkness—and Bea lifts up the rock and swings it down on the padlock hanging from the giant rusty chain. It barely leaves a dent. Sam takes the rock and tries. The padlock screams against the gates but sways away whole after the rock hits it.

"Let me give it a try," says Alice. She takes the rock from Sam—its weight drags her hands down when she takes it—and she swings it back and smashes it against the padlock and it springs open, broken, and falls to the ground. We cheer. Together we haul the gates open like the doorway to hell.

We split up and find more big rocks in the garden and carry them in increasingly muddy hands into the house. Toby and I open the doors to all the rooms and prop them open with the rocks so that the whole house is wide and inviting.

"This may well end up being the best party this year," says Toby.

"Oh yeah?" To hear that from someone like Toby is high praise.

His cheeks dimple a bit when he smiles. "Yeah."

As we work, Toby tells me about some of the best parties he's been to. The few parties we've been to with Alice got pretty drunk and disorderly, but some of Toby's stories are wild. I'm not sure I believe them all, but I'm secretly kind of impressed.

"And your parents let you go out that much?" I ask in disbelief. "How do you get away with it?"

Toby laughs. "My parents are pretty cool, actually," he tells me. "They understand that I'm eighteen and want to go out and party. Once I get the marks they expect, they let me do pretty much anything."

"But how *do* you get good marks if you're out partying every weekend?"

Toby shrugs. "I don't want to waste my teenage years," he says. "Study isn't everything. I mean, I've applied to do medicine in Trinity next year. I've got the points in every practice test I've tried so far. I study hard, but that's not all there is to me."

I don't know what to say to that. Toby's lips are full and his smile is easy. Energy shines out of him like glitter. "You're not who I thought you'd be," I say finally.

"You either."

"Oh yeah? Who did you think I was?"

Toby blushes in the light of the flashlight beams. It makes him seem less like an unattainable popular guy and more like a real person. He hands me an armful of decorations and we make our careful way down the staircase to put things up in the kitchen. Our shadows are long in the hall, but the kitchen is well-lit with brighter flashlights so people will be able to see their drinks. Martin has already brought over several cases of beer. I know better than to ask where he got them from.

"I dunno," says Toby. "More like Bea, I guess. But you aren't like her at all."

I prickle a little at that. "I think I'm a lot like Bea, actually. I think it's a great way to be."

Toby sees my expression and puts out his hands. "I

don't mean that in a bad way," he says quickly. "Just—I thought you'd be kind of . . . I don't know, weird or fake or something. You'd think people like you or Bea are posers, you know? But you're just totally genuine. Carl was right about that."

I kind of want to tell him that Carl the poser is not exactly one to talk about authenticity, but then I realize he's paying me a compliment. I reach up and readjust my mask a little nervously. "Carl?" I ask, because I'm not sure what else to say.

He turns away from me to hang some fake spiders over the shelves that are already covered in real spiders' webs. "Yeah. He's been kind of interested in Bea since Joe's party this summer, and after we heard about this party, he kept talking to me about you guys, and I didn't know anything about you, I didn't know I'd like you, but now I really do." He turns back around and looks straight at me.

"Yeah?"

Toby leans on the kitchen counter and angles himself toward me. I wonder if he ever stops smiling, then I think, *I hope he doesn't, because he has a lovely smile.* Then I wonder why I thought that. "Yeah," he says, and the littlest fingers of our hands almost touch on the counter. "You're a very interesting person, Cara Morris. A bit of a mystery."

"A mystery?" I like that. "You're pretty interesting too," I say. "I mean, I thought you were just this perfectionist

210

overachiever who thought he could get anything he wanted because he's good-looking."

"You think I'm good-looking?"

Now it's my turn to blush. "That's not what I meant."

Martin comes into the kitchen with some more beers. "Cara, are you insulting people again?" he says playfully. I aim a swat at his head and he mimes tripping over and dropping all the beer. He straightens up and puts the crates carefully on the floor instead. He looks around the kitchen for a moment and says, "I understand why you guys are so obsessed with this place." He cocks his head to one side. "It's like you can almost hear something . . ."

Toby and I turn our heads to be able to hear it too. There is music coming softly from upstairs still; there are voices—Alice's and Kim's—coming from another of the rooms. Someone is sliding a mattress across the floor in one of the bedrooms. Bea is singing to herself in the hall. Underneath that, though, I can hear the faintest whispering. I get down on my hands and knees and put my ear to the floor. Toby and Martin exchange a look, but then they crouch down with me. Our ears are cold against the dirty tiles.

"Listen," I whisper. We listen. Underneath us, the river is talking. I close my eyes. It's calling my name. It sounds like footsteps coming toward me, about to take me away. The footsteps get louder. I look up and Sam is standing at the door to the kitchen, a bunch of blankets in his hands.

"In case people get cold or need to crash," he explains. He doesn't ask why we're all on the floor. Something tells me he knows already. I wonder what the river says to Sam. He looks at me lying on the floor beside Toby and his face is hard, his expression closed off. Something twists in my tummy like a knife, but I don't move away. Toby's smile is uncomplicated and his eyes aren't sad, but mostly he isn't my brother. Sam turns slowly and leaves us on the dusty kitchen floor.

***

When the first people start arriving and the music gets cranked up—Bea's mixes filling the house like air in a balloon—I slip upstairs and take the rocks away from the bottoms of the doors to the master bedroom. I close the double doors and press my forehead to the peeling paint of the wood panels. I tighten my grip on the door handles. I whisper into the cracks. "Please be closed, please close, close."

I imagine the sound of a key in the lock, or of a bolt sliding into place, but I know that there is neither a bolt nor a key for this bedroom (or, indeed, for any other). The noise from downstairs is getting louder. More people have come. I take a deep gulp from somebody's bottle of whiskey I sneaked upstairs with me. It burns all the way down to my knees. It makes it easier to forget things.

Downstairs, the flashlights are lit. The darkness retreats

into the corners but it stays there crouching like a wolf about to strike. The music lilts and whistles like the deer the wolves are hunting. It dances about the place and no one can help but dance with it.

Toby catches me at the door to the kitchen. He has changed into his costume. His is a harlequin mask, half red, half white. The bells on the top of it jingle. He takes my hands and leads me in a dance around the room and out into the hall. We catch up with Kim and Niamh, who are drinking out of jam jars. Niamh's mask makes her look like an acrobat. It is delicate and made of something like porcelain. Kim's is a black cat. They join us and we all dance in a line—cats, acrobats, harlequins, and fairies—and pick up more creatures on the way: pigs and wolves and pandas, Victorian doll children and Venetian revelers, blank white masks like ghost faces.

The people keep coming. All those we invited and more; they come through the iron curlicued gates like a flood. They drink in the kitchen, they dance in the hall, they climb the rotting staircase, gingerly at first and then more and more fearlessly as the night progresses and the beer bottles empty. When I pass by some time later, I see somebody sliding down the banister rail.

The house likes this. All the wild dancing, the pulsing music, the slamming of so many shoes on the floor, so many drunken bodies against the walls and against each other, so many lips meeting and hands meeting other places in shadowy corners and on the dusty mattresses of the smaller bedrooms upstairs. The house revels in it. The walls beat like hearts, the floorboards groan, the staircase moans, and upstairs, the bedrooms whisper sweet nothings.

I am drunk. One minute I am with Bea in the old living room and we are telling a bunch of Niamh's friends about the ghosts, about the ceiling, about the faces in the windows, and the next I am upstairs with Joe and Carl with Toby and Martin and I am trying to steer the tipsy conversation away from sports. Then Martin and I are in one of the bedrooms and Bea is pushing Carl away from her because he's swaying too close, and then Toby and I are out on the landing talking about our families, and then I am with Kim and some of her friends on the landing and we are dancing like there's nothing else in the world but the dance, and in the hall below I think I see a girl with mousy brown hair and a Peter Pan collar peeking over the top of a shapeless sweater but when I hurry downstairs, there is no one like that around. I call out to Elsie, but no one answers except the music. Faces swim by under masks. I wander through the house looking for Elsie, but I find my friends instead. Only Sam never seems to be in the same room I'm in. That makes the forgetting easier too.

In the back of my mind I think about the changeling siblings who keep showing up in my dreams. I imagine them arriving at their party, which is very like our party, only wilder and more dangerous. There are no humans there. If I close my eyes I can almost see them, their human masks nearly gone, walking into a room full of strange, dark creatures. They see ghosts and elves and fairies and giants, they see huge half-human things, and creatures more like cats and horses and tiny dancing dogs, they see small kids with sharp teeth and red eyes. What they don't see, though, is that they are being followed. Just behind them, silhouetted in the dark door frame, is their stepfather.

After that things get blurry. Masks shift and shimmer. I can't always tell who's underneath. I sling my arm around the waist of a boy I think is Toby, but when he turns to look at me properly, I see that it's a boy in the year below me. I walk past Bea in the sitting room, but then she is standing out in the hall. I think I catch sight of a tartan skirt swishing around the corner, but when I run into the room, I see only strangers. Sometimes the music sounds like screaming. Alice is hugging me and apologizing for keeping secrets, and then there it is, the secrets booth, sitting in the front room that was probably once a study, or a library. Kim is sitting at it like she's Elsie at school and people are typing tipsy and slotting secrets into the box.

Bea sits down and types, and when she's done she takes the paper and shows it to us instead of putting it in the box. It says: *Sometimes I think my mother wishes I'd never been born.*

She throws the paper into the air and it flutters down onto the dusty floor.

"Never," Alice says. She takes Bea in her arms. "Nobody could ever think that." She kisses her cheek and the gesture is so intimate it makes me want to cry. I think about Sam's lips (I think about Sam's lips far more than any girl has a right to think about her ex-stepbrother's lips) and my heart hurts like a sprain. Can you break your heart by accident, I wonder, like you can break a wrist? If so, the accident season has me bruised and broken inside and out.

I leave my best friend with my sister and their secrets and I wander through the crowded rooms. I am still hoping to find Elsie, but I'm finding it harder and harder to remember why. There is more whiskey in the kitchen. When I get to the bottle, I find Martin and Joe. Martin's mask is half fire, half ice. Joe's is the diamond pattern of juggling balls. Toby joins us and we drink whiskey. It does nothing to help my sprained heart.

"Don't look so sad," Toby says with his ever-present smile. "You've just thrown the best party I've ever been to, and it's not even midnight. People'll be talking about this one for years."

I drink straight out of the bottle. "I'm not sad," I tell him. "I'm melancholy." Then I think of a cigarette like a shared kiss, secrets slotted into a wooden box, a heart full of the wrong kind of love. What even is love, anyway? I say, "Tonight I drink whiskey to forget."

"To forget what?" says Martin.

I giggle. "To forget my melancholy!" I shout it out and spread my arms wide, and some whiskey sloshes over the side of the bottle and onto my arm and Toby licks it off. His tongue tickles and his lips make it sound like a kiss. I block out the thoughts of pizza sauce and river eyes. Toby's eyes are an uncomplicated brown. I can see them clearly through the holes in his mask. Toby is always smiling. I smile with him.

For a while things blur again. I see Sam every so often, and once or twice we are in the same room, but mostly we are blown around like the rest of the masked dancers. The whiskey warms my tummy and the cockles of my heart. I think: *This is the best party.* Upstairs, some people are playing spin the bottle. There are clothes discarded on the floor. Skin and more skin. I turn away and dance back downstairs.

At the bottom of the stairs Toby stops me and we crowd into the hall with the rest of the dancers and he holds me close so I don't get stepped on. My wings heave in time to the music; the hot air in the hallway is blasted with cold wind every time the door opens and it lifts them like I'm flying.

Joe and Martin and Niamh and Sam are moshing in a corner. They look up and wave, but Toby and I are spinning past like music-box dancers. Under the arch of the staircase he kisses me. It tastes of whiskey, but we've drunk so much

217

of it at this point, it's unsurprising. I want to spin and dance away, but I kiss him again instead. We stay locked at the lips for what feels like a long time. It's not unpleasant (I suspect Toby has had plenty of practice), but I know deep down that it's not the kiss I want.

I pull away finally and ask Toby to get me a drink, pretend I'm going to the loo, but instead I duck into the dusty study, where Kim is still sitting at the secrets booth and people are dancing and typing and talking, and on the other side of the room Sam is punching his fist through the wall. Joe and Martin take his arms and drag him outside and I hide until they're gone.

I feel a hand on my shoulder and I think *Sam?* but when I turn around, it's Bea. She asks if I'm okay and I make myself grin wide, but she touches my cheek under my mask and her finger comes away glistening with tears. I think my grin must look strange, all tear-streaked and glittery.

"Too much whiskey," I say to her by way of explanation. Alice, who is just behind her, gives a little laugh.

"I know what you mean," she says. We are almost shouting to be heard over the music. It's pounding at my temples. It sounds like my heart. It sounds like a hundred fists punching through old plaster walls. Alice and Bea are waltzing in a slow circle around me. I look over at Kim. I want to type up a secret, but I don't think I have the words. I remember Alice apologizing for keeping secrets earlier and I want to tell her that I keep secrets too, but when I turn around, I see the wolf at the door.

"Alice," he says.

Alice turns, startled. She drops her hands from Bea's waist. "Nick?"

Nick has come dressed for the masquerade. His face is a wolf face, his leather jacket covered in tufts of hair. His teeth are sharp and I think I can see a tail swishing behind his jeans. "Alice," he says again. His voice is hoarse like he's been singing all night. Singing for Alice. Maybe he is the siren after all.

Bea moves back toward Alice and says in an urgent undertone, "I thought you said you were going to—" but Alice cuts her off.

"What are you doing here, Nick?" she says in that slightly lower, older voice. Her mask makes her gaze look dark. She lowers her voice even more. "I thought we talked last night," she says.

"I just want to be with you, love." Nick's teeth are very sharp and white in the dim room. He holds his hand out to Alice as if to dance.

"Don't worry," she whispers to Bea, her hand at the small of her scaly back. Nick's eyes narrow behind his wolf mask. His hand is out, palm up. Alice steps forward and takes it.

Bea makes a move toward Alice. "Don't," she says, but she says it too low.

"Don't," I say, but Alice is already gone.

Bea's face is unreadable. She looks pale blue in the candlelight. Or green, maybe, like the ocean. She sits down at the little desk and Kim, who has witnessed the whole scene, tries to comfort her in a way I just can't seem to do. She tells Bea that Alice is just going to talk to him, that if she hasn't ended it yet, she will tonight, that this is why she wants them to have some privacy. Bea ignores her. I think about Nick's siren voice and I wonder who is right. I think about Alice talking about his darkness. The room spins.

Bea types fast. She rips the paper out of the typewriter. Kim starts to tell her to be careful, but then she bites her lip. Bea holds out the secret so we can read it. It's all in block capitals. It says: *LOVE IS NEVER WORTH IT.* She lets the paper fall to the ground. Then she takes the box and throws its contents into the air so that all the secrets free themselves and fly around the room like big paper bats. Words come at us in the darkness.

Sometimes I think I'm losing my mind, I am a virgin, I am not a virgin, I am a liar, I don't like girls (I am a boy), I don't know if I am a boy or a girl, There is no God, There are ghosts all around us, LOVE IS NEVER WORTH IT, The wolves are real, I am in love with the wrong person, I am afraid that I am incapable of love, I haven't eaten a full meal in two years, I cut myself (no one knows), My ex-stepfather is a monster.

I trip over my feet through the flying secrets, out of the room and toward the front door. It is black as the night outside. Outside (or is it the reflection of the hall in the glass of the porch?) I think I can see the changeling siblings, watery as the rain.

They wander through the crowds, trying to find their evil stepfather before he has the chance to recognize them. They know that this may be their only chance to find him; they will only recognize him without his human mask, and this is the one night of the year in which their kind can be themselves. But their powers have weakened with every day they spend away from their home. They worry that they will not be strong enough to defeat him.

Slowly, surrounded by other changelings like them, they are becoming more themselves. The woodsprite's hair knots together like vines, the mermaid's gills pulse at the sides of her neck, the ghost boy begins to fade to black and white, and the fairy girl starts to be able to move her wings. They search through the rooms of the huge house—there are hundreds of them, some big, some small, some so well hidden, no human could ever see them. It is in one of those rooms that they find the wolf.

The woodsprite screams. "What's the matter?" the wolf boy says. "Don't you love me anymore?"

I feel a stinging slap on my skin, and my eyes open and my head snaps up and the metal man is standing right in front of me. He must have hit my cheek accidentally. When I look at his eyes, they are as hollow as an empty wolf mask. I remember that iron is supposed to be poisonous to fairies.

"You're the evil stepfather," I say to the metal man, but it comes out as a whisper.

He smacks my cheek again. He says, "It was just your imagination, do you hear me? Don't ever let me catch you saying anything like that again. You don't want to be a little liar like your sister, now, do you? Don't make me tell you again."

I nod and nod my little head. "Sure," I say, uncertain but with a smile. It's true I do have a big imagination. "Of course, Christopher."

Someone jostles my shoulder, clamoring down the stairs, and I wake up with a start. There is no one in front of me. There is no metal man. My eyes are blurry and my head is so confused. *Too much whiskey*, I think. I think, *I wonder where Elsie is.* I wonder if she's really here, in all this mess. I go upstairs, but I'm not sure if it is to look for her or to lie down. I feel like I'm sleepwalking. I don't know what's real anymore.

In one of the bedrooms a bunch of fourth years are clustered around a Ouija board. The candles flicker. I think I hear somebody scream downstairs. There are throwing-up sounds coming from the bathroom. In another bedroom a game of truth or dare is being played loudly. In a corner, on a mattress dragged off a bedframe, two people are kissing, wrapped around each other like seaweed. I think I see Carl's plastic Guy Fawkes mask dangling from a green-and-blue scaled hand, but then I tell myself that I must be mistaken. At the far end of the landing Toby and some of his friends are smoking and laughing. Toby gestures at me to join them, but I slip into the last of the small bedrooms. At this point I don't know who I'm looking for. I think of Elsie. I think of Sam. I think of Alice—and suddenly she's there, between Nick and the far wall.

Nick's head is buried in Alice's hair and his hands are all over her. The straps of her dress are torn and her chest and shoulders look too bare, too cold for this dark room. She is trapped between Nick's body and the peeling gray wallpaper, and I can tell that her arms are pinned to her sides because she is all elbows. Her mask is askew. Nick's wolf face is on the ground in front of me. Its eyes are empty sockets. It has no mouth but it is still whispering: *If you're going to do this just give me one last chance you know you want to come on if you really want to end it you owe it to me just give me one last—*

In the big black window in front of me I can see blurred reflections of the world outside. I half close my eyes and I can almost see the changelings at their own party.

They look at each other and they can see that they are weak. Back home, their powers were bright and constant like good summer sun, but here in the human world everything they feel and do is watered down. The three remaining siblings don't know if they have the strength to help their leafy sister. But they know they must try. They come up beside her; they circle her with their arms; they make themselves one creature, all together.

Alice says, "It's over, Nick, I said it's over," like she's said it fifty times before. Alice says, "Come on, Nick, stop it, please," and I run right up to him and scream straight in his ear.

The woodsprite's siblings have given her strength. She gathers up all her powers, casts off the last of her human disguise, and extends her sharpest branch and spears it straight through her wolf lover's heart. He falls bleeding to the floor.

Nick shouts at my scream and covers his ears with his hands. I grab his wrists and scream again, and he turns and runs off into the night. Alice turns to run after him, down the stairs and into the crowd. I try to catch her, to hold on to her, to hug her, but she jumps up and runs away. She runs in the same direction as Nick and I wonder if I made a mistake, if it's all my imagination (it's true I do have a big imagination). I wonder if maybe Bea is right. I think about Bea's bare, blue-painted legs entangled with another pair of legs on a mattress and a Guy Fawkes mask hanging from her hand. Then I remember that there is only one way out of the house, so of course Alice followed Nick; there's no other way to leave. You have to go down the stairs to get to the ground floor. And the girl on the mattress looks too much like the sea. She must be the changeling mermaid girl from my dream. *Love is never worth it.* She could never be Bea. My mind is a thick strange soup.

Everyone has run away and I have nowhere to go. I try the doors to the master bedroom (I remember vaguely that I haven't been in there since I closed them), but they are stuck. I push at them with my shoulder; they don't budge. I shrug and make my way back down to the ground floor, to the floor that I end up sitting on when I miss a step and fall *bump-bump-bump* down the rest of the stairs on my backside. I laugh. I laugh at my fall. I laugh at the accident season, at the accident of Alice hitting her head on Nick's mantelpiece, at the accident of the bruises on her legs, at the accident of the cuts on her arms. I laugh at the accident of the broken glass a few years ago that somehow managed to slice her wrist in a perfectly straight line. I laugh at the accident of Sam punching the wall in the secrets room. I laugh at the accident of the day I almost drowned. I laugh at the accident of my uncle's death. *Seth knew too,* I think. *That's why he pushed him in.* Then I wonder where that thought came from. I stop laughing.

I stumble into the garden, where the river runs away like I run away. The music is still loud. There are flashlights in the grass, and even though it's freezing, people are lying in the weeds. I walk unsteadily around to the back of the house, where the garden is even more wild and overgrown, and I go to the very edge of the property where the river resurfaces from underground. I crash through brambles and bushes and over to the water and he welcomes me like my only friend.

I sit on the bank and dip my fingers in the water and I remember swimming in a lake on a summer vacation, Sam and my mother back on the man-made beach, Christopher teaching us how to swim, Alice uncomfortable in her bathing suit, keeping her chin below the water. I remember asking an innocent question about something I'd seen and Christopher slapping my cheek (or maybe that is a different memory). Water filling my lungs and the hands holding me shaking. A hundred apologies afterward, and ice cream. Three big scoops in a double cone.

Then, across the water, I see Elsie.

She is holding a butterfly net and she's staring right at me. I know I need to go to her. The river is shallow here, not much more than a stream, and I splash over to the other side. When I walk out, I imagine that I look like some lost alien thing: wet and winged, masked and melancholy.

Elsie looks at me like she's not sure what to make of me. I look down at myself. My tights are muddy and my shoes squelch as I shift my weight. I am still covered in bruises. I can feel that my makeup has run from the sweat. I wouldn't know what to make of myself. I look at Elsie—her worried face, her sensible brown boots, her tartan skirt, her misshapen sweater, her hands holding a butterfly net.

I ask, "What are you trying to catch?"

Elsie gives me a very serious look. Suddenly my heart sinks. I feel like I had this one question I could ask out of all the questions I want to ask her, and I've wasted it on this one and I'll never get another chance.

Behind me, somebody calls my name. For a moment I think it is the river, but then I see that it's Bea. When I turn back, Elsie is gone, but I hardly expected her to stick around anyway. I wish I had asked her why she is in all my pictures. I wish I had asked her if anyone has the answers I'm looking for. My reflection is distorted in the water at my feet.

"Cara!" Bea yells again. There's something in her voice I rarely hear. It's almost like an edge of fear. "Cara, get back here!"

I splash back across the river. Bea is running toward me. She has my bags in her hands. Behind her, other people are running. They are all sweat-soaked and panting, they are all costumed, but some of them are more undressed than dressed up; they are all carrying bags and bottles and they are all running away. The garden is a mess of masks.

"What's going on?" I reach Bea and she grabs my arms and pulls me after her. We aren't heading for the open gates but for the side fence. It looks higher than the gates ever have.

"Hold on," I say to Bea. I try to stop her. "You want us to climb?"

"Somebody called the police," she says breathlessly. "We have to get out of here."

Now I can make out the sirens that I thought were just part of a song. I say, "Oh shit," and I help Bea to hoist our bags up and sling them over into the field on the other side.

"Where are Sam and Alice?"

"I couldn't find them. Niamh heard the sirens first. She and Kim legged it out, but I thought Sam was in the kitchen . . ." Bea pauses for breath as we start to climb. We wedge our feet in between the bars and pull ourselves up inch by inch. "But I couldn't see Joe or Martin either," she says, panting. "So they must've gotten out before me."

Her words are slightly reassuring, but then I make the mistake of looking back toward the house. The mess of masks and bottles and bags and people running and police running makes me feel sick. When we get to the other side of the fence, I throw up into the ditch. Bea and I hold hands and run home. I am wet to the skin, I am shivering and my wings are shaking. I am cold stone behind my mask. I might not be human at all.

14

Sam and Alice don't come back to Bea's house all night. We call and call their phones, but both numbers go straight to voicemail. We don't dare call my house phone in case my mother picks up and they aren't there.

Bea and I sit on her bed and talk and smoke out of her bedroom window for hours, watching the rain fall on the conservatory roof below. By morning our voices are hoarse and our lungs are black, but we are sober. I don't remember anything we talked about during the night. We fall asleep just as the sky begins to lighten and the last of the rain eases off.

***

In my dreams, at the changelings' party, the house is in chaos. Creatures run and scream in a thousand languages, there are roars and howls and whinnies. There is a dead wolf on the floor. His blood soaks into the carpet. As the huge house empties, the changelings turn and see the man made entirely of metal standing in front of the door. The people crowd past him to get outside, the surge of changelings parting like a river around his iron body. Those who touch him accidentally begin to burn and smoke. The hinges at his mouth work and he smiles an eerie smile.

The four siblings look from the bleeding remains of the wolf boy to their stepfather and a crazy fear fills their hearts. They have used up the last of their powers killing the wolf and now there is nothing left. They take each other's hands and hold on tight. They begin to realize that they are never going home.

***

When we wake up we walk to the ghost house. The way is longer than it ever has been before even though the rain didn't continue through the morning and the ground is almost dry. Bea and I meander like rivers, like we're almost afraid to reach our destination or like we wish it'd change, just for a while. Sam and Alice still aren't answering their phones.

It's early afternoon and the sky is a washed-out gray. There is no one on the roads. In the fields, the sheep bleat damply. When we get to the river, there are no workers repairing the wooden bridge; it lies there alone and broken. It's propped up by poles and beams and pulleys, but it's still completely uncrossable. Bea stands on the riverbank and her hair curls red in her eyes. She still has a few painted scales stuck to her face. It makes her look dirty and beautiful.

"Are you in love with Alice?" I ask her suddenly.

Bea doesn't answer. "You know she's probably at Nick's place, right?"

I shake my head. "No way she'd go back to him."

Bea runs her hands through her hair. "You don't know that," she says.

I think about the way Nick was crushing Alice into the peeling paint of the wall. I think about her elbows. I think about her as a little girl, bundled up warmer than October every summer, afraid of showing her body. I remember her asking me to sleep in her room some nights. "No," I say to Bea. "I'm sure of it."

Across the water, the trees whisper. It's a keening, lonely sound. "Let's not go to the ghost house just yet," I say.

We sit up on the picnic table and throw small stones into the water. I tell Bea about seeing Elsie last night. I've been searching for the faintest trace of her all week, but when I finally found her, we hardly talked at all. The whole night feels so surreal already. Then I remember something and I ask Bea if she saw anyone go into the master bedroom during the party.

Bea thinks for a second. "No," she says slowly. "Come to think of it, I didn't. And I didn't go in there all night. Not after we got changed."

"Neither did I." My stones land heavy in the water. Some

miss completely and scuttle away along the riverbank or get lost in the grass. "I asked them to close." I don't look at Bea.

"You asked what to close? The doors?"

I nod.

"And they did." She doesn't phrase it as a question. "Why?" is the question she does ask.

I shrug. I fling a stone as far as I can. It lands in the middle of the river with a satisfying splash. "I don't know," I say. "It just didn't feel right to have anybody else in there."

When I raise my head, Bea is giving me a funny look. "And they call *me* a witch," she murmurs.

I fling the next stone even harder. I remember Bea saying that every witch needs somebody to kiss on Halloween. When I think about it, I feel guilty for having kissed Toby, but when I think about it even more, I just feel angry. *I can kiss who I want,* I think. And then I remember that technically I can't. I can kiss whoever I want, except Sam, because he is pretty much my brother, and you can't kiss your brother. Except that I did. My world is so tangled, I don't know what to make of it. A tiny little voice deep inside me reminds me that Toby's kiss was less than nothing compared to Sam's. A matchstick against a bonfire.

Then I remember seeing Bea kissing Carl last night. I turn to face her. "Were you making out with Carl last night?"

Bea throws a pebble up and catches it again. She slides off the picnic table and over to the water. She flicks her wrist

232

and sends the pebble flying over the surface of the river. It skips five times. "I guess," she says with her back toward me. "I was a little drunk, maybe."

"A little drunk?" I say, like that's her excuse. The river eats Bea's next stone before it gets the chance to bounce. "Why did you do it?" I ask her. Bea doesn't answer. The river's hungry. It cries out for more stones. "Bea, what happened last night?"

Bea comes back over to the bench, but she doesn't look me in the eye. She takes out her cards. I don't want to know what her cards have to tell us. I want to know what's going on with her.

"No." I grab her arms before she can shuffle them. "Not the cards. Not the cards. You tell me."

Bea wrenches her arms away from me.

"You tell me what you're thinking," I say as she takes a few quick steps away. She winces. I raise my voice. "You tell me yourself. Don't hide behind them." I'm almost shouting now. The river's shouting with me.

Bea turns to meet it head on. She shakes and shakes her head. When she speaks, she's louder than the water flying over the tallest rocks.

"I'm a goddamn coward." She spins around to face me. Her sleeves fall over her hands. She holds out the deck of cards and points it at me. "But so are you. You're a coward, Cara Morris. You're a goddamn coward and a liar." I feel like I've been slapped.

"You're just like me," Bea is saying. "Only with you it's worse because you won't even admit it to yourself."

"What are you—?"

"Why did you kiss Toby, Cara? Why did you kiss him?"

"I don't know," I say, agitated. "I was drunk, he was nice. Why shouldn't I have kissed him?"

Bea just stares at me. I wonder if she knows. I wonder what her cards said to Sam that time he kissed her. I wonder if he kissed her like he kissed me. I jump down from the picnic table and I walk right up to Bea and I take her face in my hands and press my lips to hers. She tastes like cigarette smoke and toast and black coffee. When we break apart, she shakes her head. She turns around and walks away. My eyes are dry, but I feel like I'm crying. I don't know what I'm doing anymore.

I go on alone. There's nothing else I can do, so I pick myself up and walk on. I go to the ghost house. The gates are locked again with a big new padlock, probably put there by the police, but I climb over like last night, and at the top the gates waver and I'm not sure they'll let me through. I freeze up there—one leg on the side of the house and one on the side of the road, and I let the gates sway me while they make up their mind. They must have decided I'm okay to go through, because the iron underneath me stills for a moment, long enough to let me lift my other leg over and quickly climb down.

The garden is a wilderness. There are plastic bags and beer cans and bottles and bits of costume strewn across the grass like weeds. There are masks staring blankly up at the sky. The grass grows through their eye sockets. They look like so many ghosts. I look up at the house and it looks back at me. I can't see any faces in the windows. I wonder if I ever really did. When I open the front door, though, it groans like it always has, like it's welcoming me home.

I go upstairs. The steps are hazardous. They threaten to collapse in upon themselves wherever I put my weight. I hang on to the banister rail for guidance, but even that feels fragile. I'm beginning to realize how dangerous it really was to have the party here. I wonder where Sam and Alice are and I begin to feel afraid.

When I reach the doors to the master bedroom, I stop. I don't know if the doors will stay shut like they did at the party, but when I turn the handles, they let me in.

There is no mess inside the room. There are the flashlights we set up—dark now that their batteries have all died—and the waxy remains of candles. I'm surprised the whole house didn't burn down. There is the charred fire pit in the middle of the bedroom, and there are the dusty drapes, and there are our footprints in the dirt on the floor, but that's it. There are no bottles or candy wrappers or beer cans. There are no masks. There are just the dead candles and the silence.

I start to go back downstairs, but then I hear a little

sound behind me, and instead of turning around, I stay facing the door and take out my phone. I try to breathe noiselessly, but it feels like the ghostly person behind me is taking their breaths exactly when I take mine. I hear them only as an echo. Quickly I spin to face the middle of the room and I raise my phone up in front of my face and snap a picture. Then I leave real fast.

I'm amazed the stairs hold my weight. I'm amazed the porch is still holding itself up. I'm amazed I don't fall off the iron gates and crack my skull, but then I remember that it's the first of November and so the accident season should be finished by now. But it still doesn't feel like it's over at all.

I go back to the river and I take out my phone, but before I can open up my pictures folder, I get a call. It's Toby. I don't answer. I have too many kisses to answer for already.

When the call ends, I go into my pictures folder. I open the photo I took in the master bedroom. When I brought my phone up in front of me, there were only the walls, the candle stubs, and the moldy drapes covering the dirty windows. The light was weak and grayish and speckled with dust motes like snow, although I don't expect that to come up on the tiny screen. What comes up instead is Elsie. She is standing right in the shot like I was taking the picture of her all along. Her hair is escaping from its braid in flyaway locks and the lines on her forehead are pinched and deep. Her mouth is open like she's in the middle of a sentence.

Before I even realize it, I'm running back to the house. I run like there's someone chasing me, and it feels like there is, somehow; someone hard and fast and strangely silent on cold metal legs. My feet slap on the uneven road, and loose gravel rolls right in under my shoes, threatening to trip me up. The iron gates burn my hands and the weeds in the garden rise up to meet me. They tangle around my ankles like vines. Inside, the ghost house feels like it'll collapse around me. Or maybe I am the one collapsing. I go upstairs.

Elsie is in the master bedroom.

15

Elsie is standing beside her typewriter. In front of her, sitting on the wooden box that the secrets go into, is a complicated-looking contraption that I think might be a hunter's trap. It looks big enough to catch a small animal, anyway. It's all iron and wire and coils. It almost hums. Without really meaning to, I ask Elsie the question again: "What are you trying to catch?"

Unsurprisingly, Elsie doesn't answer me. "Do you want to leave a secret?" she says instead. I look at the trap on top of the box. I shake my head.

"Do you believe in ghosts?" she says. "In guardian spirits?"

I think about the secret I typed out a few years ago, when Elsie had just started with the secrets booth. I said that I wished there was such a thing as ghosts, like Bea believes, because that'd mean my father and Seth are still around somewhere. I also said that I didn't actually believe it myself. Now I don't know what to say.

"Sometimes I think I'm going crazy," Elsie says. "Sometimes I think I am one." She smiles, but it looks fake. "There's a secret for the box." She hunkers down and types the secret out.

"A ghost?" I ask as she is typing.

"A ghost," she says without looking up. "A guardian spirit. Something like that."

I want to ask her how she can be unsure about whether or not she is a ghost, but then I think of all the things our brains deny, all the memories they hide from us, all the secrets they keep.

Elsie sits cross-legged on the floor in front of the typewriter. In one fluid movement I join her. We and the trap and the typewriter make a circle like we're about to pray. I press the palms of my hands into the dust.

"Do you remember when we used to hang out?" I ask Elsie. She smiles. "We'd stay up in the library all break time and read these history books with lots of pictures. The ancient Greeks with their white dresses, Romans in armor, bare-breasted Amazons, Aztec sacrifices."

"All dead," says Elsie. "All gone. Like your dad."

"I guess." I want to trace the frown lines on her forehead. I can't quite decide if I am scared of her or if I want to protect her. I remember what Bea's cards said about her. *She needs us to help her find her way home.* "What about your family?" I ask. "Where do you even live?"

"My dad is dead," she says. "Like yours." She clacks that secret out on the keys. Her sweater is worn. Her hair is frizzing out of its messy braid. She looks so worried.

Without meaning to, I think out loud. "My family, we've got a lot of secrets. All of us."

Elsie writes that down too. The click of the keys is like a heartbeat. I go on: "Bea is sort of always enchanted with the world, but she's just a lost girl like the rest of us. Her dad is gone, and her mom—she spends all her time hanging around with pretentious theater folk, pretending she's ten years younger than she is, which usually involves pretending she was never married, or that she doesn't have a daughter. Bea is alone a lot." Elsie types as I talk. It feels like candles are flickering around us, but none of them are lit. The walls are all shadow anyway.

"My sister is sad all the time. She was—well, I think she was hurt really badly once, and now she goes out with boys who hurt her and sometimes she hurts herself. She doesn't need the accident season, I guess. My mother does. She needs it to explain all the bad things that've happened to her. To us all. My dad's death, and Seth—he was my mother's brother, he was her best friend, like Sam is to me, I guess, only—" I stop for a second. "Only not. Like he used to be, when we were little." I want to stop talking, but I can't. My mouth moves of its own accord and the words keep spilling out. Elsie keeps typing. She slides the bar over after every line like she's slicing a piece of meat. Shedding skins.

"Things changed really fast." I'm thinking while I'm talking, but my thoughts are running faster than what I'm saying. "Or maybe I just realized really fast that they'd been changing all along. Sam, he's—he's my ex-stepbrother, but you know that. When his father left, he was . . . blank, and angry."

Elsie's eyes are huge. She's pulling in all my words through that typewriter, like she's eating them for breakfast, like they're the only words she's heard in a year.

"Now he's still got this—this—it's not sadness, it's more like, I don't know . . . Like he's not really there all the time. Like he's flickering in and out of sight, like he's afraid he's going to disappear. Like his father disappeared."

The typewriter dings again. I know that what's going on is strange, like being in a dream, but I can't quite put a finger on why, so I find myself talking to her as if everything's normal, as if I do this every day—spill my secrets and the secrets of those around me to a strange girl I used to know; as if I didn't take a picture of an empty room and have her show up in it.

"You see a lot more than you think you do," Elsie says.

"You sound like Bea," I tell her. Then I say: "Bea is my best friend. I want to keep her close, like she's this treasure

I've found, but now I think she's in love with Alice and that makes me afraid of being alone."

"What about Sam?" Elsie says as she types. "Don't you have him?"

I shake my head. "I wish."

When I hear the words I've just said, I put my hands over my mouth. Elsie's fingers fly over the typewriter keys. I want to tell her to stop; I want to take the last inked letters back, but I can't speak.

When I tell her the next secret, my voice is a whisper. "I love him. Sam." I close my eyes and feel his lips on mine. "I'm in love with him." I touch my lips and whisper again. "But I can never tell him, and I have to keep pretending it isn't there."

"You can't pretend love away," Elsie says. She says it like someone who knows firsthand. I look up at her. She is hunched over her typewriter like she is every break time at school. Mousy hair, high-collared blouse. Her open cardigan has big red buttons running up the front. A couple of them are missing.

"Do you ever get this feeling . . ." I ask Elsie finally, when the room has grown silent after the tapping of her fingers on the keys. "This feeling that you've done everything wrong?" I press my dusty palms to my chest. "Right here. This feeling like your world's about to blow open."

Elsie's shoulders slump. "All the time."

I look down at the typewriter in front of her; at the animal trap resting on the wooden secrets box. "What are your secrets?" I ask Elsie softly. I don't expect her to reply. "What are you trying to catch?"

Elsie turns the typewriter to face me. It makes a horrible metallic screech when she pushes it across the floor.

"When I was little," she says, "before we became friends—before . . . before anything else I can remember, I remember this voice."

I look down at the typewriter and position my fingers over the keys. When I look back up at Elsie, she starts talking again. "A woman," she says. "She'd come to me and ask me things. To think of her, to remember her, to ask if I was happy and safe."

"Just a voice?"

"Write it down," is all Elsie says to me. I write it down. I write: *I have been hearing a voice since I was a child. It asks me if I am happy and safe. I am neither.*

"She kept coming to me, every week, thinking about me every day, and then she started thinking about somebody else too—another little girl. And then, later, another. Later still, a boy. She came to me with three children in her heart, and from the beginning she'd ask me to watch over them. To watch over you."

I stop typing. "Me?"

"Keep writing," Elsie whispers. "She came to me every

week, asking me to watch over you. She was too afraid. She still is, I think. So I knew that was my job. To watch over you. I look out for you. But once a year, I go away. I go searching."

"What?" I'm beginning to change my mind. I don't think Elsie is a ghost, not really; but ghost or not, I do think she's probably crazy. My hands rest lightly on the typewriter keys. "Elsie, what does this have to do with me?"

Elsie points at the typewriter, urging me to keep writing. She says it like it's obvious: "I've been watching over you all." When I look up from the little metal keys, I see that there are tears in Elsie's eyes. She says: "I guess I'm not doing a very good job."

"But why would . . . ?" Now that I can ask all my questions, I don't know what to say.

"For one month of every year I get to go away, go searching," she says. "I don't abandon you," she adds quickly. "I still try to look out for you; I'm always there in the background. I just . . . I just go away for a little while too."

When I think about it, I realize that maybe there has always been a time when Elsie's not around so much—around the accident season maybe—but then, I'm questioning my memory at the moment. I don't trust anything I think I remember.

"I didn't ask for this," Elsie says, and her words echo what I said to Bea earlier. Her voice is strange. "I'm tired," she says. "And I . . . I feel like I've failed. You and Sam, Alice . . . I don't want to fail her again. But I feel like I've failed you all."

I type out that secret. *I feel like I've failed you all.* I don't know if it is Elsie's secret or mine.

And I feel like I've failed Elsie—by not remembering her, by not finding her before now. I look at the worry lines on her forehead that have become so familiar. She looks so worried, always so worried, so I ask her, "If you've been watching over us, who is looking out for you?"

Elsie looks surprised; then she smiles. "Maybe I don't need someone to look out for me," she says. "Maybe I just need to be remembered."

Maybe I just need to be remembered, I type. When the words hit the edge of the paper and the typewriter spits the sheet out with a chime, I go to put the page of secrets into the wooden box, but the trap is in my way.

I ask Elsie the question again. "But what are you looking for?" I think about the dream catchers and the mousetrap, the flypapers, the butterfly net. I stare down at the terrifying trap in front of me. I say, "What are you trying to catch?"

Elsie sort of shrugs and gestures toward the window. "My mother always said I would catch my death out there."

She moves the trap off the top of the wooden box. It is heavy, but she's stronger than she looks. "I want you to take it over," she says.

"Take what over?"

"The secrets booth." Elsie pushes the box toward me. "If you want it."

I frown and push the box and the typewriter back toward Elsie. There's a shaking in my limbs. "It's yours," I say to her. "When we go back to school after the midterm break you'll be there, in the library, and people'll type up their secrets and you'll put them up on the clotheslines in the halls at the end of term and it'll be the same as every year. I don't know how to do that."

Elsie shakes her head. She says my name gently, like a reminder. Like she knows that I knew when she'd disappeared. Like she knows that I know that everything's changed. "I'm not going back to school," Elsie tells me. She smiles, and for once it reaches her eyes. "I'm going to catch my death if it kills me."

My laugh surprises me. "I didn't realize you were funny." Elsie laughs with me. The sound of it bounces around the room. When the laughter has echoed all around us, I whisper, "Are you really a ghost?"

"I don't know," Elsie says. "It's hard to tell."

"Is it? You'd think it'd be pretty obvious."

"Surprisingly, it isn't." Elsie pushes herself off the floor and picks up her horrible trap. It is huge in her arms and looks heavy. "Maybe I'm just this crazy little lost girl. Maybe I saw you and your lovely family and was bored with my own only-child life and so I followed you around like a puppy who wished you'd adopt her."

"But we never saw you." Elsie's walking away, but I can't seem to stand up. The floorboards creak underneath me like they're trying to keep me here. "You were in all my pictures, but I never saw you."

"There's a lot you pretend you didn't see."

When Elsie leaves, it is as if she's never been. The dust where she was sitting is undisturbed, and when I try to find the photo of her in my phone, it has disappeared like it was never taken. Maybe I've been talking to myself all along.

16

I carry the typewriter all the way home. It's balanced precariously on the wooden secrets box, and every few meters I stop and hoist it up again in my arms, and my muscles scream thinly. Rain falls on the keys like it's trying to type out its own secrets. I would read them aloud, but I don't speak the language of the rain. I'm not even sure I can understand the river anymore. It roars on beside me, but it doesn't whisper my secrets back at me, and it doesn't call my name. Maybe it never really did.

Halfway home, I slip on some loose gravel and fall to the ground. The typewriter flies out of my hands and buries itself in the mud in front of me. The wooden box lands on my foot. It is heavy with so many secrets. I can hear my bones crunch. October is over, but the accidents still seem to be happening. Nothing makes sense anymore.

I carry the secrets the rest of the way on a broken foot (perhaps it is not broken, but it feels like it is; it feels strained and pained and fragile, not a little like my heart). When I get home, the lights are on and voices are raised in the kitchen. I come inside like a storm, brittle bones and heavy secrets and all, and I drop the muddy typewriter on the kitchen table, where it clangs dimly long after it has hit the padded wood. Alice and my mother stare at me. Sam is slumped over the table, his head in his arms. If he's staring at anything, I can't see it.

"What happened to you?" My mother points at my mud-splattered clothes, the rip in the sleeve of my coat. "What's this?" She gestures at the typewriter. Her eyes are wide and the circles underneath them are the same color as her hair. I open my mouth to reply, but at that moment Sam makes a low groaning sound and gets up unsteadily from his chair. His skin is gray. At first I think it is still the makeup from his costume, but then he turns around sharply and throws up in the sink. Alice's throat chokes out a small noise. My mother drops heavily into the chair in front of her. She looks dazed.

"Sorry, sorry," Sam croaks. His voice sounds like the gravel I tripped up on earlier. He rinses his mouth out with tap water and cleans the sink without once turning to look at us. I am still standing at the table, unsure exactly what to do. My mother puts her head in her hands.

"You don't come home all night," she says into her arms. She says it about Sam and Alice, but it's like she's saying it to me. "Either of you." She raises her head. Sam bows his head over the sink. Alice lowers her eyes. I try to back away, but my mother looks up at me and I freeze.

"I get a call from the police at four in the morning about Sam and Alice trespassing on private property." Alice blushes fiercely, but she doesn't tell our mother that Bea and I were trespassing too. "Which means that you both lied to me about spending the night at Bea's house so you could go get plastered at some party." My mother's voice catches, but I can't tell if it's from anger or fear. It could be both. "And that Sam started a fight with a classmate who had to be taken to the hospital with a broken nose. His parents are thinking of pressing charges."

I drag a chair across the rug-covered floor and sink down into it. Sam still hasn't turned around.

"And he wasn't even going to tell me," my mother says to Sam's unmoving back. Her eyes are filled with tears. "*Fighting,* Sam," she says. "What are you—? What is this?" She looks around at the lot of us. Alice's face is bruised. She and Sam are still wearing their costumes. My foot is swelling up inside my boot. My clothes are filthy and torn.

My mother looks back at Sam. "What's going on, Sam?" she says. "Why are you doing this? What is this? This isn't you."

Hunched over the sink, Sam's shoulders start to shake. At first I think he's crying, but when he turns around, his mouth is set in a smile meaner than the blue streak in his hair. He laughs like there's a knife twisting in his heart.

"How would you know?" he says. "How would you know what isn't me? You're not my mother."

Alice and I have the same scared expression on our faces (I can tell because she looks exactly the way I feel). I've never seen my mother look so lost. "Sam," she says softly, "you know that . . . your father—"

"Right," Sam cuts her off. He lets out a cough of that strange forced laughter. "My father. Maybe you should call him, tell him what I've done. Right?" He stares at my mother. His hair falls in his eyes. He looks a little wild. I can see how tightly my mother's teeth are clenched by the tensing of her jaw.

"You want to call my father?" Sam says, louder. "Huh? In Borneo? Right? With his new wife? Right? Isn't that right?"

The tears don't spill from my mother's eyes. Her mouth is set like she's been expecting this all along.

"Where does he call you from, once a year?" Sam asks. His hands grip the sink like it's a lifeboat.

"I don't know," my mother says. Her voice is strange and far away. Across the kitchen, Alice has stopped breathing. She inches along the wall to the door. I want to go to her, but I can't move. My cheek stings like it's been slapped.

"What do you mean you don't know?"

My mother shakes her head. "I don't know, Sammy."

Sam's face crumples in on itself. "You're lying. You've been lying to me all along." My face is a statue. I can't even blink.

"When he—" My mother clears her throat. When she speaks, it's almost like the words are rehearsed. "Your father didn't remarry. At least, as far as I know. He didn't leave me. Us." She takes a breath. "I sent him away."

"Why?" says Sam. "Where to?" He spits out the words. "Not to Borneo."

"Not to Borneo." My mother turns around in her chair to face him. "Although he could be there, for all I know." Her hands are clasped so tightly together that her knuckles are white.

"Seth tried to tell me," she says, and it's almost as if she's talking to herself, "but for a long time I wouldn't listen because I loved him so much. I loved you both so much." The silence in the room is stifling. I can't breathe.

Sam's face is hard. "What do you mean? Tried to tell you what?" My heart is in my knees and sinking lower.

My mother stares straight at Sam, unflinching, like this is something she's been wanting to say for years. Wanting, and dreading. "Sometimes," she says, "there were things Christopher would say, or do, that were very worrying, and—"

"What kind of things?" Sam interrupts. Alice takes

252

tiny steps toward the door. My mother doesn't notice.

"Bad things." My mother touches her face as if to check for tears. "Horrible things. He'd say things about . . ." She looks over at Alice. Alice stops her inching away. "Things about you," my mother says finally. "And the girls. Very, very worrying things. I didn't make the decision lightly," she says to Sam. "But I didn't want him near you three anymore. I didn't think it was safe."

"Safe." Everything about Sam right now is blank. His gray face, his monotone voice, the way he's standing by the sink like he's about to jump into it, or disappear. But not like his father disappeared.

"Yes. Yes." My mother answers Sam's word like a question; then, when he doesn't say anything else, she goes on. "And after Seth died, I was sure . . ." But she falters again. "I sent him away. I—I got a restraining order and he never came back. I don't know where he is. I get a call sometimes, twice a year maybe, from an unknown number, and I think it's him, but he never speaks."

My tongue unglues itself from the roof of my mouth. "What . . . ?" I say. I'm not sure what to follow that up with. The word sits in the silence like a needle in a storm. There's this strange whooshing noise inside my head. I remember a slap across my cheek in a hallway; I remember hands on my shoulders pushing me down, keeping me underwater; I remember being told to forget.

"So it was you. You did it. You sent him away." Sam's voice is choked. He might not have spoken for a thousand years. My heart hurts for him. I look across at Alice. My heart hurts for us all.

"I was afraid of him," my mother says again. Repeating things is supposed to help you remember. "Of the things he said sometimes. I didn't want them to be true. I didn't want to be right, but I couldn't take that chance. I didn't want anything to happen to any of you."

There is a crack opening up in the middle of the kitchen table. The typewriter and the secrets box are too heavy for it. They're pulling the table down. They're opening up a hole in the floor. The whole room rips apart. There it is, large as life. Our lives are being blown wide open. I open my mouth as wide as the chasm in front of me and I say it: "It was already too late."

Alice's eyes are wider than eyes have the right to be. She looks like she's crumbling apart. Like she's been felled and you could count the rings of her to know how old her soul is.

"It was too late," I say again. "It had already happened. I saw him once, in Alice's bedroom." Alice shakes her head. My mother looks at Alice as if she's never seen her before. "He slapped my cheek and told me it was just my imagination. I believed him because—" I stop. "I believed him. I asked him about it a few weeks later and he—"

"Pushed you under the water." Alice's voice is a whisper.

Her eyes say she didn't know that I knew. I want to tell her I hardly knew myself. The sick, guilty feeling rises up in my throat like bile.

"Is this true?" My mother's face is grayer than Sam's. Alice looks around at us all, and before we can stop her, she bolts from the room. My mother runs after her. Sam turns to the sink and retches again, but this time it isn't because of the alcohol still swimming in his system. He slides along the side of the kitchen counter to the floor. I stare after Alice and I hardly dare to blink.

***

He was always really nice, afterward. Sometimes he brought her Pop-Tarts and Elle *magazine. Sometimes he told Mom to stop badgering her about homework. This morning he went all the way to the* pâtisserie *in the village close to the house they were renting to get her* pain au chocolat *because it was her favorite. He didn't get Sam or Cara anything.*

Alice didn't know it could be so hot in October. Sam and Seth and Christopher went around topless the whole time; Seth stocky and broad and blond, tanning as well as the locals over his tattoos. Christopher stayed pale no matter how long he stayed in the sun, and his chest hair—black as the hair on his head—stood out against his white, white skin.

Mom and Cara felt the heat too. They hardly ever changed out of their bikinis except to go to dinner in the village, when Mom put on her favorite vintage sundress and swept her hair—

dyed blue to match the water—into an effortless bun. Alice knew that Mom's hair was dark blond like hers and Seth's underneath the dye, but in all her thirteen years, she didn't think she'd ever seen it.

"Alice, come in the water, it's amazing," Mom called from a few feet out from the shore. The Mediterranean was smooth as a lake and Mom was like a mermaid floating along the surface. Farther in, Sam and Cara were screeching and splashing. Christopher was putting on suntan lotion at the edge of the water.

"I'm good here." Alice put on her sunglasses and opened her magazine.

"You'll roast," Mom said. "At least put on your swimsuit. Are you drinking enough water?"

Alice didn't look up from her magazine. "I'm fine, Mom."

Christopher got into the water, and he and Mom floated and swam and kissed. Alice kept her eyes firmly on her magazine.

Seth dropped down onto a towel beside her. He poked at her knee with his camera. "Comment alley-voo mad-moose-sell Alice?" he asked in atrocious French. "Not in a swimming mood?" he said, slightly more seriously.

Alice shrugged and shook her head. Seth nodded toward Mom swimming happily in the water. "Nice to see her relaxing a bit this time of year," he said. "Makes things feel almost normal."

"That's what Cara keeps saying," Alice said, putting down her magazine.

It had taken a fair amount of persuading to get Mom to

agree to a seaside vacation during the accident season. Seth had tried to suggest that maybe the accident season wouldn't follow them this far from home, but his theory was quickly proved wrong. On the first evening the table in the kitchen of the rental house collapsed on Cara's legs. On the second day Sam stepped on a sea urchin and Mom spent an hour pulling out the tiny spines with a sterilized needle. Yesterday Alice'd been stung three times by a wasp. Still, Mom didn't seem nearly as bad as usual this year.

Seth was still gazing out at Mom and Christopher.

"D'you like him?" Alice found herself asking. She bit her lip once the words were out. Seth gave her a measured look.

Seth was one of those grown-ups who didn't talk down to you, and who always took you seriously. He'd never pretend he didn't know who you were talking about just to make you repeat it.

Sometimes Alice thought about telling Seth. She had the words all rehearsed. Maybe it's just my imagination, but . . . I don't know if I'm going crazy, but . . . I don't know if I should be saying this, but . . .

Alice scratched at an insect bite on her leg and Seth looked back at the water.

"I like him okay," he said lightly. "He's good for your mom."

Alice didn't say anything. She knew Seth was right. It was the middle of the accident season and Mom was swimming in the sea—okay, the Mediterranean didn't have any waves or sharks or anything, but it did have sea urchins, and Mom was afraid of everything during the accident season usually. But she didn't even wince when Cara ducked Sam under the water.

Seth chuckled beside her. "And Sam's a great kid," he said.

Alice watched Sam and Cara in the water. They were twelve, but they seemed much younger. They were stepsiblings, but they looked like twins. Seth held up his camera and took some pictures. He was right, Alice thought again. She knew in the pictures they'd all look like a family. The mom and the dad, the two sisters and the brother, the favorite uncle. Everything nice and happy and normal.

Seth turned suddenly and looked at Alice again. "Why?" he asked, his eyebrows drawing together slightly. "Do you *like* him?"

Alice's breath caught in her throat. She told herself Seth was just asking her the same question she'd asked him, but something about the way he was looking at her—kind of concerned but almost not surprised—made her want to tell him even more.

Out in the water, Mom was laughing. Christopher circled Sam and Cara, pretending to be a shark. Alice glanced back at Seth, who seemed to still be waiting for an answer. She shrugged, as if it didn't matter. Still, Seth looked from her—huddled fully dressed on her towel—back to Christopher in the water, and he was frowning.

"Seth! Seth!" Cara called. "Help! The shark is going to get us!"

Seth waved at Cara and said, "Just a minute, I'll save you," *but before getting up from the towel, he crouched and looked right into Alice's eyes.*

"You sure you're okay?" he asked her.

Alice didn't say anything, but she forced a smile and a nod. Alice didn't say anything, but she thought she saw a hint of understanding creeping into her uncle's eyes.

17

When my mother comes back into the kitchen, I ask about Alice, but she shakes her head. "She needs some space," she says. "Time. Something." She looks at me, but her eyes are unfocused, so it's more like she's looking through me.

"When you nearly drowned that time," she says, as if from far away, "he said he'd rescued you. He pulled you back to shore." She can't seem to make herself say his name. "He pushed you in." It isn't a question, so I don't answer. "He . . ." My mother looks like she is about to pass out.

"Mom, where's Alice?" I ask her again.

"She's gone to . . . she needs to . . ." my mother says vaguely, "process . . ." She wanders out into the hall. Her feet tread heavily on the stairs. I make to go and follow her, but Sam speaks up from where he's sitting crumpled on the floor.

"Don't leave me alone right now," he says. His head is

in his hands like it's too heavy for his neck. Like his whole body is too heavy to even sit up straight. "Please don't leave me alone right now."

There is too much. There is just too much. Sam looks so lost. There's a big difference, I imagine, between having a father who walked out on you and having a father who is a monster. But I don't know what to say to him. I want to ask whose nose he broke, but I'm pretty sure I know the answer. And I have no idea how to feel about it.

I sit back down. I take a breath, then I take out my phone. I try Alice's number first, but she doesn't pick up. Then I call Gracie.

She guesses by the sound of my voice that something's not right. She says, "I'm coming over." A little voice in my heart tells me I'm glad that my mother has someone like Gracie to rely on. I think about Bea tangled on a mattress with Carl while Alice ran away from the wolf. I wonder who Alice has to rely on. I wonder who I have. I look down at Sam. He is looking up at me. His eyes are muddy puddles. I sit down in front of him and put my hands on his knees.

"Sammy." I have too much I want to say and too much that I don't want to say but I feel like I have to. My voice jams in my throat, so I swallow to make it come out. I don't know what to do. "Maybe we should ask Bea to read the cards for us," I say.

Sam leans back and gives me that sad, sad smile I

261

know so well now. "Bea doesn't know everything, Cara."

"But the cards—"

"Bea doesn't know everything." He says it again, with finality. "She's just another lost kid like us."

I take my hands off Sam's knees and put them into my pockets. "I know," I say in a very small voice. "I know."

By the time Gracie arrives, my mother has joined us in the kitchen again. We drink microwaved coffee and Sam starts to sober up. He and my mother don't talk about Christopher. It's like he's here, sitting at the table between us, like he's a ghost or the elephant in the room.

I remember Alice, younger, skinnier even than she is now, all bundled up in her accident clothes—hurt, but not by accident. I remember seeing Christopher with her, and it's like a scene playing over and over in front of my eyes, but not real, and mostly the girl in the scene is a foresty woodsprite and the man is all metal. Metal hands on leafy skin, metal mouth telling lies. Metal teeth, metal heart. Metal breath saying it was all my imagination. Metal arms holding me under the water. I can't fly away from that kind of thing anymore. I have no wings. I am not the little fairy girl bouncing on her silver Converse.

I knew all along. I type it up on Elsie's antique typewriter and I think that it is the biggest secret of all. Then I look at Sam, and there is far too much going on in my heart for any of it to come out through the typewriter keys.

I try to call Alice again, but she doesn't answer. I try Bea's phone with the same result. I call Kim and Niamh and even Nick—although just hearing his voice makes my skin squirm—but none of them have heard from her. Finally Sam and I decide to go look for her. My mother and Gracie stay in the house and Gracie, echoing my mother's words from earlier, tells us that Alice will come back when she's ready, that today was a lot to process. My mother looks slightly reassured, but Sam and I go out anyway. When the front door closes, Sam breathes deep for the first time tonight. The ghost of his father hasn't followed us out here.

We walk along the river. We are silent, maybe so that the ghosts and memories can't hear us. Maybe because we don't know what to say. The rain isn't heavy enough for us to put up our hoods, but little beads of water mist our hair. Our shoes slide through puddles. My left foot aches every time I put my weight on it, but I concentrate on the swing of my arms and the beat of my breath and the sound of the river, and it soon becomes bearable. The pain in my chest, not so much.

We climb down to the river walk and Sam stops at one of the picnic benches by the big stone bridge and lights up a cigarette. He takes a drag and hands it to me. I can taste his lips on the filter. My cheeks grow warm. Sam clears his throat. When he speaks, his voice is frail like cigarette smoke. Whatever I originally expected him to say, this isn't it.

"When I kissed you that night," he says. "Did you . . . did you want me to?"

I thought he'd want to talk about Christopher. That, I'm prepared for. This is a surprise. This is a whole new set of secrets.

"It's just . . ." Sam says. "I didn't want to become—" He stops, backs up, starts again. "I don't want to be like Christopher." His eyes are more haunted than the ghost house. When he holds out the cigarette to me again, both our hands are shaking so much I almost drop it.

I push past the cloud in my throat. I say, "Of course I wanted you to." My voice is a shadow, but I know that Sam can hear me even over the river and the rain. "Of course I did. You're nothing like him." My voice gets stronger. "Nothing." When I think about his kisses, my heart speeds up and fills out. I almost wish I could tell him that.

Sam says, "I'm just . . ." And he drops his hands to his sides. Between two of my fingers, the forgotten cigarette drips ash onto the riverbank. Sam looks like a lost boy, like he's lost in the woods and he doesn't know how to get home. He says: "I'm just so ridiculously in love with you." The tear in my world is getting bigger. Soon it'll blow the whole universe apart. "I try to hide it, I try to stop it, I try to bloody kill it, but it just won't go away."

I shake and shake my head. I stop thinking about his kisses. I don't look at his freckles. I don't look at the blue streak in his dark hair. "But I'm like your sister, Sam." I think: *Stop looking at his lips. Stop seeing his hands. Stop imagining his arms around you.*

"You're not my sister."

I'm so confused and turned around by all this that I laugh out loud. "You say I am!" I throw my hands up. The cigarette flies out of my hand and lands in the grass beside the picnic table. The rain quenches it quick. "You say I am all the time! You call me little sister, I tell you I'm not your sister, you say, *If you say so, petite soeur.*" I dip my head and look at him in disbelief from under my eyelashes. "It's this whole big thing."

Sam doesn't laugh along with me. My smile dies slow. He looks down at the ground and says, "That's because I have to—I try to tell myself that as much as I can." His voice is quiet. I drop my arms and take a step closer so I can hear him. "I know I shouldn't feel like this," he tells me. "I know that. So I say it to remind myself. Every time I feel—" Sam breaks off and shakes his head. "Every time I want to kiss you," he says quickly, then he sort of laughs. "Which is all the time, by the way." His voice is strange and strangled. "Every time I want to kiss you, I tell myself you're my little sister and I shouldn't want that because it's fucked-up and wrong."

The anger in his quiet voice surprises me. "Does it work?"

Sam looks right into my eyes like he's testing himself. "No."

Sam is like my brother—that's what I'm supposed to think. His bedroom is across the hall from mine. We do our homework together. My mother takes care of him when he's sick. His father was once my stepfather, but he turned out to be a monster. I want to take a step back, tell Sam to keep trying. I want to tell him that this is wrong, that he's wrong, that no one'd ever accept it and that I shouldn't either. Instead, I take his hands. Sam breathes in fast like the time I let him kiss me. Like the time I kissed him. All the secrets I'm frightened of are coming out tonight, so I unglue my lips and say it.

"I'm so ridiculously in love with you too."

I reach out and touch him, lightly, my fingertips slipping through his hair and brushing it away from his face. It falls right back down over his forehead once I take my hand away. He takes a step toward me, carefully, like he's afraid he'll trip in the mud. The rain touches us as softly as Sam's hands touch me. The side of my neck, my shoulders, the length of my arms. The scrapes and bruises underneath my coat sleeves beat with blood. I know my face is flushed. In front of me, Sam's cheeks are reddening. He puts his hands on my waist, palms wide. I run my fingers through his hair again. When I step forward, it's deliberate. I close my eyes and tilt my head.

When we kiss, the water crashes on the rocks and the wind howls. The rain swirls around us like petals and we don't feel the cold. Sam's lips are warm as swimming in summer and he tastes like forever, like fire, like wild wanting, like finally finding lost things after having waited too long. His arms pull me close and my hands grab on to him like I'll never let go and he is pressing hard against me and he is there, and real, and beautiful. There is no way I could ever not love him.

I want the kiss to last forever, but we don't have the breath for that. I feel like I'll never breathe properly again, like my heart'll never stop pounding. Still kissing, we back into the shadow of the bridge. We are hidden from the road by the slope of the ground and the stone is dark above us, and we move closer to it without letting go of each other, but suddenly I stumble on the uneven ground and fall, hard, on the riverbank just underneath the bridge.

Sam falls on top of me. I let out my breath in a whoosh. He looks concerned for a second, but when he sees that I'm okay, he smiles and kisses me lightly. Without really thinking about what I'm doing, I arch up toward him and kiss him back, a lot less lightly.

Sam leans down and our bodies press together and he kisses me, again and again, harder and deeper, and the warmth of his skin burns through my clothes and his lips on mine are like fire and soon we are a different kind of breathless. I run my hands up and down his back, his hips, back up to his shoulders. My fingers tangle in his hair, my heart beats against his. Sam rolls onto his side and pulls me with him and we lie glued together like secrets, facing each other, pressing our hands through each other's clothes. The rain falls, but we barely notice. There are rocks underneath us, but they may as well be feather beds, or the mattresses on the floor in the ghost house. We are out in the wet and the wind, but we may as well be alone at the end of the world.

We kiss like wolves, like we're ravenous, like we'll eat each other up. We can't press our bodies close enough, so we shrug out of our coats and our legs tangle like bedsheets in the morning. We move against each other until Sam takes his mouth away from mine and buries his face in my neck, his breathing ragged and raw. We build up a rhythm. Sam moans low. He reaches down below the waistband of my jeans and lower, very slowly. He matches the movement of his hand to his hips and we rock like that together, his mouth at my neck, my hands in his hair, my legs tangled with his. The stones underneath us cut in through our clothes and our breath comes harder and faster and everything builds and builds like butterflies in my tummy until my whole body is filled with it and I feel like I am going to break open like a tear in the world.

I never thought that having my world blown right open would feel so goddamn good.

When we break apart, I see something move out of the corner of my eye. A flash of light at the other side of the river. Sam turns his head and he sees it too.

"Elsie?" he says, his voice uncertain.

Our eyes meet briefly and we stand up quickly. The light flashes again, then disappears. As one we run across the bridge.

The light dips and flashes ahead of us, as if someone is holding a flashlight, and we chase it straight into the clearing where Elsie hung her dream catchers, the one with the fly-paper trees and the tiny Elsie-shaped doll on the mousetrap. When we reach the clearing, I drop Sam's hand. He turns around in a circle, staring up at all the trees, but I only have eyes for the trap on the rock in the middle of the clearing.

"Cara," Sam says.

"I know."

In the middle of every dream catcher on every tree around the clearing, and stuck to each sheet of flypaper tacked up on the branches, there is a tiny doll. Brown-haired, dressed in denim and wool, it is unmistakably Elsie, but unlike the doll in the mousetrap, these have no faces, only blank paper skin where the eyes and nose and mouth should be.

The doll in the trap is bigger. It is one of those old-fashioned porcelain dolls, the kind with red bow lips and real eyelashes over glass eyes, but the eyes have been gouged out, the nose and lips scraped away. She still has Elsie's mousy braided hair, and wears a shapeless tartan skirt and a white blouse. But that's where the resemblance ends. The doll's body has been shattered by the hunter's trap. Porcelain pieces litter the grass around the rock. When I run to the bushes at the edge of the clearing and part the branches, I see that the tiny Elsie doll on the mousetrap has suffered the same fate. The trap has snapped the doll right across her tiny chest. Little yellow dots swim in front of my eyes.

"Cara," Sam says again, and there is worry in his voice. He comes over to me and touches my shoulders. "What's happened?"

"She caught it." I don't know if I've said the words aloud or if I've only thought them. Sam wraps his arms around me. He doesn't understand. "She caught it," I say again. "She caught it."

"Caught what?"

That's when my phone rings. At first I don't recognize the noise, but Sam puts his hand into my coat pocket and answers the call. I can't believe my phone's still working after everything it's been through. I recognize Bea's voice, tiny and muted on the other end of the line, but I don't hear her words. As Bea talks, Sam's face gets paler and paler. I realize that the tone of Bea's voice is all wrong—I can tell that even from here. She doesn't usually speak so quickly. There is a franticness to the beat of her words, but Sam isn't saying anything.

"What?" I say. It comes out like a scream. "What?"

Sam takes my hand and we run. We run hell for leather and like the wind, and the rain doesn't touch us and the mud doesn't move under our pounding feet, and all we can hear are our footfalls and heartbeats sounding together, and the ragged, choking sound of our breath. I don't ask where we're going; I recognize the way well enough. I don't ask why we're going there. I decide I don't want to know. I don't want to ever reach the ghost house, but we're running too fast and soon we're around the corner. I want to slow down, but Sam pulls me after him.

When we are almost at the gates, the noises around us change. There is the rain and the wind whipping by our flying bodies, there is the beat of our hearts and our feet keeping time, there is our breath ripping out of our lungs—and behind it all, like the backdrop to a play, there is the fire.

Bea meets us at the iron gates. In front of us, the ghost house is up in flames. Sam and I stop still, and over our ragged breathing and the sound of the fire (and who would have thought that fire could be so loud?), Bea screams that she came back to get our costumes when she smelled the smoke.

"It went up so quickly," she cries. "I couldn't go in. I couldn't—" The house gives a giant shudder. One of the upstairs windows shatters. Glass rains down into the garden. I look up at the master bedroom and my heart stops beating completely. There is a face behind the drapes.

Bea says, "Alice." We run up to the porch.

The front door is open, its hinges glowing red like devil eyes looking into nothingness and smoke. We stand as close to the house as we dare, but the flames are hip-height and

271

flashing, and neck-height and choking, and they are everywhere and the heat is hotter than our bodies, hotter than the
sun, and Alice is there in the middle of it.

"Alice!" I scream into the house. The smoke swallows
my voice.

"Goddammit, Alice!" Sam yells, and he kicks the wall
of the porch and a rain of sparks falls on us from above. We
cover our heads with our arms and cry out.

"Alice, get out of there!" Bea screams. She is crying. All
of us are crying and screaming and yelling, but we just sound
like the house burning down around us.

"She probably can't even hear us," Sam says, and his face
is ashen.

"We have to do something," Bea whispers. "I've already
called the fire department, but—" She breaks off and looks at
me. We both know they'll be too late. Without a word, Bea
and Sam and I go into the burning house.

The walls are made of fire. The wallpaper curls and furls
down like wings. Everywhere, the wood is breaking. The air
is all smoke rising up into the master bedroom and we follow
it like a signal that'll lead us to Alice. The whole house is
creaking and groaning, so we step carefully, like we're trying
not to walk on a loose stair, like we're trying to be silent so
no one upstairs will hear us. Like we're afraid Alice might
frighten like a fawn.

Step by step, like someone learning how to walk, we

climb, and on one stair the wood gives way and my foot falls through into empty space and my heart jumps into my mouth and I screw my eyes shut and wait to fall, and Bea, who is below me, grabs the waistband of my jeans and pulls me back toward her in the tightest of hugs. Sam stops and turns and looks down through the stairs where I would've fallen and his eyes are wide with fear. I don't say anything because I know we all have to continue climbing.

Bea and I step over the missing stair, holding on to Sam and each other for balance, and we make it to the landing where the smoke is thick and black. I pull the neck of my sweater up to my nose and mouth like I've seen people do in films. It helps make things feel more unreal, and less danger-ous. The three of us inch across the burning landing and stand outside the empty doorway to the master bedroom and try to breathe.

Alice is inside. She's still wearing her changeling dress and she's standing before the bonfire pit, which is the only place in the house not alight. I don't know how she's still standing, the smoke is so thick. It has me doubled over with coughing.

"Alice!" we scream. "Alice!" But she doesn't move. The house is moaning like it did when we danced, but this isn't our feet on the floor, this isn't our bodies against the walls, this isn't our hearts thumping time. This is pain music, this is heat music, this is don't-care music that wants to eat us up.

"Alice!" I croak the word out. "Alice, come here." But she doesn't hear me. Her eyes are closed and she starts swaying and stamping, and her boots set off sparks wherever she stands. Each spark lights up like paintings on the walls. They pulse with orange light in the flickering, flaming darkness like they're alive. I can't tear my eyes away. A wolf reaches out to Alice and I almost scream, but the fire licking up the wall shoots out and burns it to a crisp. I can hear it wail as it falls. Bea breathes hard behind me and Sam takes my hand. The fire is killing our demons, but it isn't doing it properly. It's doing it in a way that'll kill us too.

I look over at the old bonfire pit and my whole body hurts with this incredible wash of sadness. I feel like it could almost quench the flames. I cough again and call her name, and Alice opens her eyes and looks straight at me, and she's crying so hard the soot on her face has streaks down it from the tears.

I step over the threshold and go into the room. Sam and Bea move to follow me, but like in a film, a beam falls blazing across the doorway and I'm trapped inside the bedroom with Alice and the flames. Sam and Bea scream themselves hoarse behind the doorway, but they are far away, underwater, or I am. I step carefully on the heated floorboards, toward Alice.

"Cara," she whispers. I hardly hear her over the breaking and groaning, the cracking and crackling and moaning of the dying building. I hold out my hand to help her get away, but instead of following, she pulls me deeper into the room.

From somewhere by the window there comes a great whooshing noise and a whole chunk of wall thunders to the floor. The fire sounds like the wind. It wails and screams and I can't hear Alice when she says it, but her mouth makes the movement and I understand: "Dance with me."

I pull hard on her wrists back toward the door. "Alice, come on!" I try to shout, but my words are choked. Alice sways like she's about to faint or maybe get away, so I grab her around the waist and pull her so she is facing the door and walk with her like that, in faltering, stumbling steps that make it feel like we are dancing to the sound of the flames, to the song of the screaming house caving in around us.

In the doorway Sam and Bea hold hands and cry, and the tears they watch us through burn brighter than the fire. I can almost see us reflected in them like in a kaleidoscope, like a disco ball turning and turning around the empty bonfire pit with the rest of the bedroom burning.

I am trying to run, but it feels like I'm underwater, Alice a dead weight pulling me down. The bedroom has never seemed so big. In my arms, Alice flickers and switches. She is beaked, she has wings, a tail. She is a tree, a mountain, a park bench. She's made of wood and of fire and I know that in her arms I'm flickering too; I can feel it, the shiver up my spine, the crawling of insects, the pain like needles that soon becomes too much for me to bear, and I open my mouth and scream louder than I've ever screamed and the house screams with me.

The ceiling caves in. It sends a hail of fiery beams down over us, hitting our heads and our backs like it's doing it on purpose. I lose my grip on Alice and she falls to the floor. In the middle of the bedroom, in the middle of the darkened pit, a fire starts up, lit by the plaster of the ceiling and the ghosts of the attic and the choking smoke. It burns white. It roars. It opens the house up like a mouth.

Alice's hand reaches toward me in the fiery darkness and I grab it and run toward the door, half on my feet, half on my knees, when the house starts shaking like an earthquake. Sam is retching in the doorway, bent double, hands on his knees. Bea pulls him up and out of the way as Alice and I leap over the burning beam and burst through to the landing, bringing the flames with us in our clothes and on our skin.

The stairs are shaking. We grab hold of the banister rail and cling on to it all the way down, helping each other over the missing step, coughing and spluttering on the thick black smoke. Just as Alice and I reach the last step, the banister rail breaks off and the entire staircase collapses to the floor. We topple over each other into the burning hallway.

Alice's leg goes out from under her. The bones in my foot screech together like the hinges of the front door glowing orange through the smoke. Bea and Sam hold Alice up and we stagger through the entrance hall, which has never seemed so long, and the house bows down around us, sending bits of singed ceiling, splinters of wood, embers and ashes and choking black billows of smoke down around us.

When we scramble through the front door, the fire hits our skin and we scream and the ghost house spits us out into the garden, into the rain, where we roll on the wet grass to put out the flames on our clothes and cool our burning skin. Then we crawl to the giant gates and lie down there, burned and broken, and we watch as the ghost house falls apart.

18

The changeling siblings take each other's hands and hold on tight. They stand facing the iron stepfather who has kept them trapped all these years, and as one creature, they open their mouths and scream.

From their scream there grows a forest. It pushes through the stone slabs of the floors of the house, it breaks down the walls, it rips at the ceilings like it's tearing the whole world apart. The woodsprite grows roots that burrow deep into the house's foundations and she grows like an oak to the rafters. The ghost boy begins to flicker and fade until he is almost invisible. He sneaks unseen behind his stepfather and bolts the door so he can't escape. The mermaid calls up the sea. She closes her throat, and the gills in her neck open. The water rises up through the floor of the old house; it pools across the carpets, it laps up against the skirting boards and it rises and rises until it fills every room. The fairy girl grows wings. They are huge and beautiful. They are five times as big as she is, and they are strong enough to carry her and her siblings up, up, up to where their woodsprite sister nestles on the roof surrounded by leaves.

The water fills the house—fills the stairwell when their stepfather tries to climb, fills the bedrooms, which are empty but for the body of a wolf. The siblings watch from their leafy perch as their evil stepfather flounders and flails under the weight of the water. He grabs and gasps and clutches at his throat, but the siblings are more powerful together than he is alone, and when a watery dawn rises outside the spirits' house and the sea recedes, he lies dead and drowned at the foot of the stairs.

The spell is broken. The fairy girl extends her wings and carries her three siblings over oceans and mountains, over forests and towns, across the boundaries of the human world to where their mother is waiting. Back home.

***

My mother meets us at the hospital. When she and Gracie get here, we are all salved and stitched and bandaged, and my foot, Alice's leg, and Sam's hand are in casts. Bea has borrowed a marker from one of the nurses and is already doodling on the plaster. Our burns are wrapped in cotton and gauze. The pain medication takes the edge off the worst of the blisters so that we just feel singed.

"Singed." I say it out loud. Bea writes it on my cast. *Singed, singe, sing, sang, song.* Our pain is a song. It opens us out and drops pebbles of truth inside us and then it sews us back up again. It is the end of the accident season. Bruises fade, skin stitches together, burns mend. Broken hearts become whole again.

In the car on the way home, Sam leans his head on my shoulder. We stay close. Bea and Alice hold hands. We are all together in the backseat, hip to hip to hip to hip, overlapping where we're packed in too tight. We are a little like one person: four heads, eight legs, forty fingers, five broken bones. A million miles of singing skin.

My mother looks back at us in the rearview mirror. She sees Alice's and Bea's joined hands. She sees our burns and cuts and bruises. She touches the cast on her own arm. Gracie keeps her eyes on the road. When we get home, it is she who makes the tea. She digs in under the sink for a minute and comes up with the kettle. My mother sighs and smiles.

"Tell me what's been happening here," she says when we are all sitting down. Her voice is almost normal. Gracie hands her a biscuit. We sit in a circle around the padded table like we're about to play a game. The typewriter rests on the floor beside me. "Tell me what I've missed. What I'm missing. Fill in the blanks for me."

We look at each other. For a while we don't say anything. We could tell it like a story. We could take each secret out of the box and read it aloud around the table, sentence after sentence, a spoken exquisite corpse. We could make this a fairy tale.

But we don't. Instead, we tell my mother the truth. About the ghost house, about the party, about Nick. At some point my mother starts to cry, but silently, so as not to interrupt.

The only part that is still like a story is when we tell her about Elsie. And only I know how that story ends. Secrets and guardian spirits. *My mother always told me I'd catch my death out there.* Bea and Alice and Sam bend their heads, but it is my mother who looks like she's seen a ghost.

"I have something to tell you too," she tells us. "But first I have a question."

I get nervous. There is only one secret I can think of that we haven't told her. I look over at Sam. His hair falls in his eyes.

My mother turns to Alice. She asks, "Did you set the fire?"

Alice's face is pale and pink in patches, her bangs and eyebrows burned away. Her eyes are bloodshot, her cheeks tear-stained. She stares straight at my mother and shakes her head. She looks at us all in turn. "No," she says. "No." Bea lets out a breath. I realize she's probably been wondering since we saw the fire. The thought hadn't even crossed my mind. Sam is staring at Alice as if he can see through her skull.

281

"I fell asleep," Alice says. "I went to the ghost house and I lit some candles and drank some whiskey and I fell asleep. When I woke up, the fire was all around me." Bea's hand is on Alice's knee—I can tell by the way she's leaning in her seat. Alice tucks her singed hair away from her face and takes a little breath. "But I didn't run out when I could have." My mother hides her mouth in her hands. Alice looks at Bea, at me and at Sam. "I'm glad you came to get me," she says.

"And you'll never try—you'll never do something like that again?" My mother's voice is like an old lady's. Alice shakes her head harder this time. She promises. She puts her hands on my mother's hands and promises again. Gracie puts more biscuits on the table.

"What did you want to tell us?" I ask my mother when our mouths are full of crumbs. The tea is milky sweet and comforting. It spreads warmth all down my chest to my tummy. My mother frowns and fluffs up her purple hair. It hangs around her face in tangles. She reaches out and touches the typewriter on the floor beside us.

"I don't know how to—" she says; then she breathes deep and starts over. She says, "It started with the first accident."

We all sit forward in our seats. The accident season is something that's acknowledged, sometimes spoken of, but never explained.

"It started with the first accident," my mother says again. "Three years before Alice was born."

282

Gracie's eyes are all concern. I realize that this is a story she's heard before. I don't know if I feel angry or relieved.

"When I was very young," my mother tells us, "I had a daughter. Before you, Alice. Her father was someone I met at a party once, but I never saw him again."

We all say, "What?" We don't even look at each other, we're all that shocked.

My mother suddenly looks so sad. "She died before any of you were born. She wasn't two years old. We were crossing the river—she ran ahead, the bridge collapsed. She fell in the water." My mother's voice sounds like it's completely detached from her body. It sounds like she's telling a story, like it isn't something real. "The current took her. I tried to follow, but it was too late. We found her downstream—there's this old house that the river flows under. We found her washed up on the grounds, but she hadn't drowned. She didn't wake up either. She died of pneumonia a month later. I didn't—" My mother stops. "It was the worst time. There's no other way I can say it. And then I met your father, and it was like life suddenly started again. Like a new beginning."

"Did he know?" Alice whispers.

My mother looks down at her hands. "After a few years I told him. But for you . . . I was never able to find the words. It's part of the reason I gave you girls my last name instead of your father's. I wanted to keep you connected to her, even if I couldn't tell you."

"What was her name?" I ask.

My mother smiles sadly. "Now, don't read too much into this," she says, "but it's sort of why I'm telling you this now."

"Read into what?" says Sam.

My mother puts her hands palms up on the table, like she's offering us everything. "Her name was Elsie," she says.

"Elsie." I can't tell if my heart's stopped beating or it's beating triple-time. "What river? This river?" I point at the front door; I point out of the house and down the road and through the field to where the river runs away, along the picnic-table-strewn banks, along the muddy walks, to where it hides underneath a house for a while before resurfacing on the other side of the garden. "You found her in the grounds of a house—you mean the ghost house? Where we had the party? Where I saw Elsie?" I can hardly breathe. "Did you tell her to wrap up warm? Did you tell her she'd catch her death out there?"

My mother's smile is still sad, but there's a knowing look in her eyes. "All mothers say that to their children."

"You said it to Elsie."

"Just like I'm sure your friend Elsie's mother said it to her."

I look to Bea, Sam, and Alice for support. "I don't think they're different people, Mom. I don't think so."

My mother leans over the table and touches my cheek. "Oh, honey," she says. "I understand why you'd like to think that, but it's just a coincidence." I shake my mother's hand away. "She's just a girl with the same name."

I take out my phone and open up my photos. I put the phone flat on the table and everyone crowds around.

"Look," I say. "Look." But when I swipe through the photos, I don't always see what I'm looking for.

I look for Elsie in all my pictures. She's there, yes, in a few of them. Not in all. In the class photographs, the locker room snapshots, the pictures taken at lunchtime or on school tours. Never a full Elsie, though. Just a flash of mousy hair here, a sensible brown shoe there, the hint of an ugly cardigan in the background.

"But she was there." I flick backward and forward, faster and faster. "She was in all of them."

My mother puts a calming hand on my arm. "I think the Malloys across town have a daughter your age," she says. Gracie makes a little *Oh yeah* noise. "I'm pretty sure her name is Elsie. It makes sense that she would go to your school."

"Yeah, but—"

Gracie hasn't heard me. "Sharon Malloy," she says. "She's my hairdresser."

"But—"

"They've just moved to Cork," Gracie says. "Or so I heard." My mother nods. I shake my head.

"No." I hate that Sam and Alice look unsure. "You said

she fell in the river but she didn't die until a month later. When was it? What was the date?"

My mother shakes her head. "I don't . . . It was the very beginning of the accident season. I don't know. The first week of October. But she died on the thirty-first." She says that like it's a date she'll never forget.

"But that's it—that's the accident season." I open my palms in supplication. "It's the same every year."

"Cara—"

"No! No. She was by the river. She set the traps. She was in the ghost house. She's been looking out for us, you know that." My voice rises. I don't mean it to. "She's why the accident season happens. She said that—she goes searching, one month of every year. That's why the accidents happen." I hit my hand on the table. "That's why the accidents happen." My fist thumps dully on the padded wood.

Alice grabs my arms before I can hit the table again. "Cara," she says. "So many of those weren't accidents."

I turn around in a circle. I look at the wrapped and padded house. A wildness builds inside me. I run at the walls. I rip the padding off the hinges. I tear the cloth away from the door handles. I grab the wool and bubble wrap by the fistful, I wrench it away. I uncover the table, the sharp corners of the kitchen counters. My nails split and my burned skin pulls and my broken foot in its cast feels heavy, but I keep going. I tear the padded rags apart. I rip up the afghan rugs.

I don't know when it is that the others join me, but I am in the living room baring the corners of the walls with Alice, I am pulling up the rugs in the hall with Sam, Gracie and my mother are plugging in the toaster and reconnecting the gas burners.

Bea laughs her witchy laugh and finds twine somewhere—hidden in a once-locked drawer with the carving knives—and she strings it up around the house. She winds it around all the exposed nails, she drapes it over picture frames. Then she takes the sharpest pins from my mother's sewing box and drives them through the papery skins of all our secrets. When our house is sharp and hard and dangerous again, the secrets are right there at head height, impossible to hide from, impossible to ignore.

We all stand in the hall and breathe hard. We read our secrets aloud. We count our bruises. We eat some toast. We drink more tea. When we laugh, the sound echoes. The house feels exposed and a little too real.

Soon, it is morning. The sun rises watery and weak outside the kitchen window. The trees at the bottom of the garden shimmy in the rain. We haven't slept. Outside, the bins overflow with rags and wrappings. My mother and Gracie go into the sitting room to get some rest and tell us all to go to bed.

We go upstairs and pull the mattresses off all our beds and into Alice's room again. It takes a long time because of our broken bones. Bea sits behind Alice at Alice's vanity table and cuts her burned hair. It falls onto the carpet like autumn leaves.

Sam and I lie together by the wall and watch them. I take Sam's plaster-casted hand in both of mine. There are words and swirls and secrets written on it. It is hard to the touch. I kiss the tips of his fingers without really realizing it, and Alice's and Bea's reflections look out at us and they know.

"Well," says Alice finally. "I thought so."

"The cards never lie," says Bea. Sam blushes. So that's what he asked.

Bea is smiling like she's been waiting for this all along, but Alice looks at us strangely. I decide not to pretend anymore. I say to her, "So you don't think it's weird?"

"I think it's very weird," says Alice. Sam bites his lip. "But I don't think it's wrong."

"Good," Sam says. "Because it's not." His head is high like he's practiced saying this in front of the mirror. "We're not related or anything—we just . . . we just live in the same house."

"And have the same family, and grew up together," Alice says, but she's smiling. Then she shrugs. "It'll take some getting used to. And I have no idea what Mom'll think—"

"Don't tell her." Sam's voice is huge in the room.

Alice is taken aback. "I wasn't going to, Sammy," she says softly. "But she'll figure it out."

I look at my hands on Sam's hand, I look into his river-bed eyes. I get up carefully and limp downstairs. I sit at the typewriter. I hid the secret earlier when Bea was hanging them all up, but now I write it out again. I type it carefully so the ink doesn't run.

I am in love with Sam.

I tear out the sheet of paper and pin it to the twine in the hall, just at eye level, in front of the kitchen so that everyone can see it.

***

Later, we go down to the river. We leave all our layers in the echoey house and we limp-walk-hobble down to the water like changeling things, like we're not quite used to this human skin.

I lead Sam and Bea and Alice along the bank toward the broken bridge and we stand facing the rushing river and we hold hands in a line and we scream and scream to the other side. Birds fly out of the trees. Fish hide in their hollows. Dogs bark. The river rises up to swallow us, but it takes all our secrets instead. The ones that were stuck to the roofs of our mouths. The ones that made it hard to speak. The trees on the opposite bank shake with them.

I think about the clearing that the trees are hiding. I think about the trap, about the dream catchers and the fly-papers on the trees. I think about all the little Elsies. *She needs us to help her find her way home.*

When I tell the others what I'm thinking, Bea says, "You can't cross the water with that cast." My shoulders droop. Then Bea kisses my cheek and grins. "Wait here just one second." She splashes into the river and across to the other side. The water sucks at her bare legs. When she returns, she's holding her dress out like an apron. Inside are all the dolls.

"I told you." I pick up the pieces of the porcelain Elsie. "I told you it was her."

***

A few days later, my mother shows us her grave. Baby Elsie, we call her when my mother is around, but in our hearts we know she is as old as we are. After that, we go there sometimes. We bring flowers and smoke cigarettes, we drink whiskey from hip flasks. Every time we leave, we put a tiny doll beside the headstone.

The council rebuilds the bridge: a proper, sturdy stone archway over the river. There is a small plaque in the middle with an engraving that reads: IN MEMORY OF ELSIE MORRIS.

Maybe I just need to be remembered, she said, so we remember her. Every time we cross the bridge, we remember her.

I think it must have felt like drowning, catching death that way. I think about Seth hitting his head on a rock, I think about hands holding me under the water. I think about Sam in secrets, Alice in fire, my mother in memories. I think that we all drown, in one way or another.

Every so often I look closely at a picture I've just taken and I get a glimpse of mousy braided hair, a sensible brown shoe, a lace collar, a tartan skirt. The worry lines have been replaced with half a smile. Accidents happen. Our bones shatter, our skin splits, our hearts break. We burn, we drown, we stay alive.

These days after school we walk home the long way, past the remains of the ghost house. It isn't empty anymore; there are carpenters in all the rooms. We can hear them from half a mile away. They hammer and bang and saw with electric machines that dust over the tracks our feet made on the floor. Sometimes I imagine going there and stealing a door handle or a key, a hinge or a pane of glass. But there are no windows left, and anyway, I would be too afraid. There are words there that can't be painted over.

We walk along the river and listen to the carpenters' song. We sit on Elsie's bridge and drink my mother's lemonade. In the daytime we flavor it with lavender water. Some evenings we spike it with stolen gin. Sam and I and Bea and Alice nestle close.

We raise the jam jars we use as glasses. We toast the river and we say the words together.

One more drink for the watery road.

GHOST STORIES THAT AREN'T: MOÏRA FOWLEY-DOYLE ON

THE *Accident Season*

By Shelley Diaz

Originally published by *School Library Journal*

on August 17, 2015

***

The line between reality and fantasy is so tenuous in your debut novel. Did you set out to write a ghost story? A novel with magical realism? A mystery? All or none of the above?

Ah, but *is* it a ghost story? I set out to write magical realism, and was happy to leave as much as I could get away with unexplained. Unexpected, slightly magical things happen every day, and sometimes there's a rational explanation and sometimes it's just coincidence and sometimes it's just a mystery. I love that, and I wanted to translate that feeling into fiction, make readers question what's real and what's just inside the characters' heads and what's magic, and if there's a difference, always, in the end.

What inspired you to write this story? How long have you been working on it?

I've always loved magical realism and I wanted to write something dreamy and wild and a little unsettling, but also familiar. Something I would have loved to read as a teenager growing up in Ireland and mostly reading dreamy books not set in Ireland. I wrote the first draft in less than two months, revised it over a period of six months by myself, [and revised it for] another six months with my agent, and then over a year with my editors. From the first word I wrote to the book's release date was three and a half years.

The rich Irish setting plays such an important part of this novel, from the dilapidated (and possibly haunted) house that Cara and Bea find to the eerie river scenes. How much were you influenced by the setting around you in creating the backdrop to this story?

Rural Ireland is wealthy in abandoned houses. My parents have a house (not abandoned) by a forest outside a small town in Co Mayo, [which] has a beautiful river running through it. Along the river walk you can see the ruins of old cottages and a disused factory or mill of some kind, and all around the area there are plenty of old empty houses. It's a beautiful part of the country that the story fit itself around nicely. It's pretty and understated. Not as wild as Connemara or as a rugged as the Burren, but the kind of place in which a quiet girl could just sort of slip off the page.

The romance in this work is swoony and a bit taboo. What is it about forbidden love in literature that spell-binds us so?

I *love* forbidden love in literature. I think it appeals (to me anyway) because it's different, because it's taboo, and because it's a wonderful example of emotions over-coming reason and restrictions.

Several of the male characters are not what they seem, and even turn out to be quite sinister in an almost otherworldly way. Would you consider them the villains of this title?

I think so. They are certainly the real malicious force in the book, and unexpectedly so for a lot of the characters. It might seem like the accident season itself is the main driving fear of the story, whereas actually it's events and characters grounded in reality that have had the most effect, especially because a lot of what happens is tightly tied to secrets and silence, which will always hinder the healing process. I tried to get the balance right between the sinister otherworldliness and the actual solid events involving these characters, so that the former feeds off the latter but doesn't take from its seriousness.

Secrets are a big theme here, from Elsie's secrets booth to dark family secrets. How did you plot out the big reveals without giving too much away?

By sticking close to Cara the whole time. She is fairly oblivious to a lot of what's happening around her— whether that's from lingering trauma or just her personality—and is almost willfully naive at times, so it was easy to see only what she sees—or lets herself see.

The power of friendship shines through in *The Accident Season*, especially the connections among Bea, Cara, Sam,

and even Elsie. Why do you think that it's such a marker of YA books?

It's such an important part of life, really. I think a lot of YA is concerned with finding one's place—I know that's what has always appealed to me about it, particularly when I was more Y than A—and very often that place is with the like-hearted.

What was your favorite ghost story growing up?

I've always liked ghost stories that aren't, or that might not be, or that could be something else entirely. Alice Hoffman is very good at is-it-a-ghost-story? stories, and I adore Neil Gaiman's spooky short stories.

What's the best advice that you received as a first-time novelist?

My agent, the extraordinary Claire Wilson of Rogers, Coleridge & White, has given me more good advice than I can count. One of her pieces of advice I'm trying to follow right now is to remember that the first draft is the writer telling herself the story and getting to know her characters: so let yourself write a rubbish first draft—fine-tuning and beautifying can happen in the edits!

What are you working on now?

I'm working on my second novel, another standalone, which is sort of about lost things but also has tattoos and rusty keys and illegally distilled alcohol and a lot of cycling down country roads.

ENJOY THIS TEASER FROM
MOÏRA FOWLEY-DOYLE'S NEXT NOVEL—

SPELLBOOK
OF THE
LOST AND FOUND

A lyrical, haunting, twisty story about memories that have gone
missing, people who have returned from the past, and a group
of friends who might need to give up more than they bargained
for—unless they already have.

Prologue

That night, everybody lost something.

Not everybody noticed. Some kept drinking, thinking this was just another Saturday night on the cusp of summer, a wild night spent in a field at the edge of town close to that invisible line where suburbs become countryside. It was warm because of the bonfire in the middle of the field that someone's parents had surprisingly okayed, and because of the stolen beers, the wine coolers bought with older siblings' IDs, the vodka filched from stepparents' drinks cabinets.

The night smelled like hot wood and burning rubber, like alcohol and spit, like sweat and tears. There was the hint of a strange sound in the air, which some thought might have been a trapped dog howling, but most decided was just in their imagination.

Some turned around and went back home. Some forgot things they'd always known. Others stumbled, just for a moment, not realizing that they'd lost more than their step.

Some noticed a change without really understanding what it was. Some kissed each other with cake on their tongues, rainbow icing dissolving between mouths to make new colors. Some lit up their schoolbooks and threw them on the bonfire, not caring that they still had two weeks to study for their summer exams.

Some hung back, nervous, torn between coming closer to the fire, and calling their parents to come get them. Some slipped small pills on their tongues and swallowed them with soft drinks, the bubbles tickling their throats as it all went down. Some choked on cigarette smoke even though they'd been smoking for years. Some gripped others' zippers in shivering fingers, lowered jeans or hitched up skirts. Others watched from the shadows.

By the time the fire had burned down to glowing ashes and a pile of charred wood, when everyone was dreaming deep in their own beds or lying through their wine-stained teeth to their parents or getting sick in their best friends' bathrooms or continuing the party in someone else's house, there was nothing left in the field but the things we had lost.

Chapter 1 · Olive

Silver star-shaped hairclip, jacket (light green, rip in one sleeve), flat silver shoe (right, scuffed at the toes).

Daylight is only just touching the tips of the trees when the bonfire goes out. I am leaning against a bale of hay upon which someone I don't know is sleeping.

I roll my head over to look for Rose, who I was sure was sitting legs splayed on the ground beside me. The grass is mostly muck at this point, beaten down by too many pairs of shoes and feet. My own feet—bare, the nails painted a shiny, metallic green that doesn't show up in the morning darkness—are dirty. So is the rest of me.

Rose isn't here. I call out for her but nobody answers. Not that I expect that she will be able to; sometime in the night she lost her voice from shouting to be heard over the music, from

3

singing along to really bad songs, and from all the crying.

Getting ready to go out last night, Rose told me, "My plan for the evening is to get excessively drunk, and then cry." She swiped her lashes with another layer of mascara, which seemed unwise given the aforementioned plan.

"Can we make the crying optional?" I said. "My eyeliner's really good right now." It had taken me twenty minutes, six cotton buds, and five tissues to get it even.

"Absolutely not."

I sneaked a look at my best friend's reflection. She blinked to dry her mascara. It gave her a misleadingly innocent air.

"I don't know why you want to go to this thing in the first place," I said.

This thing was the town's summer party. It's held in May every year—early enough that the weather's still miserable but late enough that the sun stays out well past nine. Until midnight it's filled with families of sugar-hyper children stuffed dangerously full of badly barbecued burgers, threatening to throw up on the rented bouncy castles. Their parents bop self-consciously to decades-old pop music blaring from speakers while the town teenagers—most of them our classmates—sneak off to nearby fields to drink.

"I told you why I want to go," Rose said. "I plan to get excessively drunk."

"And then cry," I reminded her.

"And then cry."

"Well, you know what they say," I said to the back of her head. "Be careful what you wish for."

We slept in the field, which seemed like a good idea at the time. But now there is a growing chill despite the slowly rising sun, and I don't know if it means that a storm is coming or just that I've been in the same position for far too long. I'm beginning to lose all feeling in my right shoulder, the one currently being propped up by the prickly pile of hay.

When I look down, on one bare and dirty arm I see the words: *If you don't get lost, you'll never be found.* They're blurry because my eyes are blurry; it takes five blinks for me to make them out. They run from shoulder to wrist and seem to be written in my own wobbly handwriting, although I don't remember writing them. When I lick a finger and rub at an *N,* it doesn't smudge.

For about as long as we've been friends, Rose and I have written what we refer to as our mottos on each other's arms in permanent marker. When we were younger they were mostly things like *You are beautiful* or *Carpe diem.* These days they are mostly in-jokes or particularly poignant quotes. We both got detention for a week last year because of our matching block capitals reading *DO NO HARM BUT TAKE NO SHIT.* I must have written this one during the party, although when or why, I have no idea.

My head feels fuzzy. With a wince and a sigh, I drag myself out of the last dregs of drunkenness and stand shakily up.

I take stock: I am missing a shoe (the other is half-buried in the muck beside me) and my jacket. My dress is covered in grass stains and smells distinctly like vodka. I have the beginnings of a pretty epic headache forming, and I seem to have lost my best friend.

"Rose!" I call. "Rose?"

The boy on the hay bale twitches in his sleep.

"Hey," I say to him loudly. I poke his shoulder when he doesn't wake up. "Hey!"

The boy opens one eye and grunts. He has dirty-blond hair and a carefully maintained five o'clock shadow that is heading closer to seven. I vaguely remember dancing with him last night. He squints at me, gropes blindly along the hay for a few seconds, and comes up holding a pair of slightly bent glasses.

"Olivia?" he says hesitantly.

"Olive." I have absolutely no idea what his name is. "Have you seen my friend?"

"Roisín?" he says in the tone of someone who isn't sure he's saying the right thing.

"Rose."

"Olive," he says, sitting up slowly. "Rose."

"Yes," I say impatiently. He's clearly still very drunk. "Yes, Rose, have you seen her?"

"She was crying?"

I pick up my shoe and shove it on my foot, figuring that

one shoe is still better than none. "I know. That was her plan for the evening. Did you see where she went?"

"Her plan?"

I survey the field for any sight of her. There's a blue denim jacket crumpled up on the ground not far away. I take it because I'm beginning to feel very cold.

The bonfire is ashes now, vaguely glowing. Pale blue light spills over the trees and into the field. My phone is dead, so I don't know what time it is, but it's probably close to six a.m.

I start to make my way around the fire and toward the road. The boy on the hay bale calls out to me. "Can I have another kiss before you go?"

I look back at him and make a face. *Another* kiss? "Not a chance."

"See you round?"

I shake my head and walk away quickly. Most of my memories of last night seem to have disappeared with Rose.

I make my way around the field, scanning the faces of the sleepers (averting the ones who clearly *aren't* sleeping). It doesn't take long; she isn't here. I am the only person standing.

My bare foot is cold and wet from the dewy grass. I turn around in a circle, taking in the stone wall and the tangle of bushes surrounding the field, the fence near the empty road on the other side, the small line of trees separating this field from the next one.

There's someone there, almost hidden between two trees.

It's a boy. He's wearing a flat cap, and an old, holey sweater that might be green or black; it's hard to tell in the shadows. He has a lot of brown curly hair under that awful hat, a hundred freckles on his skin, and a guitar slung over his back. He looks like a cross between a farmer and a teenage Victorian chimney sweep.

Before I have time to break his gaze, he turns and walks away, and I lose him between the trees.

I look down at myself, at my dirty dress and too-big borrowed jacket, at my one bare foot and my grass-stained legs. I could be Cinderella, if Cinderella were a short, chubby, hungover girl with smudged makeup and tangled hair. And while I'm very glad that I don't have a dead father and an evil stepmother, I'm not entirely sure how I'm going to explain my current state to my parents when I get home.

My bike is exactly where I left it, chained to the fence by the side of the road, but it takes me several tries to unlock it because my hands don't seem to want to work properly and my brain feels increasingly like it's trying to turn itself inside out. When I clamber on, my bare foot sticks uncomfortably to the pedal.

I pass a grand total of three cars and one tractor on the road into town. The rest of the time, all I can hear are quiet animal sounds—birds chirping all too cheerfully for this time in the morning, the odd sheep bleating, rustling scampering noises from the side of the road—and the swish and bump of my tires over gravel and potholes. The clouds above me are getting very gray, almost as if the dawn has changed its mind and wants to revert back to night.

My dress blows up in the breeze, but there's no one around to see, so I keep both hands on the handlebars and try to ride steady. Under the sleeve of my borrowed denim jacket I can see the tail end of the sentence written there: *you'll never be found.*

It comes back to me in a flash. Rose in my bedroom last night, staring at her reflection in my vanity mirror while pouring generous measures of cheap vodka into a bottle of Diet Coke.

She said, "If you don't get lost, you'll never be found."

We'd drunk a fair amount of the vodka already and her words were slightly slurred.

"At this rate," I said to her, "the only thing we'll lose tonight is the contents of our stomachs."

My prediction was accurate: Another flash of memory has me bent over a hay bale, throwing up the unholy mixture of slightly-Diet-Coke-flavored vodka and barbecued hot dogs that we all ate on sticks, posing for pictures holding the phallic meat like rude children. My stomach lurches at the thought and I have to pull over to the side of the road to retch again.

If you don't get lost, you'll never be found.

I hold the low stone wall by the side of the road like a lifeboat, and sigh. Without warning it begins to rain. Fat drops fall on the mess of my hair, darken my jacket, hit the dry roadside like cartoon tears. *Splat.* I have to blink them out of my eyelashes. I sigh again and drag my bike back out of the ditch.

I cycle home through pounding rain and with a pounding headache. Maybe it's that I drank too much and remember too little about last night. Maybe it's that Rose left without me. Maybe it's what the blond-haired boy said about another kiss. Maybe it's the beautiful boy I saw at the edge of the field, standing there looking like he'd lost something. But I feel like I might have lost something myself, and I have no idea what it is.